Praise for the novels of
BONNIE HEARN HILL

"*Double Exposure* [...]
romantic-suspense [...]
Bonnie Hearn Hi[...]
—[...]

"A thoroughly [...]
genuinely [...] characters."
—*Romantic Times BOOKclub* on *Double Exposure*

"Hill gets the reader's attention with a contemporary issue (is slim the only way to be?), intriguing characters and clever plotting."
—*Publishers Weekly* on *Killer Body*

"Fans…will appreciate Hill's skill in combining first-rate suspense with glamorous characters and a topical story line."
—*Booklist* on *Killer Body*

"*Intern* is a thriller that reads as if it's ripped from today's headlines."
—*New York Times* bestselling author Alex Kava

"[Bonnie Hearn Hill] creates more than enough suspense to keep readers intrigued… [a] page-turner."
—*Publishers Weekly* on *Intern*

"Whoa! Hold on tight. Engrossing, provocative and haunting, *Intern* is a riveting combination."
—*New York Times* bestselling author
Mary Jane Clark

BONNIE HEARN HILL

OFF THE RECORD

MIRA®

ISBN-13: 978-0-7783-2357-0
ISBN-10:   0-7783-2357-9

OFF THE RECORD

Copyright © 2006 by Bonnie Hearn Hill.

www.MIRABooks.com

Printed in U.S.A.

For Bob and Carol O'Hanneson,
and Sarkis, the driver:
Thank you for Half Moon Bay.

ACKNOWLEDGMENTS

Thanks to the many people who assisted with this book—most of all, my editor, Susan Pezzack, and my agent, Laura Dail, for helping me see the story that I was trying to tell.

My gratitude to Larry Hill, who put his own writing aside to read and discuss the final draft.

And to Genevieve Choate, whose friendship has opened my eyes and ears to a world I could not have experienced any other way.

And to KVPR, Valley Public Radio, Mariam Stepanian, Franz Weinschenk and Don Weaver for their support through Valley Writers Read.

And to The Tuesdays, who continue to challenge and inspire me, and make me laugh.

I am fortunate to have all of you in my life.

Prologue

KATHLEEN

Her mind was on Jesse when it happened. Out in the garden, clawing up the ground for some bulbs, she was thinking about the two of them, she and him, wondering how they could end what divorce had failed to. And they needed to end it; they must.

That's when she heard the doorbell, when she'd risen from the dirt and, after seeing the visitor's uniform, opened the door to the very enemy she feared most.

The house—her sanctuary—could make Kathleen forget anything, but not today. She'd allowed the wrong person into it. Now, not even the house—its weathered shingles, its thick green lawn, its embracing view of the ocean—could protect her.

Standing there in her gardening clothes, Kathleen studied the face before her. This wasn't just an anonymous enemy. No. In that silent moment, she realized that she was looking into the eyes of a nightmare, one she'd tried to put behind her years before.

"How did you find me?" she demanded. And then, breathless, "What do you want? Money?"

It was the wrong question. The eyes turned colder, deadly with rage. But now as they faced each other within the entryway, Kathleen knew that, even in childhood, there had been something wrong with those eyes.

"Do you think money will change what you did, Kathy Jo?"

"Of course not," she said. The mail carrier would be driving his little cart up the hill about now. If she could buy some time, she might be able to attract his attention. "I made provisions for your family," she said. "I've tried to do what was right."

"I know that."

"Then leave, now."

"Not while you're still alive."

She looked down at her hand, still holding a tool from the garden. Maybe she'd have a fighting chance. Lord knows, she'd been a fighter all of her life.

"Don't even think about it." The intruder had caught her looking at the sharp clawed teeth of the tool. But this was her only hope. She had no choice.

Hands trembling, she swung the implement like a baseball bat, felt it rip into flesh. Then, a scream, a dazed and angry form struggling to get up from the tile floor.

"Help," she shouted. "Someone help."

Fingernails dug into her ankles. Kathleen hit the floor with a jolt. Her vision blurred. She tried to get up, then fell back down. Felt herself being dragged outside. The two of them struggled to the edge of the cliffs, the edge of the view that had cost her so much to own. Fighting for her life, she realized that the view owned her now.

She gazed into the soulless eyes of her enemy. "Don't," she pleaded, amazed at the strength her voice still held.

Hysterical laughter cracked the air. "You don't get it, do you, Kathy Jo?"

All she wanted to do was make good what she'd screwed up back when she was too young to know better. She didn't want to die. She didn't want to hurt anyone else.

"You need to listen to me," she began. Before she could say more, she was shoved to her knees, her face ground into the sand.

"Killer."

"I'm not," she said, tasting the grit against her teeth.

"Murderer."

"No." She lifted her head, finally realizing what

this was all about. "All the threats," she gasped. "The accidents. It was all you, wasn't it?"

"All me. And you know why."

Blood stained the sand beneath her now, the earth and the elements that could save or destroy her. She was right to have done what she'd done. Right about Geri LaRue.

"A newspaper reporter," she choked out. "In San Francisco. Geri LaRue. If anything happens to me—"

She tried to say more, but the fingers had moved to her throat, squeezing the breath from her.

The throbbing in her head overpowered her words until it finally felt as if she were exploding. She tried to find her feet, to fight another round. She was tough. Yes. She had survived bigger battles. And, yes, she had shaken free, glaring at her enemy eye to eye. She wasn't the only one who was bloody. Maybe there was still a chance.

Hands shot out, striking her on each shoulder. Kathleen toppled backward toward the edge. She tried to scream out the truth, to beg for one more chance, but there was nothing to grasp, nothing left to halt her shuddering fall into darkness.

One

Busted.

As Steffan Kim read Doug Blanchard's column aloud at my kitchen counter that Saturday morning, I stood on the other side, too stunned to move, my right hand still gripping the espresso machine. I'd really screwed up this time. Maybe even enough to get myself fired.

"Did she jump or was she pushed?" Steffan had one of those rare voices that I could hear, but today, with my mind buzzing, I concentrated on reading his lips. "'Kathleen Fowler, who founded Half Moon Blooms and grew her nursery to a five-acre, multimillion business that supplied exotic landscaping all over California, was well known and liked in the community, where she was involved in numerous civic events. Yesterday, her mail carrier heard a scream and, after investigating, spotted Fowler's body sprawled on the jagged rocks beneath the cliffs beside her Ocean Boulevard home.'"

"I should have covered the story," I said, sickened by both the content and the very real fact that I was in big trouble with Marie, our editor at the paper. "Blanchard's a columnist. This is a news story, not column material."

"There's a sidebar on the front page," Steffan said. Then with a look that was part apology, part guilt, "Blanchard's is above the fold, though."

"He took a hard-news story and made it a column." I stared down at my purple Doc Marten boots, the same color as my hair. "I was out drinking. The only time I've ever done it, and he was able to steal my story."

"Others could have written it," he said. "You aren't the only one who dropped the ball."

"But *I* was the one scheduled to work."

"Along with a whole shift, Ger. Don't forget that."

If I'd been at my desk when I should have been, I would have heard about Kathleen Fowler's murder that Friday. Instead, I was feeling no pain, as Mama would say.

That's what you're supposed to do at Christmas-time, isn't it? Sneak away from the office early? Have a drink with your coworkers?

Except the holidays were not the reason Steffan and I had left the newspaper early Friday afternoon. Not the reason we had consumed Meyer lemon martinis like branch water at the gay bar where Steffan sang as Simply Kim. We'd left the office after reading the announcement that I'd been passed over for a position that Marie had all but promised me— for the newspaper's new lifestyle column, "Off the Record." A column that newcomer Doug Blanchard—Doug Bastard, as the staff members called him—had snagged, just as he had snagged the Fowler story.

Stretched out beside me on the floor, my dog Nathan looked up from his nap, the way he did when he sensed that something was wrong. I reached down, patted him back into a peaceful snooze, and wondered how the hell I'd get myself out of this one.

Steffan glanced over at my blinking answering machine and my drained-dry cell phone that was parked beside it charging. "I'll bet they tried to call you," he said.

I flipped the switch, and steam rushed through the espresso machine with a blast that even I could hear. That accomplished, I poured two small cups from the steamy glass carafe and handed one to him. "What shall it be?" I asked, feeling so rock bottom that I could barely manage a smile. "Bagels or cyanide?"

Two

GERI

"So?"

That was the way Marie, my editor, whom I'd recently tried to stop referring to as That Bitch Marie, usually approached me, as if in mid-conversation, on her way to catch a train, maybe. That Monday, it was the elevator. As she scrambled in beside me in those pink suede boots that went up farther than I could see or speculate, I knew that I was going to be found out.

TMB was a good-looking woman, in spite of the weight she'd lost recently. But she wasn't so good about what Steffan called *engagement*. In my case, at least, she'd gotten less good about it lately.

I can usually handle an elevator, although my lack of hearing adds to the discomfort of the closed-in feeling. "So?" I replied, trying to make it sound like a friendly question.

"Where were you Friday afternoon, Geri?"

Just what I was expecting. Steffan and I had already invented an excuse, but inside this cube, I had nowhere to run.

"Flu shot." I couldn't say more. The very lie of it filled my mouth like mush.

She looked down at her pink pointed-toe boots, then back up at me. "You were getting a flu shot Friday afternoon?" she asked.

And darned if I couldn't answer.

After an eternity of silence, the doors opened. She didn't move. "I was with Steffan," I said, and stepped out before I was trapped in there with her again.

She got off, too, and gave me an unreadable expression that was part polite and part command. "Mind coming to my office?" she asked. "We probably ought to talk about this."

Steffan was already there, just as he'd promised. He raised an eyebrow as if to warn me to stay silent. As if he had to. I wasn't sure I'd be able to speak. I hoped whatever he had to say would convince her to leave me alone.

"Good morning," Marie said to him, and I could feel more than hear the hard professional edge to her voice.

"Do you have a minute?" he asked.

"Actually, I don't," she told him, glancing at me. "I'll call you when I'm free."

She unlocked her office door and motioned for me to come inside. I did so quietly, thinking *please don't let me be fired*. I looked through the glass partitions out at the office full of people tending to any number of jobs. I wanted to be one of them, column or no column. Why had I taken off Friday without telling anyone? How did I think that I wouldn't be caught?

I was so distracted that I didn't realize that Steffan had accompanied us inside.

"What is it?" she asked him as I stood there between them beside her conference table.

"About Friday," he said.

"Geri and I were just discussing that in the elevator." She sat at the round table with its fake wood finish and motioned for me to do the same. "So, tell me, Geri."

"Flu shot," I managed.

"That's what I was going to tell you," Steffan put in, speaking so rapidly that I could hardly follow. "Geri and I realized that we hadn't gotten flu shots yet. There was a shortage at first, you know."

"That was sometime ago," Marie said, glaring at me as she answered his question. "You know that there hasn't been a shortage of the vaccine for months. You could have gotten shots at any time."

"We've been too busy," I said.

"But you weren't busy on Friday? You weren't busy right after the announcement of Doug Blanchard's promotion?"

Busted. I knew it. My lip trembled.

"Marie," Steffan said. "It was Friday. So, we left a little early. What's the big deal?"

"*You* didn't leave early," she said. "You came in at seven, remember?" Her eyes bore into mine again. "We tried to call you to cover the murder in Half Moon Bay."

"My cell phone wasn't working," I said.

"Are you sure?"

"I left it at home," I admitted. "I thought I'd be able to pick it up when we left here, but we didn't go back to my place."

"And where did you go?"

"Marie, please." Steffan interrupted.

She rose and said, "There's no point in your staying for this discussion, Steffan. You worked a full day on Friday."

He shot me a helpless look, then got up slowly and left the office. Through the glass, I could see the curious glance that Bridget, our fashion writer, gave him, then me. I stared back, blank-faced, unable to move. Steffan shook his head, and Bridget followed him toward his cubicle, her golden hair spread down the back of her turquoise sweater so perfectly that it looked as if someone had raked it.

Marie's office felt as suffocating and small as the

elevator had. Too many chairs, too large a table. The bookcase littered with framed photos and awards stretched the whole width of the wall beside her desk. She looked at me as if I were an insect, and she was trying to decide between the fly swatter and the Raid. Then, when she reached over and closed the blinds over the glass, I felt as if I were being swallowed up in the dim room. I couldn't move, not even when she came back and sat beside me.

"I swear that I remember seeing you and Steffan in the flu shot line last month," she said. "I can get the sign-in sheets if I have to."

"I'll make up the time," I said. "It was only, what? An hour, at the most? And I know I was supposed to have my phone, but—"

"So you did leave early." Her eyes grew even colder. People always said they wanted the truth, but that's not how they acted once they heard it. I should have learned that one by now.

I nodded, feeling so full of shame that I could almost taste it. "I was upset about not getting the job, and I just left. I know it was stupid, and I'm sorry."

"I didn't promise you the 'Off the Record' column," she said with an embarrassed flush that made me pretty sure she thought she had.

"I know that. But you did go on about my article about the razor killer last year."

"So, I liked the article." Her flush turned angry. "I didn't promise you the position, and you had no right to expect it."

"I didn't expect it," I said. "I was just disappointed when I didn't get it." She crossed her arms tightly across her sweater, and my blood went cold. I loved this job, needed it. "I'll make up the time," I said. "You know I'm a good employee and that I put in a lot more hours than I report."

She slammed her hands over her ears. "If you're working overtime and not clocking in, I don't even want to hear about it."

That's what we all did, and of course she knew it. Crikey. I'd said the wrong thing again, just by telling the truth.

"I'm only trying to say that I care about doing a good job," I said. I felt like crying. I'd had excellent reviews. Because of what I'd done, I'd be written up the way I used to in school when I couldn't hear what was going on in class. "Please don't write me up." *Most of all,* I thought, *please don't fire me.*

She tapped her clear nails on the desktop, but seemed to soften a little. "You have been a good employee, but rules are rules." She glanced at the pink Pucci-print band of her wristwatch. "I have two meetings this morning. Let's talk again early afternoon."

I started to say I was sorry again. Started to mumble an apology and try to be invisible the way I had for so many years. Before I could say anything, I felt the vibration of someone knocking at the door.

She sighed and gave me a look that suggested this interruption was also somehow my fault.

I caught a glimpse of Steffan just outside her office. I couldn't hear what he said. Nor could I make out her reply. Finally she opened the door wider and came to the table where I sat. Steffan shut the door slowly. As he did so, I caught the expression on his face. Incredulous is the best way to describe it. Gaping at me the way he might a stranger.

She stared down on me as if she'd caught me doing something else wrong. "Why didn't you tell me that you knew Kathleen Fowler?" she asked.

The name was familiar, but I was too scared and confused to think clearly. "Who?"

"The woman who was killed in Half Moon Bay."

Now I remembered. Crikey. Whatever was going on was way over my head. "I didn't know her," I said, really confused now. "I never even heard of her until Steffan read me Blanchard's column on Saturday."

"Interesting." She didn't move, and I wondered if she were trying to decide between writing me up and firing me on the spot.

"What's interesting about it?" I asked.

"The fact that you say you didn't know Kathleen Fowler," she said. The trace of a smile on her lips was scarier than the openly angry look she'd given me just moments before.

"I *didn't* know her," I repeated.

"Her estate lawyer's here to see you right now," she

said with that smile again. "It appears that you're Kathleen Fowler's sole beneficiary. Are you still going to pretend that you didn't know her, Geri?"

Three

A stranger had left me a fortune. Nothing in my life had been easy, and I knew that this wouldn't be, either. But, still. A fortune.

The conversation with the lawyer who'd been waiting for me the whole time Marie chewed me out left me speechless. Yes, he said, I was indeed the Geraldine May LaRue to whom Kathleen Fowler had left her estate. Yes, it was a considerable amount of money, and, no, he hadn't the slightest idea why she had changed her trust three weeks before her murder. Did I?

No, I didn't. I didn't know anything and understood less. For an instant, I thought of Mama. The word *help* actually floated through my mind. Then I had to laugh at my own joke. How could I help a woman who left no forwarding address to her own daughter?

I looked down at my Docs, a little scuffed with age. But then, I'd bought them used at a San Francisco head shop. Crikey. It hit me, just like that. I could buy new Docs if I wanted to. I could buy Steffan the giant-size bottle of Bombay Sapphire gin. He could quit his singing job at the club, put his younger brother through college. I could stuff bills, not coins, down the thin, cold mouths of those Salvation Army pots at every corner this holiday season. And yes, admit it. Maybe I could help Mama.

Stunned by the news, I stumbled back to Marie's office and her eager birdlike expression, her slew of questions. Instead of answering, I asked for a leave of absence. And she had no choice but to agree.

On the way to the HR department, she asked, "Are you sure that you never knew that woman who was killed?"

"I told you back in your office," I said. "I wasn't lying."

"I didn't mean to suggest that you were."

She was trying to be what Mama would call nicey-nice. Against my will, I thought of Mama again. If it really happened—if I really even got a little of the money—what would she say when I laid a big fat check on her? Assuming I could even find her, of course. Immediately I felt guilty. The cash that I was so freely spending in my daydreams existed only because a woman had been murdered.

"I don't know any more about this than you do," I told her. "But I have to find out. If you'll just let me have the two weeks, I should be able to get to the bottom of it."

"You're eligible for up to six months if you want it." She smiled, and that didn't quite work, either. Crikey. Had she had work done on her lips? The upper looked fuller and a little bumpier than I remembered.

Six months sounded tempting, all right, but I was afraid to ask or hope.

"What about one month?" I suggested.

She cocked her head as if looking at me for the first time and seeing a person there. "Do you really think that you can get to the bottom of that woman's murder and the inheritance in a month?" she asked.

Without having to go to a day job? Without having to deal with this woman every time I made a move that wasn't Marie-approved? I nodded and said, "Yes, I think I can."

At that point, all I wanted was out of this claustrophobic building. I was free, for a while, at least. I needed to find out why I'd been left what was, to me, a fortune. I owed Kathleen Fowler, my benefactor, more than that, however. The money, if I got it, would go to the best help I could hire to help me find out who had killed her and why. A chill spread through me.

It must have shown on my face because Marie asked, "What's wrong?"

"Nothing," I said. I didn't dare tell her what I'd just felt, or she would think I was certifiably crazy. The thought was a very simple one. Had Kathleen Fowler picked me because she knew that I wouldn't just take her money and run? Had she known, somehow, that I'd use every dime of it to find her killer?

We entered the human resources department and walked down its long carpeted hall to the conference room.

Once inside, we had to stand at the back of a long line. In front of us stood creepy Joey Reynolds. Every time I looked at him, I saw a snake—long, lanky and toxic. He'd creeped me out ever since he hit on me my first week on the job. According to the office rumors, I wasn't the first, but that didn't seem to deter his career. Since then Romeo Joe, as we called him, with his creeping bald spot and widening waistline, had slithered his way up the food chain from retail rep to ad director. He was living proof that the married man who plays around at work isn't as much of a dinosaur as most would like to think in these supposedly enlightened times.

"Hey, Ger," he said when he realized that I was standing behind him. "I heard about your good news. Wish someone would leave *me* a bunch of bucks."

If he were looking at anything above my chest, I might have believed his sincerity.

"You sound as if you know more about it than I do," I said.

"Only what I hear in the halls." He grinned at Marie as if I weren't there. "So, what's the story? Is Ger resigning?"

"I don't think that's any of your business." Had I said that? Had I really stood up to this creep?

"Well, pardon the hell out of me." He squinted those reptilian eyes, as if I'd given him a headache. "A little money, a little notoriety, and our Geri's a different person."

"Cut it out," Marie told him. "This situation is difficult enough as it is."

His smile turned lazy. "It's going to get more difficult, though, isn't it?"

My cheeks felt as if they were burning off of my face. "What do you mean by that?" I couldn't keep my voice from shaking.

"Doug Blanchard." Reynolds smiled as if to say if he couldn't get to me the first way he'd tried, that he was happy to get to me with this. "I understand that he thinks there's more to this story than meets the eye. Who knows, Ger? You might just end up in his column."

"That's enough." Now Marie was the one with fire in her cheeks.

Before she could say more, Reynolds turned and

strode out of the reception area. At the door, he met my eyes. "See you around," he said.

As I watched Marie's angry eyes, I knew with a sudden sick thud that there was more to his remark than a meaningless insult.

"What's he talking about?" I asked her.

"I can't believe someone in his position can be so unprofessional," she said. And as I continued to stare at her, she added, "Doug has asked to interview you regarding your inheritance. I was going to wait to discuss it with you."

"But Romeo Joe has already heard it and is passing it around the building." At that moment, I realized that I didn't have to take a leave, didn't have to stand there another minute. I could quit if I wanted to.

"I can't imagine—" She shook her head as if trying to shake off her frustration. "Doug must have said something."

"So, it's a done deal?" I asked. "You're going to let him write about me?"

"I know it's a little awkward," she said, "but the whole situation is awkward, and we *are* a newspaper."

And this was news, I thought. *I* was news.

"I'm not doing it." That's right. I didn't have to do as she said anymore. If she didn't agree, I'd walk right now.

She glared back at me as if gauging how much power she still had over me and guessing correctly that it was decreasing by the moment.

"Won't do what?" she asked.

"Won't give Doug Blanchard an interview." Before she could protest, I said, "I didn't ask to be where I am, but this is my life now. I'm not going to hand it over to anyone, especially not to him." I caught my breath. Never had I been this outspoken to anyone. Was Romeo Joe right? Was this what the promise of financial independence did to people?

"Fair enough," she replied slowly.

The HR clerk appeared and ushered us into the conference room to fill out my leave forms. I remembered the room from my first week here when they gave us what was called *orientation*. They also made us watch a film about sexual harassment. Of course, the mush-mouth HR director guy running the show that day, whose lips I could barely read, told us that we should report anything that resembled it. Like if I'd told him or anyone else about Joey Reynolds's pass at me, they would have taken my word over his.

I'd forgotten how blandly ugly it was in here, with the long, bare tables and the fake-scenic posters with words like *Teamwork* and *Communication* screaming from them, in capital letters. Besides, something about the room felt creepy. The windows, a rarity in this place, seemed to be open and unguarded. Maybe that was it. A kind of vulnerable indifference, one that I'd felt in other by-the-book settings in my life, filled the room.

Maria crossed her arms in front of her, the way she

liked to do, and sat down on top of the conference table.

"I won't talk to Blanchard," I insisted. "And I don't appreciate that you're going to allow him to write about me when I don't even have a clue what's going on."

"We're a newspaper," she repeated, her eyes darting toward those disturbing windows looking in on us. "We have to react to and report what's happening around us. You know that."

"But not with a guy who's already telling people like Romeo Joe that he thinks there's more to my story than meets the eye."

"That was unprofessional of Reynolds," she said, and hugged herself harder. "Also extremely unprofessional of you to refer to him by that name."

"Everyone does," I said. "And, based on my personal experience, the man deserves the title."

"And what does that mean?"

"Only that I don't like him, and I really don't like that he knew before I did that you're allowing Blanchard to write about me."

"I'm not going to tell Doug Blanchard what he should or shouldn't write about," she said, "and you shouldn't ask me to. That's why a newspaper hires a columnist. For a different voice, a different opinion."

My voice, my opinion. But Doug Bastard was the one who caught their collective eye. Or was it *her* eye? Something about her was still off. I just couldn't figure out what it was that didn't ring true.

"Bottom line," I said. "I won't talk to Blanchard."

"Then he'll write his column without your input. Is that what you want?" She crossed her arms again. I stared off into the blind eyes of the windows.

"I don't want any of this," I said. "You aren't making it any easier for me."

"I'm giving you a choice." She swung her pink suede leg up and down. "Tell you what. Why don't you sit here, fill out your paperwork and think about it? I have a meeting that's going to take most of the afternoon, but we can get back together, say, tomorrow morning?"

"I can't do that," I said. "I want to be in Half Moon Bay tomorrow."

"Well, then." She slid from the table and gave me a lips-only smile. "Fill out your paperwork. When you decide how you feel about talking to Doug, let me know."

"I've already told you how I feel, Marie."

"Your choice—" she said, stopping at the door "—I have no control over what he writes, and neither do you. I'm offering you an opportunity to tell your side." Then she strode out past me, fluffing her hair for her next meeting.

Four

GERI

Half Moon Bay was the kind of place that you could tuck yourself into and zip shut around you, the kind of place you could disappear in, even if you had no need to disappear. I loved it the moment I drove around the curved road and glimpsed the fields of pumpkins, growing like larger-than-life wildflowers for as far as I could see. I loved the safe smallness of the main street leading into town. I loved how easily this rental car of mine could find its way, in part because there were not that many choices for it or me to make.

My former San Francisco roommate, Leta Blackburn, who'd barely escaped a murderer the year before, had married her man and left me with the apartment and her half of a prepaid lease, a gift for which I'd silently thanked her every time I turned the key in the lock. Still, the affair between the city and me was love-hate all the way. The city was more sophisticated than I, and it often played tricks on me. I could lose streets I'd walked dozens of times. I could not move fast enough to jump on a bus. And my hearing made it close to impossible to keep up with the frenetic pace.

But Half Moon Bay—even the name was as laid-back as a folk song. Not as brisk as San Francisco. Not as raped, pillaged and brutal as the San Joaquin Valley, where I'd been raised. I'd never fallen in love with a place before, and I hoped for one honest second that my meeting with Annie Montgomery, Kathleen Fowler's business partner, would match the tranquillity I felt when I glimpsed the timeless streets of this town where, if the attorney was correct, I now owned an oceanfront house and half of a nursery.

For a giddy moment, I wondered if Half Moon Blooms was one of the nurseries with pumpkins scattered beside them like fat, misshapen orange globes. Then I reminded myself that I had no idea why I'd been left anything, and until I knew that, I'd better just stop speculating and find my hotel.

That was easy to do, as well. The Half Moon Bay Inn seemed to glow in a circle of sun on this cloudy day. From the California mission architecture to the wrought-iron étagère in my room, like a baker's rack

with a glass writing desk jutting out, everything about
the inn confirmed my instinct about this community,
in spite of my reason for being here.

On the balcony, a terra-cotta pot of geraniums
looked good enough to steal. I had to chuckle at the
Mama memory. If she were here, she'd probably try
to figure out a way to *kipe* them, as she called it. I'd
be tempted myself, if they didn't look so perfect in
that spot of lingering sunlight on the balcony.

I leaned on the rail, looking out at what I could
only call grounds. Lots of green, lots of flowers, even
a whimsical bench carved like a dolphin. The rooms
were angled so you could only see neighbors to one
side of you. The top floor got balconies, and the
bottom floor got sliding doors to the lush outdoors.

I breathed the sea-spiked air and glanced at the
rooms to my right. One couple holding hands. A
man in a trench coat and hat. Or was it a woman?
And farther down, almost to the end, a sheer curtain
pulled onto the balcony. Why? It was if someone was
looking at me but didn't want me to be able to look
back. Even with the sunlight warming my arms, I
shuddered.

I followed the driving directions and found the
nursery in a matter of minutes. My fantasy hadn't
been that far off. It was on the main drive into town.
Pumpkins sprouted so abundantly that they looked
unreal, as if someone had brought in a load and scattered them haphazardly on either side of the building.

I pulled in on the gravel, stopped and got out. The place was larger than it looked. Before I could survey the entire spread, a tall, attractive woman about my age with freckled cheeks and hair so carrot-red that it had to be real, marched up to my car as if she knew who I was.

"Hi," I said, taking in her Blooms shirt. "I'm Geri LaRue." My skin got clammy, maybe because she'd made it clear that she didn't want to shake hands or exchange any other unnecessary pleasantries. "And you must be Annie."

"Annette." She looked down at her dirty gardening gloves as if they were the reason for her lack of warmth. "Annette Montgomery. I was Kathleen's partner." She struck the gloves against the legs of her jeans, knocking off the dirt. "Now I guess I'm yours."

Her lips were easy to read. I was glad, at least, for that. "It looks that way," I said.

"Want me to show you around?"

"I'd appreciate it," I said, "if you don't mind."

It would be a good excuse to find out what she knew.

"What's to mind?" She gave me the same look she'd given her dirty gloves. "The nursery covers almost five acres. It's broken up into several areas. I'll have to call Glenna—she's our assistant—to cover for me in front."

Five acres? I began to tremble but forced myself to just nod okay.

"It was supposed to be mine, you know." Having said that, she shoved that glorious hair up into the baseball cap she was carrying.

"No," I said. "I didn't know that."

"Whatever," she said, and even though I was reading her lips, I could see the anger twitch in the muscles of her face.

"Why's it supposed to be yours?" I asked.

She stopped to pinch a dead leaf off something large with vibrant red flowers. "You know how she could be," she said. Then, within the instant, tears filled her eyes. "Kathleen could giveth, but Kathleen could also taketh away. She proved that she was just a little too good too to be true."

"I don't know what you're talking about," I said. "I didn't know Kathleen."

"Don't give me that." The tears stopped, and her eyes grew cold. "Why else would she do this?"

A cloud dimmed the sky, but I would have shivered anyway. "That's what I'm here to find out," I said.

"That, and take property that should be mine." She walked into the large, open building, and I followed. A faintly familiar scent made me feel warmer, protected. It came from the counter where an older man with a shock of silver hair was helping himself from a slow cooker resting on a bed of pine.

"Cider?" I asked, feeling at that moment like an eager little kid.

"For the holidays." She left me behind and approached the man as if I were not there. "So sorry for the wait, Chev," she said. "Want to try some of our mulling spices? We grow them all here, you know." She pointed out a display of small, gauzelike bags behind the counter, and her expression was warm for the first time since I'd seen her.

"Afraid not." He had a nice but not interesting face that looked as if it belonged on a computer-dating site. "Got to watch the waistline." He patted his beige corduroy pants. "I'll have the regular. I need a little color in my life."

"Orange hibiscus?" She nodded. "We just brought them indoors. Geri, could you bring the flat up from that table over there for the coroner?"

Coroner? Damn. There were lots of tables *over there*, and lots of over theres, for that matter. I headed in the direction that she was pointing, in search of anything orange. I walked through the neatly labeled rows, stopping before a table labeled *seasonal blooms*. Daisies, zinnias, marigolds, sunflowers and gaillardias, roses and eucalyptus filled the air with earthy fragrance. Some names I knew. Most I didn't.

There, off to the side, sat a flat of flowers in such an unusual burnt orange that they almost hurt my eyes to look at them. I peered at the hand-printed stake. Sure enough, orange hibiscus. I carried the entire flat and deposited it on the counter before

Annette, who was chatting up the gray-haired coroner guy. They both stopped talking abruptly, and I got that creepy back-of-the-neck feeling that they'd been talking about me.

He moved away, as if I were contagious, more gracefully than I would have guessed. "I don't want an entire flat," he said to her with an expression that stopped short of distaste.

"No, of course not," she said with a chiding look at me. I turned my back and headed back the way I'd come. Another advantage of jacked-up hearing. Sometimes, when someone was intent on giving me a hard time, I could just turn off the radio.

I realized that other than the area next to the carts outside a supermarket and the garden and patio section of Wal-Mart, I'd never been in anything remotely resembling this place. There was a logic to it, though, and I began to pick it up as I made my way toward the back of the building.

Only it wasn't the back. A double doorway led to another room. I remembered that Annette said that the nursery covered five acres. This was probably only the first of many adjoining sections.

I stepped into a room so moist and warm that it felt tropical. Rows of ferny plants seemed to bask in the oozing air. I had to stop for a moment and get my bearings. The room didn't lead anywhere, and I'd been wandering too long. I hoped that I could find my way out of this maze without too much trouble.

Annette Montgomery didn't look like the type to offer any help if I got lost.

I took a deep breath. *Now, there's a surprise.* I couldn't hear worth a hoot, but I knew marijuana when I smelled it. Just then, I felt movement behind me. Before I could turn, a hand grabbed my shoulder.

I screamed.

The big guy facing me looked ready to bolt. He jerked his hand away from me. "What are you doing back here?" I could tell he'd asked the question before and that I hadn't heard him.

"Waiting for Annette," I managed to get out, while taking in the enormity of him and the tangled blond hair that looked like a combination of dreadlocks and braids. "She's busy with a customer." My explanation didn't faze him. He moved closer to me again, and I could see the bulge of muscles beneath his lumberjack shirt.

"Waiting in the staff-only room?" he asked.

What had I stumbled into? "I didn't see a sign," I said. "Besides—"

"Besides, what?"

If he'd wanted to harm me, he would have done so by now. I decided to go for the truth.

"In a way, I am staff," I said, then stared him down for a long, silent moment.

Only his eyes changed.

"You're that woman?" he finally asked.

"Geri LaRue," I said, since he appeared to have forgotten my name. "I was just looking around. I didn't mean to disturb anything."

He turned his back on me, and I couldn't hear the rest of it. I scrambled up beside him as he went back in the direction I had come. "What I think doesn't matter," he said, when I could finally see his lips again. "You said it right the first time. You're staff."

Annette Montgomery came around a table of ground cover so fast that she almost collided with us.

"Hey," he drawled. "Who's on the counter? Glenna?"

She nodded. "I caught her leaving food for those homeless people again. No harm, I guess, but I'm not sure I like having them hang out back there." She looked at me as if I might be one of the undesirables she was describing and added "I see that you two have met."

"Not exactly," he said.

"Then let me do the honors," she said. "Geri LaRue, meet Eric Fowler, Kathleen's son."

I should have known, but realizing that this mass of hair and muscles and marijuana smoke was Kathleen Fowler's son almost took the breath from me. "Do you work here?" I managed to utter.

"Not anymore. Why would I want to bust my ass in a place I don't own a square inch of?" I've gotten my share of nasty looks, but the one he gave me wasn't just nasty. It was cold enough to freeze every plant in the place.

"I'm sure that you think I know something about why this inheritance thing happened," I said, "but I never met your mother, and I didn't know anything about her estate until her lawyer contacted me."

"So you say," Annette replied, stretching her arm around him in a move that was all about possession.

I didn't know how to ask, so I just said, "I'm a newspaper reporter. I'm going to try to get to the bottom of it." And maybe because I was a reporter and certainly because my curiosity wouldn't let me stay quiet, I tried to penetrate the frozen layers of mixed emotions in his pale eyes and asked, "Did you and your mother have problems?"

He laughed, but there was nothing funny about the tone.

"Don't answer her," Annette said, still hanging on to him in a way that made it clear that there was more going on here than business.

I ignored her and focused on him, on his eyes. "I meant what I said about trying to get to the bottom of this," I told him, "but it's going to be a lot tougher without your help. Tell me all you can, and I promise you that I'll try to find out what happened to your mother."

"Why bother?" Annette again, pulling off the cap and shaking her hair at me like a shower of red sparks. I'd shake mine back at her if it looked like that.

"You mean why don't I just take the inheritance

and run?" I asked. "Do you think I could do that? Could you?"

"That depends," she said, but I looked back at Eric again.

"Would you do that?"

"No," he said. "But my mother—she wouldn't disinherit me. She wouldn't do that, no matter what she might have said."

"So you *were* having problems?" I asked.

"Yeah." I could see how it pained him to say it. He broke away from Annette. "Yeah, I guess you could say that." I thought he was going to say more. Instead, he turned and strode to the front of the store, leaving us behind.

"Are you happy now?" Annette asked.

"I had to find out."

"So that you could get to the *bottom* of things," she said. "Time will tell what you want to get to the bottom of. In the meantime, the business is half yours now. That means that half of the responsibilities are yours, as well."

That stopped me momentarily, but I saw her point. "That makes sense," I said. "I need to get settled. I'll be back tomorrow."

"Why don't you open up?" She took a large ring of keys from her pocket, scrunched one off and handed it to me, clearly a challenge. "I'd like to sleep in for a change."

If she thought a little lost sleep was going to chase

me off, she was dead wrong. "You do that," I said. "I'll be here early tomorrow." There would be time to deal with her. Right now I had more important things to worry about, like why Kathleen Fowler picked me, for starters.

We found Eric outside standing next to a vine-covered fence leading to an old clapboard house farther back. His hair looked even more tangled in the breeze. He turned when he heard me approach. I wasn't sure if his red-rimmed eyes were the result of what he'd been smoking or tears. Both maybe.

"I'm sorry," I said. "I have trouble with my mother, too, but it doesn't change the love. I'm not trying to judge you. I just want to help."

"You want to help?" he asked, and the pain in his eyes hardened into anger again. "Then why don't you help me figure out why my mother would disinherit me to leave everything to some newspaper reporter I've never heard of?"

"I wish I could," I said, but he was already walking toward the house, his back to me.

TINY

Some nights were so cold that the best you could hope for the next morning was to wake up alive. Tiny knew how, though. She'd been waking up alive a long time in any number of places. For tonight, this old shed on the far end of a field would work just fine. The nice woman from the nursery would leave out food for them tomorrow, pretending she didn't know they were there.

Propped up beside her on the upstairs loft, Tiny's friend, Sunlight, pinched the glowing joint in her fingers, sucked the smoke into her lungs, held it as long as she could, yanked her knitted cap off her head and shouted, "*Muth*-er!"

Was she the only sane one in this outfit? "Careful," Tiny whispered. "You don't know who's out there."

"*I* know." Sunlight tried to talk around the smoke, and once she managed to, her voice was rattier than usual. "I crashed here more times than you can count. Makes it my place, dig? You ought to be thanking me right now, 'stead of bitching."

"And no one comes to check?" Tiny still couldn't quite believe it. No matter where you were, someone always came to check.

"Not as long as I've been crashing here. The rich bitch owns the place never makes it out this far back." Sunlight shoved her cap back on with one hand and stared a long time at the lifeless roach. "Just don't tell no one else about it, okay?"

"Who you think I'll tell?" Tiny asked, patting the layers of plastic packing material covering her arms. "The mayor, maybe? The city council? Those artsy-fartsies at the theater downtown?"

"Don't knock the theater." Sunlight pulled her blue cap down over her ears.

"I never had ten minutes of decent sleep in that place," Tiny said.

"Well, I have. Besides, they leave shit out after they party. One night I snagged me a case of Rolling Rock and three Costco cheesecakes."

"Good for you." That's all Sunlight ever thought about—where to snag the next whatever. Tiny just wanted a little sleep in some place warm enough, without worrying about someone coming in and chasing her out. Or worse. "Can we get some rest now?" she asked.

"What'd you say?"

Sunlight blinked, and Tiny realized that she was drifting off, anyway. Good. Tiny slid down under the plastic blankets. Finally, they could get some sleep, crunched in among these old farm tools. Agricultural implements, Sunlight had called them.

Tiny's years on the road had taught her that it was best to sleep next to another living creature—long as you trusted that creature. Did she trust Sunlight? No reason not to. She'd gotten her out of the alley behind the theater, hadn't she?

She was almost asleep when she heard the noise.

It came to her first as a squeak, then as a scrape. She'd been right. Someone always came to check. Sunlight slept right through it, but Tiny knew. She felt the presence through her whole body.

The door below crept open, and a slice of light cut into the room. Tiny glanced again at the lump that was Sunlight and prayed she wouldn't wake up right now. She held her own breath and tried to see who had just slipped inside the shed. Maybe another one of them, but she didn't think so.

Below them, someone slammed around the containers on the bottom floor. Then, Tiny heard a creak. *No!* Whoever it was had started climbing the stairs. She reached down and pulled the tarp over them. Sunlight stirred. Tiny clasped her hands over Sunlight's mouth.

It was all she could do to stop the sputtering. "Shut up," she whispered, lifting the cap and speaking into Sunlight's ear. "Someone's in here. Shut your mouth, okay?"

The head she held nodded. Good. But now what?

The steps came up closer to them. To her. If it was one of theirs, they'd know what was under the tarp. These steps slowed down before they got there.

Something rattled, a drawer maybe. Then all Tiny heard was a sigh. Or maybe she'd made it up. She could make up things she wanted to hear. She wasn't making up the steps, though, the sound of someone leaving this place.

Finally, the door below swished open. Tiny rushed to the edge of the loft and tried to see who walked through it. But this one was too fast for her. She rushed down the stairs, but by the time she got to the front window, all she saw was a long dark raincoat and the jug that had been by the door, swinging now in the pale hand beneath the coat sleeve.

"Who was it?" Sunlight stood halfway down the steps as if ready to take off in either direction if she had to. "A cop?"

"No." Tiny's skin tingled with the cold. "No cop," she said. "Whoever it was took the jug that was sitting here and hauled ass."

"What jug?" Sunlight came down the rest of the way, her watery eyes with that hungry look she always had. "You think there was booze in it? Maybe there's more."

"There's nothing here," Tiny said, peering into the cobweb curtain that covered the rusted gardening tools and a few bottles that no one had opened for years. "This is where the jug was. Right here."

"You mean that old yellow thing with the plastic handle?" Sunlight asked in a voice so ticked off that Tiny wondered if she'd really expected something of value. "I saw it when we came in. That wasn't booze in there, honey."

"I know that," Tiny said. "Who'd leave free booze in a place like this?"

"Shit." That seemed to be Sunlight's favorite word. She threw open the door, and the cold rushed in. That didn't stop Sunlight, though. "There's someone out there," she said. "Come on. Let's kick ass."

"Be careful, will you?" Tiny shuddered, unable to move a step. "I'm not going anywhere," she said, but Sunlight was already gone.

"Hang on a minute, asshole. This is my place, get

it?" Sunlight's rough cigarette voice sounded swallowed up by the wind.

Tiny closed the door but couldn't talk herself into going back upstairs. It wasn't long before Sunlight came back, slamming the door behind her, wet hair streaming down her back.

"Shit," she said. "Whoever it was knows how to hide out here. One minute I saw someone clear as day. Next, I didn't."

"Why'd you go out there?" Tiny asked. "You could have gotten killed."

Sunlight threw off her wet jacket. "I told you I don't let no one take over my places," she said. "I was here first, get it?"

"Sure," Tiny said. "Don't get all worked up, now."

Sunlight patted her right hip. "Anyone coming in here tonight's going to have serious shit to deal with." She gave Tiny a look that said that might mean her, too.

"All I want is a little sleep," Tiny said. "Could you tell if it was a man or a woman out there?"

Sunlight shook her head. "The coat was too big. Couldn't tell shit."

"You don't think they'll come back?"

"No way." Sunlight headed for the stairs, still patting her hip. "I wish they'd try it, though."

She started up the stairs, and Tiny followed. "You don't really think they stole booze out of here, do you?"

"Shit, no." Sunlight stopped and looked back at the downstairs window as if she could see the person who'd left with the jug. "I told you that wasn't booze in there."

"What was it then?"

The grin on Sunlight's dirty face almost made Tiny wish she hadn't asked.

"Not booze," she said. "Poison."

Five

ANNIE

What the county coroner's office lacked in size, it made up for in substance. Chevron Parnell never threw away anything. He had chairs on chairs. He had nesting tables upon nesting tables. He had photos. Most of all, he had photos. As Annette helped him unpack his order from Blooms, which took the remaining square footage, she wondered if there weren't regulations against accumulating this much clutter in the office of the coroner. And she tried to figure out how to ask him what she must without falling apart.

Chev fiddled with the CD player in his computer, and the sounds of a woman's voice stole into the room, bringing the blues with her. "Since I Fell for You." Heartbreak lyrics laced through a voice that belonged in church. "Coffee?" he asked in a soft-spoken way that managed to convey his appreciation that she was there. "You've got to have something after driving all the way out here with me."

"No thank you, please," she said. "That government coffee makes me cranky."

"We wouldn't want to do that."

She got the implication, although he was too refined to do more than imply, and she was too polite to call him on it. He stood watching her, a bushy eyebrow cocked, as if to see how far she would take it.

"It's not easy," she said. "Having a stranger come in and take over what I've worked for."

He shook his head and settled into his old-fashioned wood swivel chair, putting his feet out to face her. In spite of the distinguished air and white shirt and tie, his neck looked a little too long and thin, his hair a little too puffy. Something about his straight posture reminded her of a silver poodle following a command to sit pretty.

"It can't be," he agreed. "I don't know what possessed Kathleen. Do you have any idea at all?"

"Not in the least. We were partners." She spit out the word, realizing how bitter she sounded. "I could have gone anywhere, done anything, but I believed her when she said I had a future there."

"What will you do now?" he asked.

"I can tell you what I won't do. I won't give up without a fight." Chev drew back, and she realized that she'd said more than she meant to. This was not the time to lose control. She stared down at his shoes, boots really, some kind of reptile skin. "I mean that I'm not backing down," she said, keeping her voice even.

"The young woman did seem nice enough." She reminded herself that he was basically a politician who didn't really know Kathleen or her, let alone Geri LaRue. He had no idea how she felt to have half of all she'd worked for yanked away from her.

A lucky bamboo plant with a long-deflated Happy Birthday balloon attached to it threatened to take over his back bookcase. She got up and removed the balloon as much to hide her face from him as anything else.

"Mind if I pinch back this plant?" she asked.

"As long as it doesn't change my luck."

"It will probably increase it," she said. "Buy a lottery ticket on your way home tonight. What about this balloon? Can I toss it, or does it have sentimental significance?"

"It all has sentimental significance," he said, waving a hand across the office. "That's my problem. I'm a pack rat."

She glanced at the photos on the shelf. Young man, nice tush, white-blond burst of hair, spinning on roller skates as if born to it. How had that taut body melted into this one? For a moment, she envied him his framed memories. In his mind, he was probably still that boy. Annie realized that he was

watching her and said, "You were very handsome." It
wasn't a lie but a kindness. There was a softness to
him even then. Don't let him be too soft for what she
was asking.

"Thank you."

"Kathleen had a lot of respect for you," she said,
still fiddling with the plant. How phony that
sounded, even to her.

"And I for her," he said, and the doubt in his voice
was overpowered by the bluesy voice on the CD.

"I realize that," she said. "I know that you must be
devastated by what happened."

"What is it?" She turned then and saw the question
in his eyes.

"I can't do this by myself." She needed to get out
of this stuffy room and run down the hall sobbing.
But what would she do then? "Sorry," she said. "This
isn't the way I planned it."

"You planned this?" He looked taken aback,
looking from her to the plants they had carried in
that now rested on the carpet beside his desk.

She perched on the edge of the only empty chair
in the room. "I'm not saying what I mean. I'm sorry.
I still can't believe this is happening." He continued
to sit, watchful, as if trying to predict how distressed
she was. She'd planned on doing this in a casual
way—one businessperson asking a favor of another.
Now it was too late for that. "It's Geri LaRue," she
said. "She claims that she never even met Kathleen."

"Indeed?" That got his attention.

"That's right. And I don't buy it. Furthermore, if she did know her, why wouldn't she admit it? What's she trying to hide?"

"Both good questions," he said, still stroking the frame of a photo he'd taken from the shelf.

"I need your help, Chev. I don't know where else to turn. You've always been so decent, such a gentleman." *Don't lay it on too thick.* She had to cool it, look him in the eyes, be professional.

"What do you need me to do?"

"Help me find out about Geri LaRue," Annie said. "You know everyone in Northern California, and everyone knows you. I want to find out who she is, what she is, and what we can do about her."

"But I'm no detective." He replaced the photo, carefully dusting the frame with his sleeve, although it was already spotless. "And as you pointed out, I'm a public figure. I can't be involved in anything untoward."

"Please," she said. "I'll pay you." Pay him with what? she thought. But he wasn't interested in her offer anyway.

"Don't be silly," he said. "You know I'd help you if I could." *Could.* Past tense.

"That's okay." This wasn't going to happen. This man had been sitting in that wooden swivel chair in his white python boots for too many years to get off his ass for anyone. "I shouldn't have asked."

The singer with the tears in her voice was belting out "Stormy Monday." Annie stood. "Tuesday's twice as bad," she said.

"Not necessarily." He stood as well. "I told you I'm no detective," he said.

"I understand."

"But I have a friend who is."

"You do?"

"Let me talk to him," he said.

"Why?" she asked, unwilling to trust his words.

He glanced over at the photo of the boy again, then back at her. "At some point, I have to walk the walk," he said. "But you have to promise me this."

"Of course." She'd promise him anything to get his help.

"No one can know that I'm involved in this," he said. "I could lose my job. Promise me you won't tell anyone, not even your fiancé."

She didn't have to tell Eric how she was getting Geri LaRue. As long as she got her, that was all that mattered. "I promise," she said.

"You know how important it is," he said. "I retire in less than a year. If anything happened—"

She cut him off. "I know how to keep a promise," she said.

GERI

For the rest of the day, I explored. I drove past the elegant, understated home that was supposed to be mine now, but I didn't have the nerve even to knock on the door. Perched on a sloping patch of green overlooking a sharp drop to the ocean, it wore weathered brown shingles with a sense of timeless pride that felt almost New England, a place I'd experienced only through media. Could I ever live there, and if I did, would I see the ghost of Kathleen Fowler staring through every one of those porthole windows?

I not only drove the roads of Half Moon Bay—I walked the streets, as well. Somewhere here, I might find out my connection to the Fowler woman. I'd keep looking until I did, and not because I wanted a story out of it.

My tour of the town and my solo dinner in a nearby tapas place recommended by the desk clerk at the hotel reminded me of how alone I was. A tapas bar can temporarily disguise a single person within a pressed-close crowd of elbows and knees and overlapping platters of fried calamari, herbed goat cheese and prosciutto shrimp. But when the people on either side of you start talking about jazz and after-dinner drinks, and you pay your tab and stand up, no one, least of all you, is fooled, after all.

I returned to the room about eight that night, thinking that other than being odd woman out at a tapas bar, nothing can remind you of how alone you are like a bed that is clearly meant for two. I remembered that there was a bar downstairs, but I was still embarrassed about trying to order Henry Weinhard's root beer at dinner. I didn't want to repeat the affront here, and I wasn't in the mood for grown-up drinks.

No, I was sad. Sad because I was alone in a new place, attractive as it was. Sad about the separation I could feel between Marie, the newspaper and me. And, yeah, sad that I'd lost Malc, a man I could have loved, probably did love, even now.

I was staring at the telephone beside the way-big king-size bed, wondering if I dared to call him, when I heard it.

It came to me as a sound, although it had to be something else—a feeling, a smell, maybe. Something had fallen, or someone had made a noise in the bathroom just beside my spot by the phone.

Crikey. I was scaring myself. No way could anyone be in my room. Just then, I remembered looking out earlier at the guests on their balconies. One of them had been staring at me. The gaze was so intense that I'd tried to ignore the chills that had crept through me. Now I had to do something. I took off my jacket, threw it on the unmade bed and dug in my purse for my cell phone. Then I punched in 911 and poised my finger over the call button.

The bathroom door was cracked, partially opened. Was that how I'd left it? If only I had Nathan with me. He'd go into a barking frenzy if anyone came near. Now it was up to me. All I had to do was walk in there and I'd know. And what if someone was in there? What if someone had been inside my room when I'd returned? I'd better open the front door, just in case. I threw it open, then forced myself to approach the bathroom. I touched the door with my toe and it swung forward.

The light was off, but even before my eyes grew accustomed to the shadows, I knew that no one was inside. I let myself sigh and flipped on the bathroom light. No one. Nothing. I'd made all of this up, freaked myself out, with my overactive imagination.

Something had been wrong about the room, though. Something still was.

Gooseflesh sprouted on my neck and along my arms. I shuddered and realized that cold air was streaming in from somewhere. I looked up, and yes, the vent close to the ceiling gaped open. It was long, narrow, but still wide enough for someone to slip through. Someone had.

I ran outside, no longer afraid. The person who'd violated my room was afraid of me. I was now the pursuer. "Stop," I screamed, although I saw no one. And again, "Stop."

Something jumped at me from the shadows. I felt the flap of fabric like wings of a bat against my face. Before I could move, I was slammed down against the pavement. My ears rang. I tried to find my feet and couldn't. Tried to lift my head. Couldn't. But I was able to turn in time to see the tennis shoes running away from me.

Fighting blackness, I squinted and looked up, trying to focus on a face, as the form I couldn't identify as male or female bolted for the stairs.

Six

The figure watched the bearlike man, the man who said he hated this business, but loved it. Kathy Jo's son was pruning today, early, perhaps because he didn't want to be seen. He'd been there all week, except that Friday. He didn't prune then.

He reached high into the heart of a thick, tall bush, his hair pulled back, his muscular arms working the chainsaw with violent precision. The stalks fell down around the ladder, brushing the ground.

The small, uniformed figure hid behind the old house and measured how far the man would fall. This was the chase part, the toying that was almost unbearable with pleasure. Kathy Jo's son hummed as he worked. He had no idea what was about to happen to him.

ERIC

The mornings here smelled of hope, and he could use a little of that right now. As he moved the chainsaw through the overgrowth, Eric thought about Annie, about how she'd changed since his mom's death. More secretive, yeah, that was part of it, and more fragile, ready to burst into tears or fly into a rage at any time. Geri LaRue's fault. Ever since she got there, Annie had started falling apart. He couldn't blame her. None of the estate stuff made any sense, and he knew she felt responsible because of the way his mom had felt about their engagement.

He was a fool to keep coming here, but he did it for Annie, and yeah, for his mom. She had to have had a reason for what she did, and Geri LaRue had to know why.

The ladder wobbled beneath him, and he fought to steady himself, reached out for a branch, but it cracked in his hand. Something was wrong. The ladder groaned, rocked as if trying to shake him off.

"What the hell?"

His first thought was earthquake. Spiked leaves scratched his face. He dropped the chainsaw, and as he felt his feet leave the wooden rung, clung to a larger branch. The ladder crashed. He gripped tighter, but the branch burned into his flesh. He couldn't hold on much longer. Better to just let go and hope to hell he didn't break anything going down.

He heard a scream, a shout, the breaking of wood. And he let go.

GERI

The sun blinded me to the scene before my eyes— a flash of fabric disappearing behind the old house. Then, as I slammed on the brakes of my car, a body seemed to fall directly in front of me. He landed tangled in the ladder that had collapsed beneath him. Crikey. There was no mistaking the blond hair and huge, sprawled form of Eric Fowler. For a moment, I thought the worst. Then I saw him stir, and I jumped out of the car and ran to him.

Blood oozed out of a cut on his face, and his leg lay at such an unnatural angle that I was afraid it was broken. But he was moving, trying to prop himself up. Alive, thank goodness.

The chainsaw pulsed too close for comfort. It must have fallen out of the tree with him.

"How do I turn it off?" I cried out to him.

"I'll do it," he said, but when he tried to move, his mouth pinched up, and I knew that he was in more pain than he pretended.

I crouched down beside him. "You're okay," I said. "Don't move yet. Let me get help."

"Help?" His voice was harsh and broken, and the only way I could make out the words was to watch his lips. "I didn't fall off that ladder, lady."

"I know," I said, and with a creepy chill, remembered the figure I'd seen. Was that person the same one who broke into my room? "I saw someone," I told him.

"I saw someone, too," he said, and pulled himself to his feet like a man crawling out of a car wreck. "I saw you."

Then I realized what he was trying to pull. He couldn't possibly believe that I had knocked down the ladder. "The person I saw took off behind the house," I said. And before he could hit me with more accusations, "Someone broke into my room last night."

He shut up at that one, turned off the chainsaw, then touched the gash on his face with a wince. "You're the only person I saw," he said.

"And when did you see me? Not when the ladder was coming down. I was just pulling into the drive."

"Why are you here so early?" he asked with more defiance than I could handle.

"So that your girlfriend can sleep in," I shot back. "She asked me to open up, and that's the only reason I'm here."

I'm not sure if he was starting to believe me, or if he was just weary and freaked by what had happened, but he gave me something close to a smile.

"Let's go inside," he said, swiping a hand through a mat of hair that had whipped across his face. "I just put the cider on to heat in front."

The thought of it pleased me, in spite of the fact that I needed a caffeine fix far more than apple anything. I'd wiped out the coffee in my room after the intruder had gotten away. All that was left for breakfast was a couple of raspberry tea bags intended for those who take their habit less seriously than I do.

After we'd walked a few slow steps through the sugary scent of some flowering vine along the fence, he said, "Annie's not my girlfriend, by the way."

"She's not?" I asked.

"No," he said.

"You could have fooled me."

"She's my fiancée."

He looked as if he expected a comment, so I said, "For how long?"

"About eight months."

I didn't want to think about the longest I'd ever had a relationship, and I tried to keep Malc's face from my mind. "When's the wedding?" I asked.

"We haven't set a date, especially now with all that's happened."

But they'd had eight months to set that date. I looked at his pained expression, at the bloody trickling line across one eyebrow, and decided to keep that thought to myself.

"How'd your mom feel about it?" I asked.

He stopped and gave me that look again, letting the chainsaw hang at his side. "You know, don't you?"

"Know what?" I asked, trying to read his thoughts as well as his speech.

"You knew my mom or you talked to her, or she got in touch with you for some reason," he said, stepping back from the door to take me in with his eyes. "You just know too much."

"I'm guessing," I said, "that's all. I mean, you've been engaged for months. You haven't set a date. You had trouble with your mom. It was worth asking, but only a guess, honest."

"She wouldn't leave all this to you without a reason," he said. "She never did anything without a reason. What is it? Do you know Jesse? Is he involved in this?"

"Jesse Medicine?" I asked, recalling one of the skimpy details I'd managed to retrieve of Kathleen Fowler's life—her ex-husband. "Your dad, right?"

"You ever seen the dude?" he asked, all attitude and swagger. But the swagger was accompanied by a limp he was trying to hide, and the attitude was less convincing with the blood crusting on his face.

"I've heard of him." I didn't mention that I'd only heard about the wonder boy Native American painter turned commercial artist after I'd collided headfirst into Kathleen Fowler's life.

"If you'd seen him, you'd know he wasn't my father," he said. "He's only ten years older than I am." He lifted the chainsaw as easily as if it were a weight in the gym, and I was aware again of his almost unconscious strength.

"Younger man, older woman?" I asked.

"Something like that."

"Did she always date younger guys?" I asked.

"After Jesse, she didn't date anyone," he said.

"Why not?"

"You know how it goes." He shrugged. "Couldn't live with him, couldn't live without him."

"He was tough to live with?" I asked.

"For her, he was."

"And was she tough to live with?"

He nodded. "She could be the sweetest person in the world when she wanted to be. But lately, hell." He rubbed his head and squinted as if in pain.

I'd come here only because I'd promised Annette that I'd open the nursery today, and I'd already learned more than I could process.

I looked back at the ladder and the large holes it had left in the mud. "You know that I didn't do this, don't you?" I asked.

He shrugged, upsetting stray puffs of hair. "Maybe you did. Maybe you didn't. I was damn near passed out. No way can I remember what I saw or heard."

"Do you really think I could have wrestled that thing to the ground and come out of it without a hair out of place?" Once I said it, I had to chuckle. "Guess it's hard to tell when my hair's out of place," I said before he could. "We have that in common."

I was trying for a smile, some camaraderie, but he was too busy checking me out to appreciate my effort. "You don't have any mud on you," he said, making it clear that he was studying me. "You would have."

"Finally," I said. "You're starting to hear what I've been trying to tell you."

"And you really don't know Jesse? He's not involved in this?"

"Why would he be?" I asked. "Aren't he and your mother divorced?"

"Technically," he said, "but you'd never know it if you saw them together."

"I wonder how he's going to feel about all this." I gestured toward the silver-taupe planks of the nursery that stood before us, but I really meant me. I wondered how Kathleen's former husband would feel about his ex-wife's change of estate.

Eric took out a single key, and I couldn't help but notice how different his style was than in-your-face Annie with her cluster on the key ring.

"Jesse Medicine doesn't care about the bucks," he said. "He has plenty of his own, thanks to that ad agency of his. He only started the business to prove that he wasn't after my mom for her money."

"And you?" I asked.

"You're asking me if I have any money?"

I flushed, realizing that was just what I was asking.

"Not exactly. I mean, I assume the plan was for you to help your mother with her business."

"And now you've got half of the future I'd planned." He clenched the chainsaw, then tossed it beside the building. "At least she insisted that I get an education. Right now, I'm substitute teaching."

I looked at his hair and said, "Teaching, huh?"

He yanked at a pale strand. "I pin it back, okay? Teaching isn't my thing, but I'll be damned if I'll work at a place that isn't mine."

"Except to come in early for a little pruning?" I asked, in what I tried to make a nonchalant voice. Problem with not being able to hear my own voice very well was I could never be sure how the tone came out. Nonchalant to me could be smug to him, and from the look on his face, that might be the case.

We stepped inside, and I realized that I was almost happy to breathe in the scent of life that filled this place. If I had to inherit something from a stranger, I was glad that it was this and not a slaughterhouse or a collection agency.

"I'm going to call Annie," he said as we reached the counter. "You grab us some cider, and maybe our brains will work better. Annie needs to get down here, and the three of us need to talk. We need to figure out why anyone would try to knock down my ladder, and we—"

He stopped, and the look of horror on his face

made me want to run out of the door we'd just entered. "What is it?" I asked, but he was already crossing the room to a table of plants. I started to follow, then saw it, too. It wasn't just one plant—it was container after container, table after table. Hundreds. I moved closer and saw it, too. The plants that had been vibrant green and as cheerfully colored as gumdrops the day before lay bleached and limp against their beds of soil.

"How?" I managed to ask, but there was no way to stop Eric now. He bounced from bed to bed, shouting, cursing. I didn't move from the first aisle. I couldn't bear to view any more of the little murders in this place. And they were just that. Someone had murdered the plants.

Seven

JESSE

Something was wrong with the house. Something had been wrong with the house since he'd lost her. The noises of emptiness kept him awake most of the night, even when he tried to drink them away. This was different, though, something audible. Someone on the balcony.

Jesse got up and placed his ear against the wall next to his bedroom window. Someone moved steadily closer to the French doors. What might have been a human form shimmered behind the sheer drape.

In one movement, he grabbed the handle and yanked the door open.

"Who's there?" he shouted.

Not a sound. He couldn't have imagined it. Not again. The salsa garden on the balcony, the one Kath had given him and nurtured even after the split, mocked him from its clustered pots arranged to catch the morning sun. He imagined the plants and himself, at this moment, as a painting. How does a naked man appear to a community of cilantro, jalapeños, tomatoes, garlic and onions when he crashes from his bedroom at dawn, calling out to ghosts? The painting, if it worked, would speak of sanity or the lack of it. But of course, there would be no painting for Jesse Medicine, the chief of Medicine Avenue Advertising Agency, only more commercial art to crank out.

The agency was for Kath, to prove his worth, but that excuse was as much a fantasy as those in his paintings. You don't leave art for someone. You leave because— Well, that's one he wished he could discuss with Sheldon.

He was working on a layout when the woman came into the shop later that morning. She didn't make a sound, but he became aware of an encompassing scent that reminded him of something delicate, rain maybe.

He looked up from his computer, and there she was, looking nothing like her scent, but in some ways, more so. The spiked purple hair detracted from her almond-shaped eyes that were so flecked with gold and brown that his fingers ached for the right mix of paints to capture them. Her hair was manic, her unsmiling lips calm. She'd already poured herself a cup of coffee from the urn on the counter, and she lifted it to her lips before she spoke.

"Are you Jesse Medicine?" she asked in a flat voice, staring just a little too hard. What was off about her?

"I am." He got up from the computer and went to the counter, where she stood, hands clasped around the coffee cup like a kid in elementary school.

He could spot the real estate agents a mile off; the developers' wives, too, with their expressions of bored prettiness. This one didn't look like either. "What can I do for you?" he asked.

"My name," she said, "is Geri LaRue. I guess that kind of says it."

His first impulse was pain. But then, that was all he'd felt since he'd heard the news, since he'd attended that so-called memorial for Kath. Then he got mad. He'd pictured The LaRue, as he labeled her in his head, as a money-obsessed monster scheming to take over Kath's life. This little girl looked as stunned by what had happened as he was. "You're not what I expected," he said, which was at least the truth. The LaRue in his mind was a combination of talons and sneer and a face of cerulean blue. Like one of his paintings, the paintings he'd abandoned.

She gazed at his lips as he spoke, but with something more desperate than what he at first had taken for mild interest, maybe even attraction. "And you're not what I expected," she replied. "How often do you smile?"

"About as often as you do." Then he got it, just like that. Leaning close to her over the counter, close enough for her to read his lips without straining, he said, "My youngest sister is deaf, too."

The minute it registered, he knew that he shouldn't have put it that way. "Oh, I can hear," she said in a chilly voice, "but not very well. Your sister is better off being deaf, if she really is. That's a close, safe community. Better than trying to live between the two worlds."

"Easy for you to say," he shot back, not sure why he was angry, only knowing that he did not want to like this woman in the drab khaki pants and black turtleneck.

"Just my opinion."

"And," he said, as her earlier remark registered, "what the hell do you mean *if she really is?* Do you think I'd make up something like that just to impress you?"

"I didn't mean for it to come out that way." She flushed, and he realized that he enjoyed being the cause. How sick was that? "It's just that I was surprised," she said. "Very few people know that I read lips."

"You're ashamed of it?" he asked, trying to keep the contempt from his voice.

"No, I'm not." The color in her face was no longer

from embarrassment. "I don't like the extra attention and concessions that go along with having the people I work with think I'm different," she said. "Perhaps you can understand that."

"Of course I can," he said, trying to back out of it.

"And for the record, the people who matter to me know," she said. "I don't owe anyone else anything." She hit the *anyone else* hard enough to let him know that he was included in that group.

"I understand," he said, partially to end the confrontation, partially because he was beginning to like her attitude. He'd like it more if it were not directed at him. "Bad start," he said. "Let me try to make it better." Then he thought of a way to prolong their conversation without the tension. "I'm working on some signs for an event I have to attend tomorrow night," he said. "Nights of Lights. Have you heard of it?"

"Should I?" she asked. Of course she hadn't. This was probably her first trip to Half Moon Bay. Don't go there, he told himself. This was not the time to start spouting off about the natives here. Not the time to spout off about Kath.

"No big deal," he told her. "I just thought you might be interested. Several of the nursery's clients are involved."

"What is it?" She leaned forward as if sensing the invitation he was still trying to script in his head.

"Basically, the shops all stay open later so they can

make the most of the holiday traffic. There are horse-and-buggy rides and street performers, and a parade of kids wearing strands of lights." As he spoke, he knew how pathetically lame both the event and he must sound to her, and he was ashamed to admit that, money aside, his career had been reduced to this. "I also did the posters for Albee Week at the community theater." He nodded toward the one on the counter. How pathetic was that, and why was he doing his best to impress her? Time to shut his mouth.

She took her time looking at the poster for *Who's Afraid of Virginia Woolf?* and said, "I like it. I saw one for another play in front of the theater yesterday. *Albee Week, All Week,* it read."

"They feature a playwright once a year." He forced himself to stop with just that. What did Kath used to call him? Stoic? Terse? He sure wasn't today.

"And you do the posters?"

"Yeah." No reason to explain. Just keep his mouth shut. If he were more than what she saw in this shop, he'd be doing, not talking.

"And that light thing, too?" she asked, as if still not convinced.

"That, too," he said. The signs were due in less than an hour. He needed to get moving. "It will be easier for us to talk then when I'm not trying to work. I'm guessing you have questions about Kath, and I can't do them justice right now."

"Are you saying you want me to go to this thing with you?"

She didn't look thrilled by the prospect. How could he answer that one? He leaned across the counter. "We have to talk," he said. "About Kath. You know that."

"Yes?" She said it as a question.

"And since you own part of the nursery now, you need to get out and meet people. One of the reasons that Half Moon Blooms is so successful is the fact that—" He stopped himself short of saying because Kath was so willing to involve herself in the community.

"Tomorrow night's a long time away." She made it sound part promise, part complaint.

"I'm willing to wait if you are." So, he was flirting with her? Flirting was cheap, a hell of a lot cheaper than other situations he'd experienced all too recently. Besides, they did need to talk.

She shoved her rectangular glasses up and tilted her head as if trying to make the decision. "I'm on leave from the newspaper, so I don't have a lot of time to, well—"

Waste, he heard in the unfinished sentence that still dangled between them.

"But you won't work there anymore, will you?" he asked, trying to figure her out. Considering the size of the inheritance she'd snag from Kath's estate, why would she choose to work—unless she was planning to write about her experience as Kath's beneficiary? She could be taking mental notes at this very moment.

"The newspaper's all I know," she said. "Like breathing. I wouldn't know how to live without it."

He believed her. "So you're not going to stay here and run the nursery?" he asked. That's what Annie and Eric had told him. How wrong could they have been, and where were they getting their information?

"I don't know anything about nurseries," she said. "Besides—"

"What?"

She shook her head. "I need to get going. I know you're busy."

He was busy, all right, with the numerous projects that now defined him as much as a portrait could. Real estate brochures. Nights of Lights. Who's Afraid of Edward Albee?

"You are what you art," Sheldon had told him once, in true mentor fashion when Sheldon had gotten him the gig helping him etch glass in Las Vegas casinos. *You are what you art.* He was then, and he was now. No illusions in an industry, and even an office, full of them. He'd thought of Geri as The LaRue, a monster that would try to take over Kath's life. Now he didn't know what he thought.

She had turned her head to look at the photo of Kath and him that he kept on the counter. His shaved head gave him a fierce look that Kath said he used to keep people at bay. He liked this photo because of his eyes, because of how full of love they were. Looking at his face, at hers, brought back the love, if only for a moment.

Geri glanced from it to him and said nothing.

"See you tomorrow at six," he said as she headed for the door.

"What?"

He'd forgotten. He waited until she had turned completely and could see his lips. "Six o'clock, tomorrow," he said. "I'll pick you up."

"I'll meet you there," she mouthed back, as if he were the one who couldn't hear. Then she started to turn toward the door and stopped, her gaze riveted to the painting. "Oh," she said with a little gasp as if she'd stepped inside it and felt the emotion. "Who did this?"

"Native American artist," he replied.

"I don't know much about art." She moved closer, turning her head at various angles and then back to him. "Tell me about this. Why is the animal's face blue?"

"I don't know," he said. "There's a primitive vein in many Native American artists that makes them paint semi abstractly."

"And this one is—" She looked back at him with an unreadable expression. "The signature is 'Medicine,'" she said.

"Imagine that."

"You painted this?"

"A long time ago."

"It's wonderful. You know that, don't you?"

Of course he knew it. What more was there to say, what more to mourn?

"See you tomorrow," he said. "The parade's starting at the newspaper office. I'll meet you there. Once it's under way, we can get a drink or some coffee, whatever you like."

"Fine," she said, but she didn't look fine. She looked disoriented.

"What is it?" he asked.

"I don't know," she said. "I need to go now."

But she wasn't walking right. Something had slowed and wobbled her step. He thought of Kath. He couldn't help it. If he'd been there that day, if he hadn't moved out, she might still be alive. "What's wrong?" he asked.

"I think I'd better sit down."

He got to her just in time and eased her into a chair. Her face had turned the color of ashes, and her skin felt as if she'd just stepped out of a sauna. When she looked up at him, her pupils were pinpoints, almost invisible.

"I'm sorry," she said. "My head. It feels like it's exploding."

Not again. He had to take action right now, anything to try to help.

"I'm going to call emergency," he said.

"No, please. It's not that bad. I think I can get up."

"Don't even try."

She began to shudder. "Please don't call anyone. I'm okay. I really am."

"I've got to," he told her, crossing the room for the phone. "You just stay right there, and I'm going to get someone to come help you."

"So sorry." She pulled her knees up close to her chest and curled over them. "I don't even know you. You shouldn't have to do this."

"Take it easy, will you?" he said. "Just be quiet."

He called the emergency number and was comforted when the dispatcher answered with his address.

"That's it," he said. "Please get them here as fast as you can. My friend's really sick."

With that, Geri moaned and tried to pull herself out of the chair. "Your friend?" Had she been able to read his lips, as sick as she was? Before he could ask or try to calm her, she struggled to her feet and almost made it to the door before she crumpled on the floor.

He was afraid to lift her, so he crouched beside her on the floor, making sure that she could see his face. "You are going to be okay, Geri. They will be here any moment."

It was a little-kid face that looked back at him. "Now you're making me scared."

"Don't be." He stroked her face, tracing her eyebrows, imagining that he was erasing pain with every touch. "Don't be afraid. I'm right here."

He no longer cared if she heard him or if she understood. He didn't even care that she'd come into his life because of Kath's death. All he cared about right now was that he was going to save this woman.

Eight

GERI

Had Jesse Medicine really been so kind to me? So concerned?

I woke up on my stomach, smelling the bleached hotel sheets the next morning, with those questions in my mind. My right hand dangled from the side of the made-for-two bed, searching for Nathan.

Nathan, who was still staying at Steffan's place.

Staying at Steffan's because I'd thought I'd be back in a day or two.

Because I didn't believe that any of this estate thing could be real. It was real, and if figuring it out was to be a long-term job, I needed Nathan with me.

Had Jesse Medicine really been so darned nice?

It had been one sick night, and even before it got

sicker, the medical folks Jesse had summoned said my symptoms were similar to poisoning. Luckily, I hadn't ingested enough of the poison, if that's what it was, to have my stomach pumped. In California, you have to be on death's doorstep, as Mama would say, or have great insurance to end up in a hospital. I was out before I was in, but now I was woozy. As I got out of bed, I tried to figure out how I could have been poisoned enough to impair me but not enough for the medical folks to determine the source.

I'd tried harder than they had and had come up with three possibilities. There had been the cup of raspberry tea in this very room from this very basket where I was contemplating choosing another. There had been coffee at Jesse's office, and before that, cider at the nursery with Eric. That was all I'd had.

I stood on wobbly legs and surveyed the sealed tea bag. No way could anything bad get inside that package. Just to be on the safe side, not to mention because I so needed a hit of caffeine, I replaced the tea in the basket and ordered two espressos and a bagel from room service. Maybe, if this morning played out a shade better than yesterday, I'd drink just one. Yeah, right.

While I waited, I tried to call the nursery and got a recorded voice, which I knew with certainty the moment I heard it was Kathleen Fowler's. It stunned me so that I called back, just to listen to it again. I couldn't trust my hearing, especially with an answering machine, but to me, she sounded young. She sounded confident. And, yes, there was a rich, deep warmth to her voice that I could hear even through the fuzz. I don't know what I expected, but it wasn't what I heard.

I called back one more time, just to try to see if I could recognize anything familiar in her tone. This time, a real person answered. Annette.

"It's Geri," I said, paranoid about my voice on the phone. Just enunciate. That's all I had to do. Just slow down and say what I meant. I hated myself for always having to go through this ritual when I talked to a new person on the telephone for the first time.

"Where the hell are you?" I didn't have any problem hearing that one. "I was here by myself until closing yesterday. We had a terrible mess. Hundreds of plants destroyed."

"I know. I'm sorry."

"I meant exactly what I told you," she said. "If you own half of this place, you can do half of the work or let me buy you out. If you force me to get an attorney, I will, you know."

"You should have one, anyway," I said, refusing to let her threaten me. "I planned on coming back, but something happened. I can be there in thirty minutes if that will help."

"It won't help much. And it sure isn't going to fix what you pulled when I needed you here."

A knock on my door was followed by a hearty,

"Room service," the two best words I'd heard all morning.

"I have to go," I said, and then realized that I was saying it to a dial tone. Annette Montgomery had hung up on me. So much for restraint. This was going to be a two-espresso morning.

Annette hadn't warmed up much by the time I reached the nursery. She'd pulled her orange-red hair back into a ponytail, and if her freckled face was any indication, had not put on the makeup she clearly didn't need. In spite of her trendy crewneck gray shirt and matching yoga pants, she looked as if she hadn't had much more sleep than I had.

"Thanks a lot for yesterday," she snapped the moment I stepped inside. "I guess I shouldn't be surprised."

"Just one minute." I faced her over the counter, partly so that I could watch her lips, partly to let her know that I wasn't afraid of her. "I was sick yesterday. I hadn't planned to be, okay? Furthermore, you're not my boss. I came to open up for you as a courtesy. I really did plan to return, but it didn't work out that way."

"A courtesy?" She almost came over the counter, at me. "You're half owner, the same as Kathleen was. You've got to do something for your half." She cast her gaze down for a moment, then back up at me. "Unless you want me to buy you out."

So that was it. And maybe not such a bad idea. I looked around at the tables of plants. Whatever she'd done had made the place come to life again. Would I be happy as a permanent part of this environment? Would I miss the adrenaline-driven newspaper and the diverse neurotic personalities that gave it life? Could I be content with plants indoors, and outdoors, a community that felt like somebody else's childhood?

The answer was clear. There could be no answer until I found out why Kathleen Fowler had chosen me as her beneficiary and what she wanted me to do with that power.

"I can't make any decisions right now," I said. "If you want me to help you, I will, but what will really help both of us is if I spend the majority of my time trying to find out why your partner did what she did with that trust of hers."

That seemed to soften her, but not enough to erase the cynical curve of her lips. "Do you think you can?" She cocked her head as if evaluating me. The sneer I could handle; that belittling once-over I couldn't.

I thought of the easy pride that lit Jesse Medicine's troubled expression when I'd told him that his painting was wonderful, and tried to draw on it. "I'm good at what I do," I said. "I don't know if you know this, but I played a part in solving that razor killer murder case last year."

"The one in San Francisco, where those men were killed by that female stalker?" I could tell that caught her off guard. She reached for the cider and ladled some into her cup. "I didn't know that," she said. "I don't really know anything about you."

"Then I wish you wouldn't judge me before you get a chance to."

She didn't respond at first, just looked down at the cup in her hands. The spicy scent drifted into my nostrils, reminding me of cinnamon candy, maple syrup, stomach aches, worse.

"Want some?" she asked.

My stomach churned. "No thank you," I said. "I got really sick yesterday, and I'm still a little queasy. That's why I couldn't come back when I said I would."

"What do you mean?" Her cheeks went pink. "Sick how?"

"Sick as in disoriented," I said. "Sick as in paramedics. They thought—"

"What?" she asked, her eyes too wide and too scared. I didn't mean to do that to her, but now it was too late.

"That I'd been poisoned."

"Like the plants," she said, and although her eyes filled with tears, it wasn't pain I saw there, but anger. "Like Eric."

"Eric?" I felt my skin crawl.

"That's why I had to work alone yesterday," she said. "Eric checked himself into the hospital, so ill he barely knew his own name."

Her words and the spiced apple scent had brought back the fear of the day before.

"What was wrong? Do they know—" I couldn't finish. She watched my face with guarded eyes.

"Poison," she said.

"Poison?"

She nodded. "I never got around to drinking my cup, but Eric—" She put her hand over her mouth, and whatever she said next was lost to me.

The plants. Eric. Me. And as the day progressed, four customers—all of them big-time pissed off—reported that they'd suffered from abdominal cramps and disorientation after drinking the cider at the nursery. I needed to figure out the connection. Whoever poisoned the cider couldn't have wanted to wipe out all of us. There were easier and more certain ways to accomplish that.

Eric turned over the jug and the rest of the contents to the police. He and Annette filled a smaller simmering pot with dried lavender leaves that soothed away the lingering reminders of apples and spice like a balm. Eric insisted on spending the day at the nursery, although he looked as if he belonged in bed. The two of us sipped peppermint tea, each dunking our own pouches into safe, separate cups as I mourned the lack of caffeine almost as much as I appreciated the safety.

"I'm doing all of this for my mom," he told me. "I don't give a damn about this place."

"I can tell." I looked up from the miniature roses and ferns we'd brought in from the outside to replace the rest of the damaged ones. We made our way past pale purple Chinese wisteria climbing like bean stalks, and pineapple-guava shrubs, to the herb section. Potting the rosemary, chervil and lemon basil cleared my head as the lavender infusion had earlier.

Eric looked up at me from his cross-legged position on the ground. He'd pulled his hair back, and without it clouding around his features, I could see a sweetness about him, a combination of blue eyes and little-boy pout that didn't fit his size, his muscles and his big talk. "Hand me that flat, will you?" he asked.

I took it from the shelf and eased it down to him. As he took the other end, he met my eyes with his and asked, "Do you think the police will be able to tell what kind of poison that was that got us?" My question exactly.

"I don't know." At closer inspection, I could see the watery red rimming his eyes, the same as I'd seen in my own mirror this morning. "I do think that we were poisoned, but I don't know what they'll be able to find out."

"Why not?" he demanded, taking the flat from me. "Tell me how someone can come in here and poison my frigging cider. Tell me why the cops crawling all over this place can't figure out who did it."

"Because nobody died. Nobody even got very

sick." I voiced what had been worrying me since Annette had told me that Eric and I had suffered similar symptoms and that those symptoms might well be connected to the poisoning of the plants. "This wasn't meant to kill us. It wasn't enough to kill us, only enough to make us violently ill for a very short time."

His pale eyes narrowed, and in that moment, I wondered if he thought I could have been responsible for whatever had been put in that cider. "Why would someone just want to make us sick?" he asked.

I sat down next to him on the ground, but not all neat and lotus-legged as he was. I wanted to be on his level when I said the next part. "Someone wasn't trying to make us sick," I said. "What happened to me was an accident. Only Annette knew that I'd be here early."

"So?"

"So, that cider was left for you, Eric."

"That's crazy." He kicked himself out of his yoga pose and jumped to his feet. "How the hell would anyone know that I'd be the one to fix the stupid cider in a nursery I don't even own?"

Still sitting, I asked, "How many days a week do you come in early and heat the cider?"

"Shit." He was stalking now, back and forth in front of me. "Sure, I come in now and then before we open. In the winter months, that includes starting up the cider so that Annie won't have to when she gets here. I did the same thing when my mom opened."

"Someone knows that," I said. "If they can get in to poison the cider, who knows what else?"

He stopped in his tracks. The hair had clouded down again, drifting in puffy rows toward his face. "Who?" he asked. "Who knows that I come in here early?"

"You tell me," I said. "Maybe we need to make a list."

If he'd do it, maybe I could find the connection I was trying to seek. But not as I had thought, between the poison and me—the connection we needed to find was between the poison and Eric.

We propped against the wood back of the planting bed and began the list on the back of a package of sweet pea seeds. Glenna Teague, the nursery's assistant manager; Annie, of course; a few street people whom Glenna fed and who sometimes slept in the shed out back of the nursery. "And Jesse Medicine," Eric said. "That's everyone."

I don't know whether or not I made a noise, but he looked at me as if I had. "Why would Jesse Medicine know your hours?" I asked.

"Because he knew my mom's hours." He put the list we'd been making on the ground beside him, and as he ended his connection with it, I could feel him ending his connection to me as well. "Jesse's a weird dude," he said. "Way obsessed with my mom."

"Because they continued to spend time together

after their divorce?" I asked, trying to sound sane and steady.

"They everythinged together," he said, "but Jesse still kept sliding into that dark side of his. No way they could work it out. I heard them yelling at each other the day before she was killed."

"What did they say?" I asked, my need to know balanced against my need not to.

"Doesn't matter now." He turned away from me and busied himself with a plant.

We worked in silence for a while. In my mind, I went over the list of people who would have known he'd be at the nursery early.

"Tell me about the assistant manager," I asked.

My question roused him from whatever funk he'd settled into. "Glenna Teague," he said, and shook his head. "Kind of an old hippie. She always says that my mom saved her life. She wouldn't hurt me or anyone else."

"And the homeless people?"

"They hang around here because Glenna sneaks them food. They've never caused any problems."

Just then, a shadow fell over us like a cloud.

I looked up into the wild eyes of Jesse Medicine.

Handsome was too small a word for him. I don't know how I'd failed to miss that the day before. Sure, he was good-looking, in terms of form and symmetry, but his were not textbook good looks. His stark, shaved head and unsmiling expression created that same ferocity in his face that I'd seen in his painting. This guy was all big brushstrokes and color.

"Don't," he shouted.

I froze. "Don't what?" I asked, but before I could say more, he reached down and swiped the cup out of my hand.

"Just a fucking minute," Eric shouted back. "I'm not my mother, dude. You can't pull that shit in here."

"You'd better believe I can pull it." Jesse glared at Eric, who'd jumped to his feet. I sat staring at my smashed cup, the contents soaking into the flower bed. "What are you trying to do," Jesse demanded, "trying to kill her, too?"

"You best watch your mouth," Eric said. "I overheard your last fight with my mom. I'm thinking I just might get me a lawyer."

Jesse paused only for a moment, but long enough for me to catch it in that way that I could often catch silences more than words. "You tried to kill Geri," he said, looking down at me. "One of you did, or both of you did, and I'm going to find out. I'll tell you that right now."

"You are so off your ass," Eric said. "What's wrong? You started drinking your breakfast now instead of just your lunch and dinner?"

"No, asshole. I went to work. That's all I did. And one of my part-timers came in. She was poisoned, too." He looked past me to Eric. "My part-timer came here, drank your cider and had to go to the hospital with what she was told were signs of poisoning. How long are you going to pretend that she didn't get that poison here?"

"I got sick, too," Eric said. "I don't know how the cider got poisoned."

"But you heated the cider," I reminded him, feeling clammy just talking about it. "Remember? The cider was already hot when we came back inside."

Eric drew back, and I wondered if his sudden hostility was for Jesse, for me, or for both of us. "So, you think I'd poison myself just so I could get you and a few of Annie's customers while I was at it?"

Instead of apologizing, I kept my gaze steady on him. "Why would you do something like that?" I asked.

"You tell me, lady. You're the one with all the questions." And to Jesse. "My mom's dead. Get your ass out of this nursery, and take this chick with you."

"What's the matter?" Jesse shot back. "Are you afraid your efforts to override Kath's trust are going to fail and that it's easier just to kill Geri and pretend to poison yourself?"

I trembled as he said it, but the caught-redhanded look on Eric's face was way worse than I felt.

"How?" Eric demanded, and in his eyes, I saw *How do you know?*

That was all it took. I stood up and knew that it

would be my last time walking out of this place. Before I did that, I stared into Eric's darting, probably lying eyes, and said, "You're trying to break the trust?"

"I don't owe you any explanations," he said. Although he didn't move, I could feel him squirm, as if he itched all over but didn't dare scratch.

"Damn right he is," Jesse said, taking my arm. "He and Annie are trying to break it. Trying to discredit you, too."

"You're a liar," Eric shouted, but Jesse wasn't through.

"They've even talked to a newspaper reporter in San Francisco," he said.

"Doug Blanchard?" I asked, and felt ill again.

"We can talk to anyone we like." Eric had gone from almost friendly to confrontational, and all it had taken was for Jesse Medicine to appear.

"And I'm so sure you'll tell the truth," I said sarcastically. But my stomach sank. I'd come to Half Moon Bay to find the truth behind my inheritance and Kathleen's murder. Now I was material for the man who'd gotten my job. If I was killed, I'd be giving him even better material for his column. That would be reason enough for making sure I stayed alive.

"Oh, I'll tell the truth." In spite of his injured leg, Eric looked ready to charge Jesse. "I'll tell anyone who wants to listen that I don't believe my mom intended to leave one dime to you. I'll tell them about what happened with the ladder yesterday, too."

"What ladder?" Jesse asked.

"You be sure to tell him." Eric followed as we walked out into the parking lot.

"You know that I didn't have anything to do with that," I told him. "I'm not the enemy, you know. If we worked together, maybe we could find out what's going on."

He said nothing, standing there with his arms folded as if to bar me from this nursery that was legally mine.

"What ladder?" Jesse repeated once we were out of earshot.

"Someone pulled his ladder out from under him when he was trimming some bushes in the back yesterday morning. He thinks I did it."

"That's crazy." He leaned against his truck, and for the first time since he'd come crashing in, his expression relaxed. "I'm sure glad you're okay."

There was something lazy and sexy in his smile that embarrassed me. "And I'm glad you're concerned."

"Let's talk about it at breakfast," he said. "I'm hungry, aren't you?"

He went around and opened the pickup's passenger door. Although I knew that he had not asked for and I had not accepted a breakfast date, I said, "Yes. I am."

Nine

Chev left his office and took Highway 92 past the 280 interchange and followed the signs to Half Moon Bay. In a few minutes he was on Kelly Avenue heading for the Francis Beach entrance gate. After parking his van, he walked through the well-paved entrance road to the weather-beaten asphalt of the beach trail.

A dark cloud cover had stretched across the afternoon sky, but he had wrapped an olive-green alpaca scarf around his neck the way he used to as a younger man. Probably made him look like a duffer, but he couldn't worry about that. Just being on the trail he used to skate daily reminded him of how it had felt back then. The wind lifted his hair, his best feature. He wasn't being vain. That's just the way it was.

Women had loved him back then. Men, too, not that he was wired that way, but he welcomed the admiration from every camp. A long time ago. Such a long time ago. If it were a song, blues diva Mickey Champion would sing it. Since Ginger's death, much of Chev's life had been about the blues.

Low sand dunes extended between the trail and the beach, at some places low enough so that he could see the ocean. A shame that money going to useless amusements wasn't funneled to improve this trail. But maybe that was the way it should be. If it were improved, everyone would use it. Chev had struck out heading toward Francis and Dunes beaches when he saw him.

He smelled him first. As always, the cigarette smoke went straight to his nostrils. He shoved the scarf up around his throat, and Lester Brown laughed his familiar hack.

In the year or so since Chev had last seen his former neighbor, Lester had aged. His eyebrows were more gray than black now, although his hair still shone glossy and thick. In the long, black leather jacket and with the amused scowl, he could still pass for Johnny Cash's younger brother.

Even when Chev had been Lester's son's coach, Chev and Ginger had kept their distance. It was only after the break-in and Ginger's murder, when Chev had crumpled over her body, that Lester had taken charge. While Chev was still caught in the numb, surreal cloud of shock, Lester had burst into the house, chased the intruders through the backyard and down the row of houses. When it was all over, he'd shot and killed both men, crack addicts looking for money. And he'd almost saved Ginger's life. Almost.

Lester crushed out his cigarette and strode onto the path. "Still scared of secondhand smoke?" he said, shoving out a hand. He made it sound unmanly.

"Of course not," Chev replied. "Thanks for coming."

"No one will see us out here. That's for sure." He made a chortling sound. "You wouldn't want to be seen with the likes of me."

"Better to err on the side of caution," Chev said. "It's good to see you. How's Junior?"

"Doing better than his old man." Although his voice was gruff as always, he couldn't hide the look of pride on his face. "Going to college."

"Does he still skate?"

"Hell, no. That was just one of those phases when he was in school." He coughed and added, "Not that I got anything against it. I never told my kids what to do."

Like hell, Chev thought. "Well, give him my best," he said. "He's a good kid."

"How you doing?"

"You know."

"Yeah, I do. You ever get that gun?" Lester asked.

"No."

"Damn it, man, what do I have to do, read the crime stats to you? What's going to happen if some more sonsabitches break into your house again? Whatcha gonna do? Call 911? What if there's a national emergency? There will be sooner or later. Who's gonna save your ass then?"

Chev wanted to tell him that he didn't care, but instead, he kept walking and said, "You're right, Lester."

"Then listen to me before it's too late. If you're worried 'cause you don't know how to shoot, I know guys who could teach you. There's a place not far from your office."

Chev began to move along the asphalt again, and Lester huffed next to him, smoke spiraling up to meet the fog. "Did you find out anything?" Chev asked.

"Yeah, I did. Mind my asking your interest?"

"Doing someone a favor," he said. "She's willing to pay."

"You know I never charge my friends."

"She's more like an acquaintance. Just a nice lady in a bad situation." Chev thought the trail might slow Lester down, but the big man was more agile than he looked in the bulky jacket.

"A lady?"

"Not like that," Chev said. "A young woman. She's engaged to the son of the woman who—"

"Kathleen Fowler," he said, strictly business. "I got all that. This Geraldine LaRue—she goes by Geri—is a newspaper reporter in San Francisco. Before that, she was a computer librarian at a daily in Pleasant View. Worked her way through college as a stock clerk at ServeMart, night shift. No kids, no boyfriend, far as I can tell. Hangs out with some crossdresser singer, a Korean guy who also works for the newspaper."

Lester gave Chev the glazed look that usually sparked a monologue about how the country had gone crazy, how men were no longer men, women were no longer women, and how law enforcement had wimped out.

"Good work," Chev said, hoping to distract him. "What about her family?"

"None, as far as I can tell. Zip." He gestured with his cigarette. "She was raised in the foster care system, so who knows what she's all about."

"The foster care system?" He hadn't expected that. The fog settled in and hid the ocean from view. "Is she some kind of orphan?"

"Could mean anything," Lester said. "Parents could be dead, but usually it's something dirtier. Drugs, maybe. Violence in the home. Abuse."

It wasn't exactly the makings of a con woman, but there had to be some reason Kathleen had named the LaRue girl her heir. "Can you find out more?" he asked.

"Buddy, I can find out anything." Lester paused beside a tree, gasping. "Hey, slow down, will you? We're not as young as we used to be."

To tell the truth, Chev was a little winded himself. "We might as well go back," he said. He loved this path, but it was getting more overgrown and tougher and tougher to walk. As they made their way back, he wondered how much he could tell Lester. How much could he trust him? "I really appreciate your doing this," he said.

Lester waved him off. "It's what I do, man. You were good to my boy, and I don't forget. You want me to find out more about the girl?"

"If you can," he said. "And there's something else." Lester looked at him expectantly, and he added, "Can you investigate Kathleen for me, too?"

"That's easy," he said. "She's dead."

Sometimes Lester's humor was difficult to tolerate. Chev knew if he laughed or even smiled, that he'd encourage more of the same. "I'm interested in anything you can find out," he said. He'd done everything else he could think of. Maybe this volatile friend of his could help where he had failed.

Lester rubbed the side of his chin, as if trying to rub away the dark shadow of stubble. "This part of that favor you're doing? Or is it more personal?"

The bastard was a walking lie detector, always had been. The fog had thinned, and the sun reflected off the ocean like a mirror. He yanked off his scarf and let the cool air hit his throat. "Guess you could say it's personal, but you might find a connection."

Lester hadn't moved. Although sweat sprouted along his forehead, he made no attempt to remove the long black coat. "How personal?" He gave Chev a grin that was both weary and victorious. "Why do you care about Kathleen Fowler?"

"She was a nice lady, a good person." That was true enough. "It's not right what happened to her. Someone needs to pay for it."

Lester rubbed his face again. "But, why do *you* care?"

"I don't know," he said. "Maybe it's just time I cared about something again."

"Maybe." But he still hadn't moved, and the sun was beating down with the intensity of a heat lamp. "I want you to promise me that you'll buy that gun, now. Okay?"

"Okay," Chev said. "What kind?"

They went back the way they came, and he avoided any more questions about Kathleen Fowler by encouraging Lester to go on about his favorite topic. And that's how they left the path—with Chev pretending to listen as Lester explained about firearms and how necessary they were in these violent times.

Ten

GERI

If I could have canceled my meeting with Jesse that night, I would have. After learning that Eric had been in touch with Doug Blanchard, I didn't feel like going anywhere. I especially didn't feel like going to the event that Jesse had been so embarrassed to promote that I could barely read his lips through the shame.

As soon as I got back to the hotel that day, I called the newspaper and left a message on Marie's voice mail. I'm not sure what I intended to say, but I wanted to hear it from her that she'd okayed whatever hatchet job on me that Blanchard was planning with Eric.

"Tell me about this Doug Blanchard guy," Jesse Medicine asked that night.

"We call him Doug Bastard at the paper, and the name kind of says it." I wasn't sure how I'd allowed myself to get talked into the buggy ride with him, but at least we had a little privacy, except for the driver and the horse, both of whom had clearly made this little trek more times than I ever would. "He writes a column for the paper," I said finally. "A column that I wanted to write. For some reason, he has it in for me."

"Why?" He kept his face focused on me as he spoke, the way only someone used to dealing with people who can't hear well would do. It was a secretive, intriguing face, too, and not just because of the shaved head and thick, inquisitive eyebrows. I, who hadn't as much as checked out a single male since Malc and I parted, found myself studying it, feature by feature. "He got the job, right?"

I nodded, glad that most of the clop-clop-clopping and the Christmas music was only a soft blur in my ears. My focus was Jesse. "He got the job with an essay that changed my editor's mind about him," I said. "High-drama stuff. About his murdered fiancée. I couldn't compete."

"So, you should be the one who has it in for him, not the other way around, right?"

I started to come back at him, then realized that he had my number, as Mama would say. I started thinking like her only when I was stressed—at the end of my rope, another favorite of hers—reaching as far back as I could for something to anchor me. Then, before I could worry any more about how I felt, Jesse Medicine flashed me what must have been his version of a smile, and I didn't know what I was.

"So maybe I dislike him," I admitted, unable to stop the grin that was as much from watching Jesse as realizing that I'd been busted. "Okay, I guess I do dislike him, but not because he got the job I wanted. Because he's arrogant."

"And why does he dislike you?" he asked.

Another good question. Blanchard had the job, the column and Marie's undying approval. What did I have that he wanted? "I don't know," I said.

"You have to find out." His eyes seemed to darken as he spoke. We passed beneath a canopy covering the street, and then I couldn't see his eyes at all. The clop-clop of horses' hooves grew louder, his voice softer. We must have been approaching the end of the ride. "Did you understand what I said?" he asked in a louder tone than before. Then before I could answer, "You've got to find out why he has it in for you. Don't you see? That's the only way you'll be able to beat him."

I'm not sure what it was about that statement that made me tremble. Maybe it was the cold, secretive look in his eyes. Maybe it was my own knowledge of Blanchard. He'd beaten me once. Now he was working with Eric. Would he beat me again? And if he did, would I care about this crazy trust thing the way I'd cared about that column that had almost been mine?

"Heavy thoughts," Jesse said. "I can feel them."

Before I could answer, we were back where we started, and the next couple was ready for their turn on the ride.

I realized, as we climbed down from the buggy, that we hadn't talked about Kathleen, that I'd been putting off the subject. I had to push Doug Blanchard out of my mind. I had to push whatever it was that I was feeling for Jesse right behind it. And Jesse and I had to go over as much of Kathleen's history as he was willing to share with me.

It wasn't going to be easy. He was bombarded by a petite, blond-streaked chamber of commerce person named Sandy the moment we returned to his office.

"We need you, Jess," she said, and I stepped back, seeing the cringe, watching the embarrassment color his face again. He hated this job, felt both above and below it. I saw it all in his expression, and I almost forgot the reason I was here with him.

So I walked along with the blonde named Sandy and him and the people who joined them. I observed. I planned what I would ask him about Kathleen once we could speak in semiprivacy. But then I got interested in watching him operate, how he both engaged with his clients but kept himself distant. At one moment, when he looked up from the client he was addressing, with a guarded expression, into my eyes, I realized who he reminded me of. He reminded me of me.

Finally, we got a chance to return to his office.

"Coffee?" he asked, reaching for the pot before I answered.

"You know my addictions."

He opened the cabinet and pulled out a bottle of Irish whiskey. "And you know mine," he said.

I started to protest, then decided not to say anything, since he'd already poured a good-size splash into each mug.

"No whipped cream?" I asked.

"Next time." He clinked my mug as if toasting that possibility, and I didn't need the coffee to warm up.

We drank it outside his office sitting at a wrought-iron café table. Posters for the Albee plays lined his windows. *A Delicate Balance. The Zoo Story. The Ballad of the Sad Café. Tiny Alice. Who's Afraid of Virginia Woolf?* No trace of the real art I'd seen inside. And only one Albee play—by way of Richard Burton and Elizabeth Taylor—that I'd seen. Live theater and Spanish-language channels. The two areas where my hearing loss interferes most with my life.

"What are you smiling about?" he asked.

"Spanish-language films, believe it or not. Your sister would understand."

"I already know," he said. "You think at first that something's gone wrong with your lip-reading equipment."

I knew few hearing people who got my situation as well as he did. "Right," I said, and sipped at my bitter, boozy coffee. In a burst of courage, I added, "I like the way you are. You get close enough to people so that they trust you, but you don't risk your life."

"You're right." I didn't know if I was hearing his laugh, reading it, or both, but I liked the feeling. Better yet, he didn't try to make the excuses I expected. "My sister says the same thing," he said. "You have to meet her."

I wanted to ask if it was because we both had hearing problems, or if he just wanted me to meet his sister. I didn't dare ask for clarification. Instead, I said, "You know, we were going to talk about Kathleen tonight, and we haven't."

"Because we've been talking about you," he said. "And that Doug Bastard guy. And me."

"And way too much about me." I put my mug on the table, feeling like a gambler spreading out his cards. Then I rose to my feet. "You've got to tell me what you know, Jesse. It could make all of the difference."

"It hurts like hell," he said with eyes I wanted so much to trust. "But I know you're right. Most of all, we've got to find out why Kath changed her trust. Do you think Eric's behind what happened to her?"

"I didn't," I said, "especially not after what happened with the cider. But after what you told me, I don't know."

We walked without speaking. Finally, he said, "I knew her heart. She wouldn't disinherit her own son, regardless of their problems. It's not like her."

"But that's what she did," I said. "At least, it's what she appears to have done."

We neared my car parked not far from his pickup on the opposite curb. No amount of shuffling around in the cold darkness could distract me from that.

"So," he said. "Are you as hungry as I am?"

The question stopped me for a moment until I realized that I was ravenous. "Kind of."

"Then let's take my truck," he said.

"Where?"

He looked down, and if he said anything, I couldn't hear it. When I could read his lips again, he was saying something about salsa, chips, steak, Mary. No, make that Bloody Mary.

"I can't go to your place, Jesse."

"I didn't mean it as that kind of an invitation."

"Besides," I said, searching for a better excuse. "Don't you have to be here?"

"No," he said. "I just do the collateral for the night. The actual events are handled by a woman who runs a PR firm in the city."

The chill that froze its way through my body had nothing to do with the weather. I knew all too well which leading San Francisco PR firm specialized in promoting chambers of commerce and special events. Maybe I was wrong. Maybe there was more than one firm with Adrienne's appeal.

"Oh," I managed.

"Revell," he said before I had a chance to ask him to provide me with more details. "Revell Promotions. Adrienne Revell, the owner, is here tonight. She made it clear a long time ago that she doesn't want me underfoot."

Malc's new woman. My replacement. I didn't know how to handle it. "Adrienne?" I managed to choke out. "Here? You know her?"

"I don't have any choice," Jesse said. "She's in charge of the budgets for a lot of the local events." He pointed toward a joined-at-the-hip couple moving our way down the sidewalk, the woman in drifty, skinny white, the guy in a fisherman-knit sweater over jeans. "There she is," Jesse said. "Adrienne. Her boyfriend's a shrink. Piercy, I think. Yeah, that's it. Malcolm Piercy."

It was Adrienne Revell, all right, ash-blond, ash-thin, ash-perfect as always. And beside her, make that, attached to her, was Malc. My Malc. No. Not my Malc, not for a very long time now. He looked at me. I looked at him. His hair, only slightly darker than the sweater, sprouted from his head in unruly tufts my fingers could remember smoothing down. I took in the gray-green eyes and borderline-bushy eyebrows, and my legs turned to rubber.

Adrienne spotted me and tried to guide Malc in

the direction they'd come. It might have worked if Malc and I hadn't already seen each other. He came toward me as if I were reeling him in.

I couldn't do it. I didn't know how to play the game, to be friendly to Malc and Adrienne, to treat him as the new Malc and not the old. It didn't feel honest, and it didn't feel right.

"You know," I said, turning to Jesse, unable to sound as excited as I knew I should, "I am hungry. Why don't we go to your place, after all?"

"Works for me," he said, but by now they were ready to collide with us. I could tell that he felt my confusion and distress. He took my arm and raised his hand to both of them with a casual, "Hey, how ya doin'?" Then he guided me across the street as fast as the two of us could walk.

"What was that all about?" he asked once we were in his car. His breath was warm with coffee and whiskey.

"What was what about?"

"You know what," he said. "What's going on? You have a problem with Adrienne Revell?"

"I met her only once," I told him. Why couldn't I lie just once in a while? "Well, maybe I talked to her a couple of times. But I didn't have a problem with her. Still don't." And then, just because I could, I turned the tables and asked, "Do you?"

"Do I what?" We pulled into a drive leading to a tidy-looking two-story house bordered by enough foliage to make me wonder if it were a mini-nursery.

But of course. Kathleen was probably responsible for the garden.

"Do you have a problem with Adrienne Revell?" I repeated.

He turned in a defiant way that made it clear he wanted to be sure I read what he was about to say. "Yes." And when I didn't respond and his face hadn't moved from mine, "I guess you could say that. I dated her briefly after Kath and I first split. It didn't end well. And you know what, Geri?"

"What?" I asked, reminding myself that I was here to talk about Kathleen, not bash Malc's new woman.

"You're a lousy liar. I think you have a problem with her, too."

"You're wrong," I began. "Why would you say that?"

"Because," he said, his eyes as vibrant and scary as the ones in his painting. "Because seeing her changed your mind about coming with me tonight."

And because I didn't want him to probe deeper, I said, "You're right."

He clicked something on his visor, and the garage door opened. I almost gasped when I saw the meticulous insides, angry, vivid paintings on every wall, as if it were a gallery and not somebody's garage. To the sides, where normal garages would attempt to conceal garbage bins and old magazines, I could spot smaller canvases. The ones that faced forward looked like portraits of people I should recognize.

He turned off the car and said, "Someday we'll

compare notes on Adrienne, once we know that we can trust each other." Warm breath in my face again. He said it in a way that suggested that day was close.

I wanted to ask how it had ended with Adrienne and why she might not be the perfect woman I'd thought she was. But I was afraid.

I was also attracted in some stupid animal way to him, his eyes flashing little promises that I shouldn't, if I really still cared about Malc, be able to pick up on. Maybe it was the alcohol. Why else would I be so reckless as to invite myself home with him?

I stared at the door leading from the garage to the house, then back at the one offering freedom. If I walked with Jesse Medicine through that insignificant-looking door tonight, I would end up in his bed sooner rather than later. I knew that he knew it as well as I did. We sat there for a moment, and I could feel his thoughts, as heavy as mine.

"I'm sorry," I said. "This isn't a good idea."

He nodded and asked, "You sure?"

I looked at the doors again, the one in and the one out. "I think so."

He touched my cheek, then slid his finger under my chin and lifted it in a slow, sexy way that promised kisses. "Be very sure, Geri. We may never have a moment like this again."

That decided it for me. The loving gesture started to feel manipulative. His words felt just a little too much like pressure.

"I hope we will," I said, comfortable with the truth again. "But as for tonight—"

I didn't have to say more. He was already backing out of the garage.

He drove me back to the site of the festival, and this time I could hear the loud bells and Christmas music.

He parked in front of my car, and when he looked at me, it was with reluctance. "I hope we see each other again," he said. "You're my only connection to Kath now."

So was that why he was willing to bed me? I wanted to accuse him. Instead I gave him one of my don't-care shrugs. Then I placed my right hand on the door as if ready to jump out. "Who killed her?" I asked. "You must have an idea."

"I don't have a clue. Everyone loved her." He reached over and pulled my hand from the door. "I can't tell you how many people she helped turn their lives around and how many causes she supported," he said.

"No enemies, I take it?"

"Not until those last six months. That's when whoever was harassing her first contacted her."

"Did she tell you that?" I asked, surprised to learn that someone had been contacting Kathleen before her murder.

"She didn't have to. I was her husband, I mean, her ex-husband."

But his eyes didn't look like ex anything. They looked haunted. When they finally landed on me, I cringed. "So her behavior changed?" I asked.

"Everything changed. I told you that I knew her heart. I could sense the change in her, the fear." He slammed his palms against the steering wheel. "Damn, I should have done something."

For the first time, I noticed the strength in those hands. And the anger. I needed to go, to leave Jesse with his ghosts and his regrets. There was no place for me unless he could tell me something that could explain Kathleen's actions.

"I know this is personal," I said, "but you obviously cared for each other. Why did you ever—"

"Don't go there, Geri."

"But you don't even know what I was going to ask," I persisted.

"I know, all right, and I'm not going to discuss it." He touched my cheek again, but this time, his fingers were so cold they made me shiver. "I'm not going to talk about Kath unless it's something that I believe will help. I'll tell you anything you want to know about what happened those last few months, but that's it."

My instinct was to press on, but I knew that to do so would only anger him more.

I leaned back and folded my arms, trying to distance myself. He was not easy to define, and neither were my feelings just then. "Okay," I said. "Tell me."

"She had some strange accidents, including an intestinal attack after we'd eaten dinner one night. Only, I didn't get sick."

Crikey. I thought of my own poisoning and caught the acknowledgment in his eyes.

"Exactly," he said. "And at the pumpkin festival in October, she went back to the car for something and on the way back was nearly run down by a truck."

"Did anyone see it?" I asked.

"No one could identify anyone in that crowd. Kath said it was probably an accident, but I could tell she didn't believe it. The next day when she was driving to work, she realized that someone had tampered with her brakes."

"Was she hurt?"

"No," he said, "but she started to distance herself from me, and she wouldn't talk about it. When I insisted, she refused to see me at all."

"But Eric said you were together at the nursery the day before she died."

"I wanted to know what was wrong," he said. "I demanded that she talk to me. She told me to get the hell out. We could be like that. I have a temper, but she could match me."

His expression was pure regret. It reminded me of every remorseful replay of every mistake I'd ever made. There was a sad humor to the way he said it, as if even remembering their mutual anger was a comfort now that he had nothing else.

"Where do I come in?" I asked, and the minute I said it, realized how it must sound to him.

"I don't know." The tenderness in his expression embarrassed me. "I can't figure you out."

"No," I said, unable to look at him. "I mean where do I come into this whole story? Why did she leave everything to me?"

Now he was the one who looked embarrassed. "I wish I knew," he said finally. "She never mentioned you to me. Not once."

"It's not likely we'd know each other," I said.

"No. She wasn't from around here." I started to say that I wasn't, either, but instinctively forced myself to shut up and listen. "She was raised in the San Joaquin Valley," he said. "She didn't move up here until she was twenty or so. She'd already had Eric by then."

I felt as if I'd been slugged. The Valley was a big place, but all of a sudden, I felt it shrinking around me.

"Where was she raised?" I asked, trying to appear calm.

He studied me as if trying to decide if answering would cross the line he'd already drawn. "Different places," he said. "She started with nothing."

"Do you know what city?" I asked. "Maybe—"

"Foster homes. One after another."

I kept very still, knowing that my voice would betray me if I attempted to speak. *No* was all I could think. *No.*

"That's why she didn't ever want to move from here," he continued, obviously unaware of what his words were doing to me. "You can see how important having a secure home base would be to someone who was raised like that."

"Yes," I managed, fighting memories, fighting tears. "Yes, I can."

Eleven

GERI

I'm not sure how I was able to say a civil good-night and get the hell away from there. No more fantasies about Jesse Medicine. No more Irish coffee or visits to his studio. I'd been attracted to the man and had wanted to keep that going. He'd been a fascinating distraction from Malc. But now I had a bigger distraction. His dead ex-wife had apparently been raised as a foster child in the same system that I had been.

I forced myself to do something I thought I'd never do again. I visited the fosters in my mind, trying until my head hurt to remember a Kathleen. I couldn't remember the girls, could barely visualize one little boy. Kathleen would have been older, a teenager. My mind filled with shadowy faces, most of them missing names, some who probably never had them to begin with.

Corcoran, Hanford, Tulare. The towns rolled through my mind like stops on a train. The memories and the fosters were supposed to be behind me. I'd gotten out, hadn't ended up like a lot of kids. Stubborn, Mama called it, but Mary Haskins had said it was stick-to-it-ness. *Mary Haskins.* A chill crept over my skin. Where had that name come from? And now I had a face of sorts, and a shape—large. A social worker, although I may not have known that then. How many years had she been lurking around in my memory? She couldn't still be working. Just in case, first thing the next morning, I called the Department of Social Services in Hanford, California, and asked.

Retired, just as I'd thought. But would it even occur to a woman like the one I remembered to request an unlisted telephone number? I gave it a try just as I pulled out of Half Moon Bay on my way to Hanford.

I'd left a message at the nursery, telling them that I'd be back in a few days and that I was concerned— there was the word again—about Eric's decision to speak with Doug Blanchard. That's where I should have been heading—the newspaper office to confront Marie in person. First, though, I had to take this trip I dreaded. I needed to go back to the Valley, to Hanford, and try to find anyone who remembered my early days better than I did.

A call to information confirmed that an M. Haskins lived on Lincoln Drive. When I stopped for a bagel and a jolt of caffeine, I called the number. The voice that answered brought me back. I could see her, that giant form rising out of a pair of white oxfords. I couldn't hear her but I could smell something sharp. Peppermint. It was all I could do to say, "I'm trying to locate a Mary Haskins."

"And you're going to tell me I won the lottery, right?" Her voice was loud enough for me to hear without straining, but it wasn't exactly friendly. "I'm sorry but I don't take solicitation calls. I'm supposed to be on that no-call list."

"This isn't a solicitation." I spoke carefully, doing my best to keep her on the line. "I knew you when I was a foster child."

"You don't say? What's your name, girl?"

I let out a sigh at her change of attitude and reached for my coffee.

"Geri LaRue," I said.

A pause. "My memory's not as good as it used to be. Not gone, though. I remember all you kids. It just takes me a little longer these days."

"I'm a newspaper reporter," I said, and I realized that it was a knee-jerk reaction to being grouped with *all you kids*. "I need to talk to you."

"What about?" she asked. "What kind of story are you writing? I'm not going to speak out about the system. I'll tell you that right now. It may not be perfect, but it's the best we have."

Maybe it was better to let her think of me as a journalist. "I'm going to be in town today," I said. "Is it possible for us to get together?"

Another pause. "I've been retired for almost ten years now," she said. "There's not anything I can tell you that will make any difference in whatever you're writing."

"Maybe not, but give me a chance to find out." I could hear the panic in my voice and was sure that she could hear it as well. "Please."

"You sound as if it's serious."

"It is," I said, my lips so dry that I could barely speak. "If you want to check me out, I can give you the contact information of people who know me in San Francisco. The HR department at the paper will verify that I work there."

"Now, why would I want to go to all that trouble?" she asked.

"So that you'll know I'm telling the truth," I said, feeling like an awkward kid trying to impress an adult. I didn't like the way this conversation reduced me to something less than I was, but Mary Haskins was the only link I had.

"I don't need references for that," she said. "I'll know if you're telling the truth the minute I see you."

She was going to see me. She'd as much as said it. "Where can we meet?" I asked.

"Well, I'm going to have my grandbabies this morning."

"After lunch, then?"

"That's when I go to the seniors' center."

"Why don't I meet you there?"

"It's hard to find. You know where the old courthouse square is? The seniors' center is right behind it, past the fountain, beside the veterans' building."

"I'll find it," I told her, and said the fastest goodbye on record before either one of us could change our minds. Then I sat there, looking down at my shaking hands. I took the coffee in small sips until finally I could taste it again. Maybe this wasn't such a brilliant idea, after all, but what choice did I have?

I found the courthouse square, across from an ice cream parlor just about the time the intermittent rain let up. The fountain was there, right where she'd said it would be. At the northern end of the park was an auditorium with its eight massive columns and imposing facade. It reminded me of a junior high school I'd briefly attended. It would be pretty to most people, but something about it frightened me then and now. Looking at it made me think of being sent to the principal, of being called names I couldn't hear but knew were bad.

I passed the fountain and made my way to a cluster of offices. The seniors' center was on the other side. I caught a whiff of metallic cafeteria smells—chili beans and baked-apple something—and stopped outside the door. Inside, Ping-Pong balls flew. Cards were dealt. I focused on the actions more than the people as I got used to the place, then realized that I was standing in front of a table with a cash register on it, and an older woman who'd probably been staring at me as long as I'd been staring at the room.

She was pretty in that patina kind of way that women who've made surgical adjustments to their features are at first glance, and her streaked hair was what Mama would have called brindle. "May I help you?" If she was a senior, it was just barely.

"I'm looking for Mary Haskins," I said.

As if she'd been anticipating my arrival, a large black woman swept across the room in my direction. In spite of her size, her movements were so graceful that she might as well have been dancing. She wore silver-gray slacks and a matching sweater with a sequined Christmas bell on front that, as she drew closer, I realized matched the smaller bells dangling from her earlobes.

"Looks like you've found her," the woman at the counter said. "You're a popular lady this week, Mary."

"Popular all the time." Mary Haskins made it to the desk and put out her hand. I shook it. Neither of us spoke for a moment. I was aware of patina lady at the desk watching us with a curious tilt of her head.

"Maybe—" I began as Mary and I eyed-to-eyed each other.

"A little walk?" she suggested, patting at the gray

hair she'd pulled back from her face. I nodded, and we went out into the dim afternoon. "Been spitting rain all day," she said. "Let's hope this sun stays for a little while." I wondered how long she'd go on like this, but then, the moment we'd wandered past earshot of the woman at the front table, she stopped, completely business, and said, "Okay. What's this all about?"

Crikey. Now it was my turn. "I was in the foster care system here," I said, not certain how else to start.

"You told me that on the phone. And I told you I'm retired."

"I know this is going to sound strange, but I can prove it," I told her. "Recently someone who was also in the Kings County foster care system about the time that I was died. I didn't know her, but she left most of her estate to me."

"My." Mary kind of chewed on the information, then said, "The obvious question is why?"

"That's why I'm here," I said. "I didn't have a clue, until recently, that she was also raised in the San Joaquin Valley."

"So, the story you're writing," she said. "It's about the woman who left you the money?"

I looked away, knowing that this experienced reader of lies could see the one stamped all over my face.

"Not exactly." I looked back up at her. "I am a newspaper reporter, though, and this woman—her name was Kathleen Fowler—she did name me her beneficiary."

Kathleen Fowler's name didn't generate any more recognition in Mary's face than mine apparently had. She motioned me to sit down beside her on a stone bench protected by an overhang. "What exactly do you want me to do?" she asked.

"Try to remember me." I don't know why, but I wanted desperately for her to say that she did. "Anything at all about my past or Kathleen Fowler."

"There were so many of you." She squinted as if she could see past my eyes to the emotions I was trying to hide. "Do you remember *me?*"

I nodded. "Your name, at least. No, I think I remember you."

"How long were you in the system?"

"On and off," I said. "From the time I was four until high school graduation." I realized that I'd peeled the polish from my thumb. It lay in flat blue strips across the knee of my pants.

"Oh." Her eyes changed, and I wondered if there was a special sympathy in social workers for kids who don't leave the system until they're pushed out of it. "Can you remember any of the families?"

I hadn't wanted to, but now I let myself try. "Nichols," I said, wondering where I'd been hiding that name. "Chuckie Nichols."

"He was the son." She nodded as if I'd given her the answer she'd been seeking. "We placed lots of kids with the Nichols family over the years. You wouldn't know that unless—"

"I'm telling you the truth," I said, rising to my feet. "Please help me."

She stood, too. "I told you, I'm retired. Besides, I've still got a good nose on me, and I'm not smelling the whole story here."

"You want the whole story? Okay. Kathleen Fowler didn't just die. She was murdered."

That stopped her. She hugged herself as if to soften the blow of my words. "Tell me the truth, 'cause I'll know if you're lying. Were you involved?"

"Not in the least," I said. "I wasn't anywhere around. Then I found out that she named me sole beneficiary."

"And you think I can help you find out why?" she asked. "That's way too big a job for me."

"You could help me find out where I was placed," I said. "The homes. You must have records."

She stroked her chin. "I could get my hands on them. I need time to think about it, though. And you're right. I've got to check you out. The last thing I need is some newspaper reporter trying to get me to do something unethical."

"This isn't about ethics." I reached into my bag and took out the business cards I'd had the presence of mind to bring. They looked battered from knocking around with lip gloss, pens, credit cards and the other useless stuff I kept there. I should have listened to Steffan and taken the time to put them in the brushed chrome-and-black case he had given me. I selected the least dog-eared and handed it to her. "Please believe me," I said. "You're the only person I can remember. I don't know of anyone else who can help me." Tears squeezed out and slid down my cheeks. I pretended not to notice, and so did she.

She looked down at the card, pressing her thick thumb along its surface as if she were ironing it. "We'd better go," she said in a voice almost too low for me to pick up. "It's started to rain again."

I hadn't noticed. That's how distracted I was by her, and most of all, by my attempts at remembering.

I followed her in the direction from which we'd come. The patina lady was still at the table flirting with a couple of men wearing Santa hats. Up close, her suntan foundation looked as if she'd applied it with a trowel.

"You have a local number?" Mary asked me.

"I'm driving to San Francisco tonight," I told her. "Call me on my cell, and I can be here in a few hours."

She nodded. "I'll call you one way or the other."

One way or the other. Meaning whether or not she decided to help me.

I made one final attempt to connect with her, something out of left field I didn't even consider until the words were out of my mouth.

"One time—and I can't begin to remember when—you told me I had stick-to-it-ness."

She paused, patted her hair again, although it

didn't need smoothing, and studied me with renewed interest. "That's a word of mine, all right. Used to be, at least."

"I'm sure you said it to me," I said. "I must have been really young. I never forgot it, though. There were times when just knowing someone believed that about me kept me going." It was the truth. I just hadn't remembered where I'd heard it, although I carried the stubborn pride of it all of my life, especially during the tough times.

"Didn't say it to every kid." She peered at me as if trying to recognize a face in a blurry photograph. "Too many of those kids didn't have it. The rest didn't know that they did."

"So you reminded us." My voice got shaky, and I could tell that she'd picked up on it.

She gave me a smile I almost remembered from before. "If you're trying to sweet-talk me into something, little girl, you're doing a good job of it."

"You mean it?" I said. "You'll help me?"

"Nothing better to do," she said. "Why don't you stick around town tonight?"

"I could do that," I said, trying to control my impulse to hug her. "What then?"

"Work," she said. "I'll get hold of those old records of mine, and we'll get on them first thing tomorrow. Won't take us long to pull out the stuff you need."

"Thank you," I said, and threw my arms around

her. She didn't return the hug but didn't pull away, either. "Thank you," I said again.

"Don't thank me yet." She gave me a scowl that must be a way she tried to keep clients at arm's length. Except I wasn't a client, not anymore.

"See you tomorrow," I said.

Even before I finished speaking, she walked away from me, humming a Christmas carol I couldn't make out but still remembered as she unleashed her umbrella and stepped into the rain.

Twelve

MARY

The girl had gotten to her. Lord, she could be a pushover sometimes. Couldn't help it. In spite of the hair color and the attitude, the girl's face reflected the hurt she'd lived with so long that she probably didn't know any other way.

Geri LaRue. Geraldine LaRue. Yes, Geraldine. What was it about that name? She drove back to her apartment, trying to remember. She had to be careful, though, pushover or not. Couldn't say anything to a newspaper reporter that would hurt the good she'd done over the years.

She'd always meant to move from the apartment not far from where she used to work in a part of town whose rotten core she dealt with daily. The place wouldn't let her go, though, never would. It felt like home, was safer than the tall gates implied, and the neighbors kept an eye out for one another. What else did she need? Even the small backyard was a plus, making it easy for her to watch the grandkids. Now she was glad that she never got around to that move.

At the curb, a man in a Santa costume stopped and asked her for directions to Seventh Street. She gave them, and he got back into his car with a wink and a "Merry Christmas."

She straightened the huge green wreath on her front door and inhaled its Christmas tree scent. Kind of brightened her mood and put the past out of her mind. She turned up the volume on the CD of carols and took the pins out of her hair.

Knitting still relaxed her as much as a shot of good bourbon. She'd start with the one, then graduate to the other. She couldn't relax, could still see the girl's desperate expression.

Geraldine LaRue. Yes. There had been a little girl, something wrong with her. And a little boy.

Doorbell. How long had she been sitting here? Dozed off, maybe. With a groan, she pulled herself out of the chair and glimpsed the uniform of the person on the other side of the door. Always good to check first, even with the gate. She opened the door. Said, "Good evening."

"Happy holidays."

"Same to you," she said, and unlocked the security screen.

Before she could react, the intruder was inside, the door kicked shut. A gloved hand slammed over her mouth.

She tried to scream, to bite the thick leather, but the intruder, although smaller than she, was strong. Still she struggled. She was a big woman, and right now, an angry one. It had to be money. Damn burglars would dress up like anything to get inside someone's home.

She kicked and heard a grunt. Good. She needed to break away, to explain where she kept the money.

"Recognize me?"

She didn't expect that. The burglar was someone she knew. The eyes narrowed and blurred as she tried to breathe. But familiar, yes. There was something familiar about them. Something long ago. She thrashed and kicked. Lord, she still held her knitting—the scarf, the circular needle. If she could only lift her hand high enough.

She used all of her strength to drive the needle deeply into the uniform. A shriek tore out of the intruder, louder than the music. Someone would hear. She jerked away from the hand, gulped air, then as soon as she was free, a streak of fire burned her gut. Her own needle tore into her flesh.

"Bitch."

Fists smashed into her face, and she crumpled

into a heap on the carpet. Help would be here. People looked out for one another in this place. She tried to open her eyes, fought to stop the rush of panic.

The hazy figure knelt down beside her, their faces close, the gloves around her throat. "Do you recognize me?" Tears filled her eyes. This wasn't a robbery.

"I never forgot you," the intruder said. "You shouldn't have forgotten me."

She tried to speak, but the angry hands turned her words into gurgles. The fire in her gut spread through her. She couldn't die, not at Christmas, not with the grandkids still so young. She had to plead, to beg.

She twisted her lips, made herself mouth *please,* although there was no sound left, no hope. She felt the last of her life being pressed from her throat. As she began to let go, to let the darkness take her, she glimpsed a vague shape, something silver and square, moving closer to her face. A click, and then a voice, an echo now through the thunder in her ears.

"Smile for the camera."

GERI

I spent a weird, wired night in a motel too new to have been in Hanford the last time I was. That was the way I wanted it, but even that knowledge didn't help me sleep. Of course, the back-to-back coffees didn't help, either. Nor did the sailors from the nearby Lemoore station screaming drunken chants all night long.

I'd called Steffan the night before, and he'd confirmed that rotten Doug Blanchard was off to an interview with Eric Fowler. Another reason for interrupted sleep.

I'd tried to explain to Steffan about my conversation with Mary Haskins, but I couldn't tell if he got it or not. It wasn't just about finding my connection to Kathleen Fowler, as important as that was. It was about finding my connection to the past I'd tried to bury. It couldn't have been all bad with people like Mary Haskins in it.

I thought about calling Jesse Medicine, too, but didn't know what I could say. The shred of good sense I still had told me that I needed to find out my link to his ex-wife before I could deal with him.

When Mary still hadn't called my cell by nine the next morning, I knew I couldn't spend another minute in the hotel room. I could always take myself to breakfast, maybe drive around until I found a decent-looking coffee shop. That was like a heroin addict driving around until finding a decent-looking needle.

My car solved the problem for me. Soon, I was in an older part of town, following the streets as if by memory. No cul-de-sacs here. Everything was symmetrical right down to the lined-up stop signs and broken strip of sidewalks.

The house I was trying to find was located next to

a church and across from a grocery store off Irwin Street. *Redwine's*. The name appeared in that magical way the past can materialize from the curtain of memory. Redwine's Market. The grocery store had been replaced by a gas station, but just as I was ready to drive past, I realized that the church and the house were not gone; they had just changed. I hit the brake and sat there staring at my past.

The two-story house looked small, almost dingy, its yard, green as the shutters beside the upstairs windows, divided by a concrete walk. A girl of elementary-school age sat on the cement slab that served as a porch, wearing jeans and an acid-green sweatshirt and drawing on the sidewalk with a tangerine-colored piece of chalk.

I was too far away to read the slogan on the front of her sweatshirt, but not too far to see the fear reflected on her pale face. I'd lived with the same uncertainty every time a strange car pulled up, every time an official-looking person spent a little too long checking me out.

The girl must have sensed me watching her, because she looked directly at me, got up and dashed inside the house. A potbellied man in a white T-shirt stopped his lawn mower and squinted at me.

I wanted to take off, breaking every speed limit, to barrel back to the relative safety of the motel, but I knew I couldn't. I'd braved Mary Haskins yesterday. I could brave the Reverend Coy Nichols right now.

Crikey. There was his name. I didn't even have to struggle for it. I got out of the car and crossed that street, and it was getting easier and easier to remember.

"Hi, Reverend," I said as I approached the yard. He'd already turned off his mower, and I could feel his uneasy appraisal of me. I guessed from the way his pale eyes were fixed that his scrutiny had stopped at my hair.

"Do I know you?" He had one of those southern accents that was difficult for me to read around, but his back-pew-reaching voice compensated for it.

"I'm Geri LaRue," I said, and when it became clear that I could just as easily have said Howdy Doody, I added, "I was a foster child here when I was four years old."

"You don't say?" He wiped his hands on his pants and reached out to shake my hand, but his expression remained wary.

"I just happened to be in town," I said. "I saw Mary Haskins yesterday."

At that, his smile grew more genuine. "A fine lady," he said. "S'pect I'll see her at services tomorrow. She never misses, whatever the weather." He glanced up at the gray cloud cover threatening his lawn mowing.

"I didn't realize she attended your church," I said.

"She always has," he said. "That's how we got started with the foster kids in the first place. They didn't have enough real homes for them, and some of them went to group homes. Mary couldn't stand the thought of that and talked us into taking our first. We're still doing it."

I tried to remember what life had been like under the Reverend's green-winged roof and came up with nothing. It was as if my memory were playing it cagey, giving me his name and nothing else.

"I can see that you are. A little girl was sitting on the steps when I drove up."

"That would be Kayla," he said.

No wonder an unfamiliar vehicle in front of the house scared her. "Did you ever have a Kathleen Fowler here?" I asked.

He began dragging the lawn mower toward the side yard, speaking over his right shoulder. "I'm not as good at remembering as Mother is," he said. "She remembers all the kids, no matter how long ago we had them."

I could tell by the way he said it that the Mother of whom he spoke was his wife. I couldn't even recall a Mrs. Nichols, so her memory must be better than mine.

"Is Mrs. Nichols here?" I asked.

He shook his head and crouched to adjust the grassy-smelling attachment spilling over with his cuttings. This contraption looked ancient enough to have been mowing his lawn since the days of my fosters. I tried to remember it, but only his name convinced me I'd ever lived here. "Mother's in Texas right now," he said, gasping from the exertion. "Our son's wife just had a baby."

"Chuckie?"

He nodded, and my heartbeat quickened at having another sliver of memory confirmed. "That ugly little whelp married himself a beauty," he said, looking up at me. "Smarter than his old man, too. He's working for a big frozen food company in San Antonio." After that bout of fatherly pride, something dark as the storm cloud above us crossed his face. "They don't usually come back," he said. "I mean, not unless something's wrong."

Instinct told me to keep from telling him what I'd shared with Mary. "Nothing's wrong," I said. "I work as a newspaper reporter in San Francisco, and I thought it would be interesting to come back and try to remember those days."

"Reporter?" He scrambled awkwardly to his feet, like a bear tearing his way out of a patch of stickers. I'd intended to impress him a little, not scare the hell out of him.

"Not on assignment," I said quickly. "I grew up here. I just wanted to return. I don't think that's so odd, do you?"

"No, I guess not." He looked at my hair again and said, "San Francisco, huh?"

"What?" I asked, ready to go to the mat if he decided to start gay bashing or talking about heathens.

"Nothing," he said. "I just wish Mother was here. She'd be able to tell you anything you want to know. I'll wager she has a picture of you in one of those albums of hers upstairs. You kids were all blessings to us, every one of you."

I got the feeling he was picturing himself in the pulpit just then. If I were such a freaking blessing, you'd think he could remember my freaking name.

"When will she be back?" I asked.

"Monday. Why don't you come back then? Of course, you're welcome to join us at church tomorrow, too." He squinted as if trying to picture me there. Before I could answer, a large white duck waddled past. It stopped to give me a lidless stare, reminding me how much I feared anything with wings and beaks. "Quack-Quack, get on in the back right now," the Reverend said with a stomp of his foot.

The duck gave him a *bite-me* look and took his time heading back down the overgrown lawn.

Quack-Quack. I stared at the duck's strut, remembering again a flash of something. "That can't be—" I began.

"There's always been a Quack-Quack," he said, his expression sheepish enough to reveal fondness for the duck. "We keep a little pool in the back for him."

There'd been a pool before, too. Another image struck me. "You don't still…?" I couldn't finish the sentence or the thought.

"No," he said, as if as horrified as I. "Mother doesn't think it's good for the kids. Besides, I've kind of lost my taste for fowl over the years. Can't even eat chicken anymore."

"Oh," I said, trying to nod politely.

"Besides, this little guy has grown on me." He watched the duck with such affection that I wouldn't have been surprised to hear him burst into an all-things-wild-and-wonderful sermon.

I reached for my bag and pulled out another business card, caring less about its dog-eared condition than I had about the one I gave to Mary. "I'm not going to be able to stay past today," I told him. "Could you have your wife call me when she gets back?"

"I'll do that," he said, his ruddy face reflecting sweat and relief.

As I left and he went out back loudly calling for Quack-Quack, I wondered what he'd expected from me and what had made him so guarded at first. I also wondered why I could remember so little about the house with the green shutters.

Once I was in the car, I took out my cell phone to be sure it hadn't run out of juice, which had happened more times than I'd like to admit. It blinked back, all color and illustration, as if to ask what was my problem.

Good question.

My problem was that I still hadn't heard from Mary Haskins. I called her number. No answer.

Please, don't let her have changed her mind about helping me. I couldn't believe she had. She'd been too definite. Maybe she'd gotten waylaid at the seniors' center. At least, perhaps someone there had heard from her. I decided to drive over.

From the rearview mirror, I took a final look back at the Rev's house—the clean, clipped lawn shining green under the dipping clouds, the mower, the shutters. Nothing in that scene reminded me of even a distant memory from my past. Only the Reverend, only Chuckie, only Quack-Quack. I shoved the mirror into a better position and headed for the seniors' center.

Thirteen

The rain picked up again as I parked my car at the curb of Courthouse Square. I crossed the lawn past the fountain, pulled my coat collar up and tried to shield my head. Purple hair was one thing. Even I had to admit that when wet, it was not a pretty sight.

My visit with the Reverend Coy Nichols, not to mention my glimpse of Kayla, the little girl who reminded me of me as a kid, had unnerved me, and I'd been popping Altoids all morning trying to take the edge off. I wondered about "Mother" Nichols, if she would remember me the way her husband promised, the way Mary Haskins couldn't quite. This lack of impression I'd made in my early years had left me feeling invisible. But I had *stick-to-it-ness,* then and now, I reminded myself. They'd soon find out that I wasn't invisible anymore.

A couple of nuns crossed in front of me, scurrying to get out of the rain. An old man with a cane inched along in the same direction I was going, protected by the overhang. I passed him on the wrong side and got a splat of water on my forehead.

When I turned the corner toward the seniors' center, I knew that something was wrong.

The patina woman held court at the front table surrounded by many of the same group members I'd seen yesterday. The two men who'd been vying for her attention when I left Friday now stood holding their Santa hats and shaking their heads. She was dressed in jeans and a gray T-shirt, and rivers of ruined makeup.

She dabbed her swollen eyes with a wadded-up tissue. "Terrible," I made out as I watched her lips. "It's the worst thing that ever happened to me."

This time I saw the nameplate on the table. Joyce Hardcastle.

"Joyce," I called, and she looked up.

"Oh, *there* you are," she said with a theatrical gesture in my direction. "You were here yesterday, weren't you? I told the police that, but I didn't have your name."

"Police? What for?"

"They want the names of everyone she saw last week." Joyce flicked tears from her eyes. If I weren't so worried, I'd be amused by her flair for the dramatic.

The group around her moved back, making room for me to approach the table. "She, meaning Mary Haskins?" I asked, my throat aching. Please, no. Not Mary. Don't let anything have happened to her.

"Oh, God. You haven't heard yet, have you?" Joyce said, tears flowing anew. "Mary was killed last night, murdered. And I was the one who found her body."

I couldn't react. I could only think of Mary—those eyes, that voice so rich that even I could hear. Stick-to-it-ness.

"What happened?" I managed to ask.

Joyce had retrieved a small gold compact and was patting more color onto her face. "Somebody murdered her, strangled her in her own home." That brought on a new wave of sobs that streaked her cosmetic repairs. I wanted to tell her to just leave it alone, that it didn't matter, but I had tears of my own, and it was growing increasingly difficult to keep them inside. "I'll need your name," she said again.

I took out my third business card in two days and dropped it on the table. She picked it up and absorbed the information almost greedily. "You're a newspaper reporter?"

"Yeah."

"Oh, my goodness. So's the other one."

"What other one?" I asked, but the compact was out again, and the nose and forehead were being covered, as if I had a photographer waiting just outside for a shoot. "Damn it," I said, raising my voice a tad more than I meant to, "I asked you a question."

She jumped and pulled back at the same time, as if I were more dangerous than just your basic purple-haired newspaper reporter ready to burst into tears. "And I was trying to answer it. You didn't give me a chance."

"Sorry." I sucked in a deep breath. "Tell me about the other one."

"I told you that Mary was popular last week," she said slowly. "Three people, not counting you, called to see when she'd be in. One was a newspaper reporter. That was all I meant."

"Male or female?" I asked.

"Male." We let the word settle between us. "Are you satisfied now?" she asked, and in spite of the drama-queen stance, I could see that her long-suffering smile was pure victim.

"What about the other two?" I asked.

"Women," she said. "That's all I know. I wasn't Mary's keeper, but I did stop by for coffee sometimes. That's what happened today. We were going to have some coffee and those corn muffins she makes." Her face caved in again, and this time, I believed that the grief was genuine. "Made," she said. "Mary made fabulous muffins. Crème de menthe bars, too. Oh, God."

"Do they know who did it?" I asked.

She shook her head. "No one knows anything, but it had to be someone she knew. Whoever it was walked right into her apartment. When I got there this morning, the door was unlocked."

We exchanged a few more words, although I could feel her energy diminishing as mine did. There was no way that this blathering woman and I could figure out who'd killed Mary Haskins. I left the center wondering where I should go next. Back home to San Francisco? To my new home, that palace on the cliffs of Half Moon Bay?

Yes, Half Moon Bay, where Jesse was. In spite of my earlier resolve, I had every intention of phoning him when I returned to the car. But when I took my cell phone out of my purse and looked at the call log, it wasn't Jesse's number waiting for me, but Malc's.

Fourteen

GERI

I beat my printed-out computer map's estimated time by about thirty minutes. The Bay Bridge never looked as good as it did today, stretched there above the fog. I breathed in the welcoming, sea-fresh energy of it and turned off onto the Fremont exit just before three o'clock.

I'd called Malc a couple of times from the car—make that a couple of dozen times—and gotten no answer.

His voice mail message on my phone had said only, "Malc here, Geri. Get back to me as soon as you can."

That wasn't unusual for him. He knew that long messages were difficult for me to understand, even on expensive state-of-the-art cells. He also knew that I lost, destroyed, ran over and, on one occasion, washed and dried cell phones, so preferred to purchase cheap ones that I could demolish relatively guilt-free.

Why was he calling? He had looked as uncomfortable as I felt when we ran into each other in Half Moon Bay. He had to have heard about Kathleen and the inheritance by now. Yes, that was it. He was calling to offer me support. Why did I care? What did I want? Maybe just that, I realized. Just his support. Anything else was out of the question for both of us.

Saturday afternoon, soon-to-be night. I could guess where he was. With damned Adrienne. No, that wasn't right. I felt guilty thinking about her that way when she'd never done anything to me but take my man once he was no longer mine, and by mutual consent, at that. Still, I knew she was the reason I kept getting his voice mail instead of his voice.

Malc was a man who worked hard but who, when work was over, had no problem turning off his cell. I guess therapists had to learn that or forever be on the other end of someone else's crisis.

I'd leave my phone on, just in case, and make an attempt to reclaim my real life, the one that had been replaced by the life in Half Moon Bay. As I pulled into the underground garage of my apartment building, the phone beside me on the seat, I flirted with the idea of calling Jesse Medicine. Now, why would I want to do that? I still was no closer to finding the connection between his ex-wife and me. And I'd sworn to swear off of him until I did.

Okay, I was scared. I was lonely. I was confused. And I didn't want to think about Malc.

Not one of them a good reason to call the man in Half Moon Bay, Geri.

Right again, self.

I'd already phoned Steffan in a last-minute attempt to see if we could get together. I missed him, and I needed Nathan back with me, tonight, for sure. His doggish presence would soften a lot of the ugliness that had claimed too much of my time since Kathleen Fowler's murder and my unwilling part in the aftermath.

Steffan wasn't answering, either. I left a message along with my estimated time of arrival. Told him I missed him. Told him I missed Nathan. Told him I loved them both.

I took the elevator to my floor, feeling safe with the familiar in a way I hadn't felt safe in Kathleen Fowler's perfect town or the perfectly charming hotel in which I'd tried to exist while there. I got off the elevator and almost skipped down the musty paisley carpet to my apartment. Finally, here was something solid, something that would help me focus and figure out where I needed to be and what I needed to do.

I expected to see the door, the silly, over-the-top iridescent Christmas wreath that Steffan had insisted

I place on it. It was there—the door, the wreath—and so was he.

Malc—all hazy hair and tailored clothes—leaned against the wall outside my apartment like an elegant stranger waiting for a cab.

Only he wasn't a stranger.

He saw me the moment that I saw him, and we both just froze. I could feel my heart beating like hell. I could almost feel his. That's how it had been with us. How it still was.

He wore that chamois-colored jacket he'd had on the first time we met more than a year ago, the one that complemented his gray-green eyes. His wild curls were tamed and closer to his head, and I wondered if it was due to an earlier rainfall similar to the one I'd experienced in the Valley, or to his new woman's idea about men and hair. As I recalled, Adrienne's former husband had cropped his to the skull of political correctness.

So here we were, finally. A tiny little victorious voice in my brain whispered that he'd shut off his phone, not because he was with Adrienne, but because he'd been waiting here, in this poor-cell-reception hall, for me. How long had he waited, and what did I do now?

Did I run into his arms? Did I walk slowly to him and shake his hand? We were no longer lovers, would never be again, but I was so freaking happy to see him that I wanted to release the tears I'd been holding in since Mary Haskins's death, maybe a whole lot longer.

"It's about time you got here." I'd forgotten how easily I could hear his voice, how it was one of the few that didn't have to pass through imaginary cotton balls in my ears to go straight from sound to words.

"You knew that I was in the Valley, right?" A lame-ass greeting, but the best I could do.

"I didn't know where the hell you were," he said. "Steffan thought you'd be home today. He doesn't know where you were, either."

"I left him a message on his home voice mail." I tried to control my quivering lip. "There's been a lot going on this weekend."

"I gathered that." He took a step forward. "I'm glad you're back, Geri. I was going to wait out here all night if I had to."

This time I was the one to take the step. "Really?" I asked.

"Yeah."

Crikey. I couldn't think of anything else to say. I took another step, and my feet began to move faster. My body pitched forward. His seemed to do the same. Before I knew it, we were face-to-face, and one of us—I'll never know which one—pulled the other into an embrace that almost made me forget the time and space between us.

The moment we connected, we both jumped

back, and I'm pretty sure that move was unanimous. Maybe the first one was, too.

"I'm sorry," he said, as sandalwood danced in my nostrils and my memory. Just like him to take the blame. "What the hell happened? Why did Kathleen Fowler name you her heir?"

He was going too fast for me, switching from what had just happened between us to what had happened to me following Kathleen Fowler's murder. I pinned my arms to my sides, the way I would in a strong wind. "I don't know." I looked at the once-safe door to my apartment with all of its Steffan-inspired cheer. I couldn't invite Malc in there. "I'm sorry," I said, knowing that I didn't need to say any more.

He frowned, deepening those two diagonal criss-cross lines between his eyebrows. "I was thinking that maybe we could walk down the block for a beer," he said.

It was three blocks, but I was so grateful for the suggestion that I would have walked a hell of a lot farther. We stepped out of the building and onto the street—the chilled air was scented with shish kebab, soy sauce, garlic and fast-food grease. I didn't want to go to the bar we used to frequent when we were a couple. That might be almost as bad as inviting him into my apartment, but it was too late to reconsider now.

He must have shared my reluctance, because he didn't move, either. "We could take a drive," he said.

"Okay." Another thing we used to do together. All of those patient Sunday afternoons when he'd be my tour guide, pointing out where one district ended and one began. Telling me which ones were okay to walk alone and which ones were not.

The car felt safe, and I turned to watch his face, trying to figure out how a year could have changed everything between us. I had loved him. I knew I had. But now I didn't. I was just conjuring the memory of the love, and that was the loneliest feeling of all.

He focused those deep-set eyes on me and said, "Okay, Geri, can you tell me about it?"

His question seemed too abrupt, more like a demand. "Not yet," I said. "First, you need to tell me. How'd you hear about what happened?"

"Adrienne." He didn't sigh, but it was there in his voice. "She knew Kathleen. I knew her, too. I mean, I'd met her."

"So Adrienne told you about the murder?" I asked.

He shook his head. "The inheritance," he said. "She heard about it from the son. Kathleen was her client. They were good friends."

I hadn't counted on that one. Hadn't counted on Kathleen and Adrienne knowing each other let alone being friends, make that good friends. "Jesse Medicine said Kathleen was a foster child from the San Joaquin Valley," I said. "Did Adrienne know that?"

"I don't think so, but you can't believe anything Medicine says."

I stiffened. "Why not?" There was something just a little too smug in the way he casually attacked Jesse's credibility.

"Because Jesse Medicine is a—well, let's just say he's a guy with a lot of demons," Malc said. "I don't understand why you'd want to spend time with someone like that."

That one stopped me. Malc had demons, and I'd sure as hell spent time with him. He had Adrienne. How dare he question my relationship with Jesse? Not that it was a real relationship. At best, it was an attraction of convenience. How could Malc question something I hadn't been able to figure out myself?

"Back off," I shot back. "Jesse and I aren't a couple. I can spend my time with anyone I choose."

"Of course you can." For a moment, I thought I might have one-upped him, as Mama would say. Then before I could celebrate even that small victory, he added with the sunlight glinting in his hair, "I'm asking only because Kathleen told Adrienne a lot about Jesse."

"Like what?"

"That he's a loose canon."

"What is that supposed to mean?" My heart began beating way too fast. I'd only wanted to find some sympathy and solace from Malc, maybe even a teensy little connection to our past. But now I was more upset than I'd been when I stepped off the elevator in my apartment. "This ride was a bad idea. This whole everything was a bad idea."

"I'm sorry," he said. "I'm trying to help you."

"I don't need—"

"You do need, damn it." I could see him trying to control his voice. "Let's stop and have that beer," he said. "I need to make you understand about this, and I can't drive and do that, too."

He parked somewhere off Union, and I tried to calm down. He didn't mean any harm, but I didn't need help from someone who only wanted to bad-mouth Jesse.

We got out of the car and walked in front of trendy post-Starbucks storefronts and cafés. This entire part of town smelled like coffee, my drug of choice. Before I could suggest some, Malc pointed toward a flicker of neon. The sign read only Bar. As I squinted I made out two overlapping cocktail glasses and smaller neon scrolled lettering that blinked from red to green—Cosmopolitan, Appletini.

"That place looks new," Malc said.

"I should say so."

Appletini, Cosmopolitan.

Cosmopolitan, Appletini.

Green and red; red and green. I'd been known to get hypnotized the rest of the way out of the world of the hearing by less, but right then, I knew that his goal was the same as mine. In short, avoid emotion.

Appletini, Cosmopolitan. If I could hear it, it would be a waltz in my ears.

I wasn't into designer martinis, whatever the color or flavor of the vodka, and I knew that he wasn't, either. But that wasn't the reason we were standing there together, staring at the blinking lights with something close to desperation.

"You think it's too…?" he asked, unable to specify the *too* to which he was objecting.

"No, not at all," I replied, unable to define it, either.

He looked relieved, and for a moment, I wondered if he might be worried about running into Adrienne and having to explain. He wouldn't have to worry about it at this place.

On the way in, we passed a man and a woman, both about my age with hair styles to prove it, engaged in what sounded like a drunken argument over two singers.

Malc raised an eyebrow, but neither of us stopped.

Once inside, I settled into the dark anonymity of the place. It smelled a little too much like disinfectant and not enough like the old wood and leather of our regular dive, and I was glad for that. No memories to be made or missed. The woman and her boyfriend were gone, arguing somewhere else, disrupting someone else's evening.

The circular booth was large enough for four or five people. Malc slid to the center and ordered two beers, and my monkey mind tried to scramble out whether the plural of one Heineken was *two Heineken* or *two Heinekens*. Monkey mind always jumps in for a reason. In this case, I thought it was probably because I was trying to forget that it was still daylight outside, and that I never drank or swore until after five. What I didn't try to forget—what I reminded myself from the get-go—was that I was sitting in this dark booth in this dark bar with another woman's man.

Our beers arrived, and I inched away from him toward the edge of the booth.

"I'm sorry about upsetting you," he said.

"That's okay." The next words out of his mouth would be that I needed his help. I might not be in love with him, but I wasn't exactly over him, either, and I didn't want anything from him. "It was the gossip about Jesse that did it."

Malc lifted his glass the way someone who plays chess might make the final move. "I was only repeating what I've been told."

"Then you were told a lie. And Adrienne told you, right?" Then, hating the loyal sheepdog expression stamped on his face, I said, "With all due respect, Malc, your lady friend was as wrong in her assessments of that matter last year as she is with this one."

"She gives you full credit for finding the razor killer," he shot back, clearly pissed off. At that moment, I resented him, not for being right, but for trying to defend Adrienne's case with the disgusting mix of logic and passion. Most of all, passion.

As I took a swig of the beer, I realized that this was a good thing. Malc had been the fantasy man every woman regrets and revisits in her mind. He'd just proven to me, over a solitary Heineken, that he wasn't worthy of the title.

He loved another woman, the bastard. He believed in another woman. He'd taken me out for a beer only to convince me of his loyalty for said woman.

A good thing. A very good thing to figure out all of this right now. So why was I ready to burst into tears?

"What's wrong?" he asked, as if it were his fault. For a crazy moment, I saw only his eyes in the dim light and remembered how similar they were to right before we were going to jump each other's bones. Never again, I reminded myself.

"You don't believe what I'm saying," I told him. "I understand that you believe Adrienne. You should. She's your woman."

He shoved his back against the booth. "As you would say, Geri, it's none of your business. That's not why I'm here."

"Then why *are* you here?" I asked.

"Because I thought maybe we—that maybe Adrienne could help you find out what's going on."

At that moment, I had to remind myself that I wasn't the violent type. Otherwise, he'd be wearing the beer.

"Thanks for the offer," I said. "Still, if Adrienne doesn't even know about the fosters, I don't know how much help she'll be."

"She might know," he said. "She just didn't mention it to me."

"But she did mention that Kathleen said Jesse was a loose canon." I couldn't help myself from doing it, and I felt something close to pleasure as I watched him draw back. We'd never been cagey with each other, and I could see that I'd taken him by surprise.

He took a slow swallow of beer. I could almost hear him counting: one thousand one, one thousand two, one thousand three.

"That doesn't really matter," he said. "What matters is that she might know something that you don't."

"I appreciate the offer," I said. "But you could have told me that with a phone call."

Another swallow of beer. Another count to one thousand three. "You're right," he said. "I guess I wanted to see you."

"Why?" *Beg, why don't you, Geri? Really humiliate yourself while you still have the chance.*

"To let you know that I'll try to help if I can." I kept watching him, trying to see what he really meant. "Okay," he said. "I was curious. Seeing you with Jesse was a surprise, to say the least, especially considering that Kathleen had been his wife."

I felt my skin slowly burn and hoped it didn't show

on my face. "There's nothing between Jesse and me."
Not a lie. Not even close to a lie.

"I also wanted to tell you," he began.

"What?"

He looked at me with an expression so helpless
that I wanted to wrap my arms around him. "I'm just
sorry about how everything worked out."

It was more than I could have asked for, more
than I deserved, but that was like him. He was ultimately and always decent before he was anything. It
wasn't his fault that I hadn't been able to trust him.

"I'm sorry, too." I couldn't say more.

"If it's true about Kathleen and the foster homes,"
he said, "you'll have to go back there, won't you?"

I nodded, realizing that he had put on his shrink
face. "Already have."

"Are you going to be able to handle that?"

I thought about Mary Haskins and trembled.
Thought about the Reverend. About Quack-Quack.
"I don't have any choice." This time I couldn't stop
the tears.

He didn't turn away from them. That was another
thing I remembered about him. He wasn't threatened or embarrassed by emotion. Good thing, too,
because that's about all I was just about then.
"Another woman, a social worker, was killed," I said.
Then I began to sob, my body shaking as I fought to
control it.

He waited. And when I could finally breathe evenly,

he said, "It's not going to be easy for either one of us, but you are going to have to let me help you on this one."

"I don't know," I whispered. But even then, I did. I needed a professional to figure out the *why* behind the murder and the inheritance. Like it or not, I needed Malc's expertise.

Without admitting that he was right, I asked, "Is there any way you could profile the kind of nut who kills like this? Throwing someone off a cliff? Strangling a senior citizen?"

"I'll need to know more." His movements were cautious, as if he was afraid he'd chase me away. "Revenge killing is my first thought, but I can't be sure. Usually with such cases, the revenge takes place over a long period of time. It—"

"What, Malc?"

He covered both of my hands with his. "Just for now, back away from Jesse a little, okay?"

I jerked my hands away. "For how long?" I demanded.

"A week or two, until I can do some checking."

I stood up from the table. "Adrienne must have done a real number on him," I said.

"Sit down."

"I don't want to stay here."

"As you wish." He tossed some bills on the table and we walked to the car, not looking at each other, and I remembered that Malc once told me that anger was a secondary emotion. I had no idea what primary one was driving mine.

When we got to the car, I couldn't hold it in any longer. "What?" I asked. "What did Adrienne say about him?"

"You really like him," he said, and I wanted to slap the smug analytical frown off his face.

"I think I know him better than you do," I said, climbing into the car. "I think I know him better than your girlfriend does, too." Then I slammed the door.

He stood outside his own car, looking in for one moment. Then he yanked the door open again. "Did you know that he physically abused Kathleen?" he asked. "Did you know that he threatened to kill her?"

Fifteen

Raining again. It ran through her clothes like water through a sieve. She and Sunlight dashed across the field, Tiny trying to protect herself by pulling the plastic bag down around her ears.

It was the kind of night that could send you straight to a shelter. The kind of night that could make you swear to find Jesus, kick booze, get a job or any of the other promises people like her made when they knew that they'd end up back on the streets soon as the sun came out.

But it was okay now. She and Sunlight rushed through the door, screeching like kids. Tiny had to admit she'd had the warmest nights she'd been able to remember in this shed. Sunlight hadn't been lying when she said she protected her spaces. And now that Tiny was Sunlight's friend, she got protected, too.

Even two nights in a row at the same place felt like forever when you were on the streets. Four nights in a place with no one crashing in on you either meant you were dead or you'd lucked out. Tiny had lucked out.

Not that Sunlight didn't have her problems. Dope smoking for one. Stealing and cussing like a stevedore for two and three.

She was going to be able to sleep tonight and probably wake up alive in the morning. That was what did matter. She wasn't sure why being alive mattered anymore, only that it did.

She yanked off the plastic bag and fluffed her hair almost dry. Then she followed Sunlight upstairs. Did she want to sleep under the tarp tonight? Probably. After that first night, no one had come near the shed when they were there, but you never knew. Sunlight's place was too sweet to stay secret for long.

Tiny propped up her gym bag under her neck and watched Sunlight smooth the frayed blue cap over her head.

"You doing okay?" Sunlight asked in that voice that was bigger than she was.

"Doing fine," Tiny said. "I just wonder what happened with that poison jug. The one that used to be downstairs."

"Who knows and who cares?" Sunlight fired up a joint, the way she did every night. "One minute I saw that raincoat flapping 'round whoever it was. Next minute, I was looking at a tree."

As smoke crept into the space they shared, Tiny tried to close her eyes and think about the last time she'd felt safe. Never like right now. How can you feel safe in the rain, trying to sleep in an alley behind a theater downtown? Now she had Sunlight and whatever it was Sunlight patted on her hip each night. Their protection.

The friendly smell of dope filled the loft. "Take a hit," Sunlight said, her sleepy voice rising as she held down the smoke. "How come you never get high with me, girl?"

"I'm allergic," Tiny said.

"Shit. That's what all the addicts say when they're trying to go straight."

"I'm not an addict." Now, that pissed her off, that Sunlight could know her and think she hadn't told the whole truth about herself. "I'm poor. I'm homeless, but I'm not no addict, and, yeah, I'm allergic to dope, okay?"

Sunlight propped herself up against a big orange industrial fan she'd wrapped with enough plastic to make it look like a pillow. The blue knit cap she never took off covered her head to the ears, and her long hair hung down her back. Its color might have been light enough to earn her the name of Sunlight once, before the gray got to it. Probably, though, it had been her eyes. They looked younger than she did, and even when she was stoned, they were alive in the way the rest of her wasn't. Her lips pinched around the joint, and when she sucked down the smoke, Tiny could hear the anger in it. "Fine by me," Sunlight said, but Tiny knew it wasn't.

"I'm probably high just breathing the same air as you," she said. "Bet I am."

"Breathing the same air as me probably saved your dumb-ass life." Sunlight patted her hip again, and Tiny could almost see the gun there. "You were like a baby in that alley by the theater. The others already had a plan about what they were gonna do. Me, I took pity on you."

"You know I appreciate it," Tiny said. "I wish I could do something to pay you back."

"You gave me the money. That's enough."

A couple of bills to pay for dope. Tiny was ashamed that she didn't have more. Sunlight was right. If she hadn't stepped in at that alley, Tiny would be dead— or would wish she were dead—by now.

There was comfort in Sunlight that she didn't feel with others at any of the shelters or on the streets. Sunlight wasn't a dyke, but she could fight like one. She wasn't a drunk, but she could drink without passing out. And even though she was as homeless as Tiny, she could find the best places to crash. This loft was the best of the best.

"I'm tired as hell," she said. "You sure we're safe here?"

"I already told you that." She patted her hip.

"Is that a gun?" Tiny finally asked.

Sunlight choked out a laugh. "Better than a gun. You turn a gun on some bastard, he can turn it back on you. Same with Mace. That's just a brand name for tear gas. Does the same thing. Sometimes it makes them meaner."

"So?" Tiny didn't know how to ask more.

"I'm going to sleep now," she said. "The rain wore me out."

"Cool," Tiny said. She knew Sunlight was in Dopeland already. A good time to check out. So good to feel warm, to feel safe. To try not to feel anything else.

She could sleep now.

No, not yet. What was rousing her? There. A click downstairs. She'd heard it before, that night the poison had disappeared.

And now another click, a noise like a door closing. No mistaking that one, especially when the cold air shot straight up from the downstairs.

"Sunlight," she whispered.

"Huh?" Sunlight jerked herself out of Dopeland, patting her side. "What?" she asked.

Something creaked on the stairs. Tiny's heart beat so fast that it hurt to breathe. "Get your gun," she said. "Right now, damn it."

"Who needs a gun?" Sunlight pulled out something that looked like a cell phone. "Pepper spray," she said. "The best in the country. Ten percent, just like the cops use."

Another creak. Someone was definitely walking up those stairs.

Tiny lifted the tarp. "Someone's coming," she said. "Don't do anything crazy. Get under here so they don't see us."

"No way." Sunlight was already on her feet, facing the door, the pepper spray aimed like a gun. "This is my place." She wasn't even whispering, wasn't afraid. Tiny couldn't imagine how that would feel. Not to be afraid.

She slid under the tarp, scared, but something else, too. She felt as if she were falling down something dark and narrow. Dizzy, she clapped her hands over her mouth to keep from crying.

Sunlight laughed and called out in a hoarse voice. "Don't think you can scare me. Anyone can hide behind a getup like that."

What was Sunlight talking about? And why wasn't anyone else saying anything? There wasn't a noise. Everything was quiet as death. Then Sunlight yelled again. "Get out of my place. Get out, or I'll use this."

Something crashed next to where Tiny hid. A scream, higher pitched and more hideous than anything that could come from a human shot straight to Tiny's bones.

"I warned you," Sunlight said. "That hood of yours ain't no protection against this stuff. Now, get your ass out before I shoot this again."

Instead, there was a struggle, all grunts and thumps, nothing that made sense to Tiny. No one screamed or shouted out. Maybe Sunlight's pepper spray had done the job.

The grunts melted into one fading moan, a scream-choked gurgle. Then heavy boots, marching boots, coming toward her. She flattened out, even thinner than she was. *Don't think about the people who try to hunt out the homeless for medical experiments or just for fun,* she reminded herself, thinking about all of the lectures she'd heard at shelters. Be quiet. Be almost dead, so that you don't have to be really dead. Pray that these boots will soon leave the way they came.

Instead, they kicked at the tarp. She felt the sharp impact to her butt and was glad she'd wrapped in the extra blankets, even though she'd felt almost too safe for them when they'd gotten here tonight. A tiny bit of the tarp had been lifted by the kick. She saw light and a long plastic-looking coat, dark blue. *Please,* she thought. *Please just go.* No, instead another kick. She drew back, taking a boot tip in her chest.

Someone laughed, a high-pitched laugh like something you'd see on a cartoon show, not hear from a real person. Couldn't have been Sunlight. Had to be this maniac who'd invaded their place. She closed her eyes and tried to remember how to pray.

Even in partial blindness, the figure in the uniform continued to laugh. Couldn't stop it. Slowly, it made its way back, carrying the rain hood, squinting the eyes that felt as if they'd been doused in gasoline. The homeless woman had been right about that. It was no protection from whatever she'd sprayed. But the homeless woman had gotten what she had coming.

The rain washed away some of the fire. A baggy sleeve wiped the eyes, and the world returned, blurred but there. The figure reached into the pocket and patted the cell phone. Poor vision but good photos. That was all that mattered.

A sudden noise electrified the hairs along the figure's neck and arms. Someone else was out here, walking through the brush toward the shed.

The figure crouched beneath the bushes, and, yes, there was someone moving closer to the shed. The shape grew bigger by the moment. A big man with long, bushy hair paused, as if sensing a presence. Then he moved toward the shed and stepped inside.

Even with blurred vision, the shadow darted through the trees, boots pounding the muddy soil.

Eric Fowler heard the noise but couldn't identify

it. Too distracted. At least maybe he'd find some peace out here where no one would come looking for him. He took the joint out of his pocket and opened the door. Walked inside. Just a little peace. That's all he wanted.

Sixteen

GERI

I regretted seeing Malc. I especially regretted thinking that I could be rational about anything he said. There was only one way to deal with Adrienne's gossip. Ask Jesse. And I intended to. Malc parked in front of my apartment.

"Geri?" he asked.

I didn't invite him up. I didn't continue the argument I'd never win. "Good night," I said.

The moment I stepped off the elevator in my apartment building, I could smell the sesame/soy scent of *bulgogi* down the hall. *Steffan,* I thought. *Nathan.* And I began to run. How long had they been here?

It hit me as I yanked open the door that this was the happiest I'd been all day. That alone should tell me all that I needed to know about my feelings for Malc. Sure, they flared when he was around, but right now, all I could think about was what waited inside for me. A friend who wouldn't question, a pet who would love me unconditionally.

They were there, both of them, Nathan inhaling a piece of meat he'd just been tossed, Steffan at the cooker, and the scent and smoke of *bulgogi* filling the place.

Steffan had brought over his dome-shaped cooker for the specialty that was his version of a Korean barbecue. As he tossed the marinated meat up against the sides, he blew me a kiss.

I knew not to disturb the master at work. Besides, there was Nathan to contend with. He covered the room in two bounds.

I wanted to cry. Instead, I said, "I am so happy to see you two."

"About time you got back," Steffan said as Nathan jumped me again.

"Baby dog," I said, and hugged Nathan. "I missed you so much."

"And we missed you," Steffan said. "Are you okay?"

"Far from it." I couldn't lie to him. "A social worker in Hanford was killed last night. I think it's connected to Kathleen Fowler's murder."

He lifted the *bulgogi* cooker from the burner and crossed the room, joining Nathan at my side. "Why would those two things be connected?" he asked.

"Because we were both fosters. This woman was my social worker, and I think she was Kathleen's, too."

He patted Nathan absently. "Guess that's about the same as going to the back of the book for the answers, isn't it, boy?"

"Her murder is connected to me in some way," I said, "and I think it's connected to the fosters."

"How much can you remember from back then?" Steffan asked. "Anything, you know, weird?"

"It was all weird," I said. "Most of the memories are about being alone and out of place. I wasn't just a foster. I couldn't hear, either. The whole time pretty much sucked."

"But you grew up in foster homes," he said. "You must remember some of the kids you knew."

"Some when I was older, but not many when I was young." The concern in his face made me love him even more. Steffan understood in a way that Malc had not.

"I'm lucky to have you for a friend," I said, "but I just can't remember that much."

"Are you sure?" he asked. "I can." And before I could admonish him, he said, "But then, I was raised in a relatively happy home."

"And with the same people," I told him.

"The same people. Yeah, that makes a difference, all right."

But I could tell he wasn't convinced, or that there

was something else he wasn't saying. He seemed distracted, maybe just concentrating on his cooking.

"What's the matter?" I asked.

Steffan tossed a piece of steak to Nathan's ready jaws, and slowly made eye contact with me. "Doug Bastard," he said. "His article is printing tomorrow."

"How do you know?"

"Don't ask."

I managed to say, "I can't believe it."

"We knew it was just a matter of time." He opened the refrigerator and dug two frost-covered Henry Weinhards out of the freezer. Then he sat beside me at the counter, our root beers in front of us.

"I knew it, but I didn't know it would be this soon."

"The son's apparently vindictive," he said.

It wasn't the word I would have used to describe Eric, but I didn't know him, either. "I just hope he didn't lie." I gulped the Henry, which was so cold that it had pieces of ice in it. The bones between my eyes burned, as if I had a margarita headache.

"I don't think it's a good idea for you to be pursuing this case. The social worker's murder just proves it."

"Proves what?" I closed my eyes to squint away the pain shooting to my temples.

"That there's a crazy out there killing people, and you'd better drop out of sight." He slugged down several swallows from his bottle, and I thought he'd give himself a margarita headache, too.

"It doesn't matter what I do, Steffan. I can't get away from this case because I'm involved in it."

As I said it, I realized with a sick tightening in my chest how right I was. I had volunteered to be involved, and I wouldn't be able to get up and leave the way I could leave the theater in the middle of a bad film. The murders were part of me, and I was part of them. Now I'd have Doug Blanchard's column to deal with, too.

Steffan squinted at me in a way that he did when he wasn't wearing his contacts. "Two women have been killed," he said. "You might be involved. You might not. But why not just kind of disappear for a while? Let the crazy focus on someone else."

"It's pretty difficult for me considering Doug Blanchard will probably paint me as some kind of money-hungry con artist," I said.

He contemplated it as he stared at his bottle. Finally, he said, "Why not let Malc help you?"

"Malc?" I shot up, nearly tripping over the bar stool. "You talked to Malc?"

"He cares about you, Ger. He wants to help. So does his girlfriend. What's her name? Angela?"

"Adrienne. And please don't butt into my life. I just saw Malc."

"You did?" The look of relief that washed over his face made me want to hug him for caring. "I knew he was trying to connect with you. And I'm glad you had a chance to talk. He told you, I guess, about Kathleen Fowler's ex?"

I slammed my glass on the counter. "How do you know anything about Jesse?"

"Calm down," he said. "Malc just asked if you were seeing him. I told him I didn't think you were seeing anyone. You aren't, are you, Ger? You don't want to get involved with someone like that."

"I'm not involved with anyone." This time his look of relief did not make me want to hug him. I'd have slammed out the door, Nathan with me, if it wasn't my apartment. "Not anyone, understand?" He'd plotted with Malc behind my back, tried to spread dirt about a man he'd never even met.

"I understand that you're pretty upset about this," he said. "You've been through a lot."

"Let's drop it, then," I said.

"You're not mad at me?"

How could I be mad at my only friend in the world? "No." I got up from the stool and pecked his cheek. "I love you. You know that."

His look softened. "You ready for some dinner, then? I know Nathan is."

I couldn't stand the thought of food, not after living on Altoids and caffeine all day. "Sure," I said.

In our relatively short friendship, I'd always insisted that the day I couldn't eat Steffan's *bulgogi*, I'd be dead. I was wrong. Every time I tried to savor the sweet/hot meat, it was all I could do to swallow.

I kept seeing Mary's face, her humorous yet skeptical expression. I could see Malc, too, the anger and conviction in his face when he slammed Jesse. And although Steffan and I did not discuss it, I kept thinking about Doug Blanchard's article. How could Marie, my editor, allow a column about my private life to be published?

Steffan and I had said all that we could about it. I tried to show appreciation for the meal and his presence. He tried to entertain me with newspaper gossip about Romeo Joey Reynolds's newest and not-so-secret affair with a new reporter.

"Why would he look at her?" I asked.

"She's needy, my dear, and predators like Reynolds love needy."

He speculated. I reacted. We gossiped about the last two people in the world who mattered to us. Sometimes that's the best friends can do—pretend to go on as usual when life is anything but. So we sat at my small glass-topped bistro table, Nathan patrolling beneath us, and did the best we could.

The phone rang before we'd finished eating.

"I'll let the machine take it," I said.

"Better not." His look was wary. I'd already figured out that I'd be an idiot to trust any call right now to voice mail or even the new amplified phone that I'd purchased along with a bed shaker that actually shook me awake so that I could answer said phone.

I could hear almost anyone on this state-of-the-art

monster in the nook beside the kitchen. I got to it on the second ring. That's when I saw the caller ID. MEDICINEAVE, it read.

I yanked the phone off the cradle, no longer caring what Steffan thought.

"Where are you?" I said.

"Nice way to greet a caller," Jesse said. I could hear him as clearly as I had the last time I'd seen him.

"Sorry," I said. "I'll explain when I see you. And I hope it's soon."

"What about now?" he asked.

A tiny shudder crept along my arms. "Tonight?"

"Tonight," he repeated. "Geri, I'm standing outside your apartment right now."

Seventeen

TINY

She didn't know what to do, still couldn't believe what was happening. From the moment she saw Sunlight, her body sprawled up against the wall, she'd known she was dead. The murderer had done it like a joke, the way you'd prop up a scarecrow to frighten birds. There was nothing funny about the bloody gash in her chest.

Tiny had been too afraid to scream or cry out. Still, tears had run down her face like water. She'd reached out to touch Sunlight, and her body had toppled forward. Tiny gasped. The blue cap flopped to the floor, along with several bills. The cap. That's where Sunlight had hidden her money. She hadn't trusted Tiny enough to tell her that.

What the hell was she going to do now? Maybe rent a room, even for a night, anything to escape before what happened to Sunlight happened to her.

She'd gathered up the bills, then not sure why, took the cap, too. The can of pepper spray had rolled next to it. Tiny picked it up and ran out into the night.

She still wasn't sure how she'd gotten to the motel. But she was here now, safe for just a little while. When the money ran out, she'd figure out something. She kept thinking about what Sunlight said about a hood. Her killer had been wearing a hood. Something about that creeped her out in a way that didn't make sense. What kind of person wore a hood without getting noticed? Astronaut? Firefighter? Trying to figure it out made her too scared. Now she knew why people like Sunlight did the drugs and the alcohol.

Tiny got out of bed and turned up the heat. The people inside had no idea how good warm could feel to someone who lived outside most of her life. She knew, though.

The shower in the bathroom looked like a grout-less slab of concrete, but to her, right now, it looked like heaven. She'd already taken one shower, but maybe she should take another one, or two or three, just to feel that sweet, warm water on her back.

She was ready to step into it when she heard the noise. The walls in this place were like paper. She could hear the scratching at her door as if it were in the shower with her. She grabbed the pepper spray and went straight for it. Shoved her eye into the peephole. Couldn't see anybody.

Okay, then. She'd call the front desk. Took a long time for the phone to pick up. "Someone's trying to break into my room," she said.

"We'll be right there," the man with the accent replied. "Do not open the door unless it's one of us on the other side."

As if she could tell the difference. As if. Better put her clothes back on and hope for the best. If not, she still had her gift from Sunlight.

The motel lights played with her mind. How could she let her friend be murdered while she hid? The knock at the door was so loud she knew it must be the man from the front desk. Still, she hesitated.

"Ma'am," he shouted, as if the door were made of something a hell of a lot thicker than it was. "There's no one out here."

Ma'am. That'd be a hoot if it wasn't so sad. She inched the door open. "Are you sure?" she asked. As if anyone would hang around waiting to be seen.

His dark eyes met hers. His violet tie was so bright that it sucked the light from the room and washed out his features. "We looked all over the place. We've got good security, too."

Then she saw the man behind him, in his ironed crisp security guard uniform. She'd dealt with rent-a-cops before. Most of them didn't even carry guns.

"Just keep a watch on my room, will you?" she asked.

He edged inside, and she caught a whiff of his scent, like incense or cheap candles. She didn't want him in her room. Before she could close the door on him, he narrowed those eyes on her and asked, "Have you been drinking?"

"I don't drink, and I don't do drugs," she said. "Now, get out of my face."

He backed off, but the smell of him stayed. "Sorry. It's just out here, renting the rooms by the hour, we're never sure about who we get."

At least it wasn't the streets. She had to remember that. "Keep a watch over it, anyway, will you?" she asked. "I promise not to do any drug deals while I'm here, but I do want to feel safe, considering I paid for the place."

"No problem," he said, ignoring the dig about drug deals. "My man here will take care of it. Won't you, Evan?"

"Sure thing." The security guard spoke for the first time. At least he was big enough for the job. The ones around the shelter were pretty wimpy.

"I'd appreciate it," she said. For a moment, she thought about stepping out there so that she could see both of them better, maybe explain to them what had happened to her. She wanted to, and as they started to walk away, she called out again, "Wait."

"What is it?" The guard this time.

"Nothing," she said. "Sorry."

The two men walked away, and she could swear that she heard one of them—the guard, she thought—saying, "Fruitcake. Nutty as hell."

She wasn't a nutcase, though. She just needed to get help, someone she could trust to listen and help her figure out what to do. When she tried to think, only one person came to her mind.

GERI

As flattered as I was about Jesse Medicine's sudden appearance, I soon learned that he was in the city to deliver costumes for some of his clients at the Dickens Fair at the Cow Palace.

Between Scrooge, Father Christmas and some chimney sweep attire, there wasn't much room in the truck for me. I squished in, anyway.

I didn't know much about the Dickens thing, except that it was a place to buy gifts and have holiday parties and basically spend a bunch of money. Malc and I had been there once ever so briefly to visit an old-fashioned photo parlor sponsored by one of Adrienne's clients. How connected Adrienne had always been to our short relationship, and I hadn't even seen it. I wondered if she'd sensed our problems and just waited around to catch Malc when I dropped him.

Odd how that dropping thing goes. You hope they'll bounce back up to you, but that's the chance you take, the chance I took when I dropped Malc. People aren't yo-yos. Sometimes, when you drop them, they bounce into someone else's lap.

Now I was with Jesse, but I kept remembering my brief time here with Malc. Although the Cow Palace had been difficult for me to navigate in an auditory way, Malc and I had hung around long enough for me to buy him a silver snuff box, and for him to pick out a Victorian corset for me. Crazy the things relatively rational people do when they're falling fast for each other. I didn't want to go back to the Cow Palace with Jesse.

I felt as if I were holding a large, stiff child, then realized that the chimney sweep's hat was slipping into my lap. I shoved it and the rest of the costume a little closer to the door. "Jesse," I said. "A social worker in my hometown was murdered Friday night."

"Your social worker?" he asked.

"Yes, I'm sure of it, and maybe Kathleen's, too."

"That's all I need," he said, but his lips were difficult to read, and his voice had dwindled to something below my register.

"What's wrong?" I asked.

"Let's get this over with first," he said.

The moment we pulled in, I recognized the Dickens scene. Costumed characters patrolled the front. I spotted booths for wheat weaving, doll fashions, rum cakes and feather masks.

I helped him carry in the costumes to the main office. For a moment, I thought Adrienne Revell would be there, waiting to deliver her nonjudgmental smile and give me a nod of her taffy-colored hair. No Adrienne. Admit it. I was relieved.

Before I could think of Adrienne another moment, I felt a warm arm around me. His. "All done," Jesse said. "Want to have a drink? Dinner?"

How do you answer "all of the above" to a question like that?

Then I remembered that he was here for a reason, and so was I. Malc insisted that Jesse had abused and threatened Kathleen. I didn't believe it. Maybe this was the time to ask.

"What do you have in mind?" I asked.

He gave me that dark, distrusting stare that I remembered from our first encounter. "I need to talk to you. You name the place."

"What's wrong with right here?"

That struck him wrong. He stepped back from me and said, "Safety in numbers? Is that what you want?"

"It was just a suggestion," I said. "What do you want?"

"I want to talk to you," he said. "And I'd like to spend some time with you." He gave me that gruff face and said, "I thought we dug each other."

Dug each other. If it could only be that easy. "I don't know what to think," I said. "My life is pretty crazy right now."

Behind me, I smelled the scent of sugar being burned into colored candy canes. I turned, and sure enough, there was a glass-faced machine tended by a man in a fancy, feathered costume.

Jesse touched my arm. I jumped. Even after he jerked his hand away, I could feel the heat of his fingers. If nothing else, we had chemistry, but I'd had chemistry with Malc, too. I knew how long that stuff lasted. I knew how long it didn't. "My life is pretty crazy, too," he said. "And it seems to be getting crazier."

I'd fallen in love with Malc. I knew that now, and I was pretty sure he'd felt the same once. This was different. With Jesse Medicine, I was falling into some kind of enchantment. He couldn't have done what Adrienne said he had. But why would she lie? Why would Malc?

"So, let's talk," I said.

"Good," he said, nodding stern approval. "Why don't we get out of this zoo and go to dinner? On the way, I'll tell you about the cops."

"What cops?"

"The ones your buddy the shrink sicced on me." He headed for the exit, and I hurried to catch up with him.

"Do you mean Malc?" I asked, unable to believe what he was telling me.

"Malcolm Piercy? You'd better believe it." In spite of his calm, almost stern presence, the anger glittered in Jesse's eyes. "Thanks to him, two cops showed up at my studio with all kinds of questions about Kathleen."

"I can't believe that he would do that." Even as I said it, I remembered how Malc had talked about Jesse to me.

"Well, he did," Jesse said. "He told them I abused Kathleen. Physically."

Finally, it was out there. "What did you say?" I asked, my mouth so dry I could barely speak.

"What do you think I told them? That it was a damn lie, that's what." We stepped outside into the cold. The mist felt good on my face, and I could have danced the rest of the way to the car. I hadn't realized how much Malc's accusation had been eating at me.

"Why would he say something like that?" I asked myself as well as him.

"And why would he have it in for me?" he asked. My expression must have changed, because he stared at me for a long moment with those penetrating eyes of his, as if he were trying to figure out how to paint me.

"What?" I asked finally.

"Do you know why he'd go after me?" he asked. "You do, don't you?"

What did I say? How did I explain? And was it too crazy to believe that Malc would try to harm Jesse because he thought he was involved with me? Too many questions. "Let's talk about it at dinner," I said.

The curt nod he gave me made it clear that I wasn't going to avoid telling him the truth about Malc and me. But that still didn't explain why Malc would want to send the police to question Jesse. The only way to find out why was to ask Malc, and that's exactly what I was going to do.

Eighteen

I couldn't sleep that night. Still, Malc was right. I needed his help. And if I needed Adrienne's help as well, I'd just have to suck it up and talk to her.

My new phone toy vibrated under my pillow early Sunday morning. My first impulse was not to answer. I was barely awake, in my own bed, with my own dog butted up to me, and it was way too early to talk to another human being.

The vibration stopped before I could reach a decision, but then it started up again. No escape for me. I picked it up if only to shut up the vibey device under my pillow.

"It's about time you answered."

Not the friendliest voice I wanted to encounter. Half-awake, I recognized it. "Good morning, Annette. I'd ask how you are, but I can guess that."

"You'd better get back here," she shouted into the phone. "There's been another murder. Cops are all over the nursery. I need your help at the counter."

"Who?" I asked, thinking for some ridiculous reason of Jesse.

"Some homeless woman. Eric found the body. Just get back here, okay?"

I thought about Malc, who'd offered to help. About Jesse and our dinner last night. I thought about Steffan crashed in the front room, and of Nathan, heavy and warm at my side.

"How soon do you need me?" I asked.

"Right away. As soon as you can get here."

This was a woman who'd treated me like shit, a woman who'd as much as called me a liar. Now she needed me. How mean could I be? How much revenge could I extract? Then I remembered what she'd said. A homeless woman had been murdered.

"I can be there by noon," I said.

I arrived at Half Moon Blooms a few minutes before that. I knew that Annette was surprised to see that I'd kept my promise. Her hair was tied up in a white turban thing, a few wet auburn bangs dribbling over her pale forehead.

She was conducting business like this?

She caught my eye, and I felt as if she'd heard my question. She crossed the stones that separated us and said, "What the hell's going on? How does a woman get killed on my property?"

"*Your* property?" I asked.

The look she gave me could have frozen my ears off. "Okay. Maybe I'd better rephrase. How could this woman be killed on our property, the property that *you* own, and *I* work?"

I got the dig and didn't care. "Tell me about the woman," I said. "Who was she?"

"Sunlight, no last name." Annette pulled her navy raincoat to her, and I could almost feel her shudder. "A homeless woman. Most of them hang out in the alley by the theater. This one...she..." Annette steadied herself as if unable to say more.

"How?" I asked.

"A knife."

More than I wanted to know, but, yes, she was doing the right thing, for the first time, to tell me what she knew.

"Thank you," I said, and hoped that she knew I meant it. "I have to go check in pretty soon."

"Check in where?" she asked. "Where are you staying?"

"A hotel not far from here." Did I really want to go back there after what happened the first time? "I haven't registered yet."

"Why not just move into the house?" she asked. "Considering that it's yours."

I didn't know how to tell her that I was afraid of that house. More than that, I was afraid of overlapping into any more of Kathleen Fowler's life. I was already attracted to her ex-husband. I already felt some kind of weird pity for her son. Would I lose myself if I moved into her home?

"Let me think about that one," I said.

"While you think, remind yourself that the house payment is due." She started to walk away from me, then turned before she could hide the anger in her eyes. "I'll give you the statement. It's your house now, so you can pay the mortgage. Or not."

"And you don't care, do you?" I don't know what made me feel so mean, maybe all that payment-due stuff.

"Not in the least," she said.

I could have guessed that response. "I'll move in tonight," I said.

"Tonight?" Now she was the one off center.

"It's my house now," I said. "I'm moving in."

It was easier said than done. The house had been closed since Kathleen's death more than a week ago. A pile of newspapers littered the porch. Furniture hadn't been dusted. Thankfully the recent rain had saved the outdoor plants. Only a faint smell of wax penetrated the mustiness of the first floor.

But the ocean gleamed with the last rays of sunset from the front windows. I was moving in. Once I got those details handled, I was going to see Jesse Medicine.

I unpacked my bags in Kathleen's immaculate

bedroom with its reversible black-and-white comforter. It would be easy to sink into this bed, this life, easy to pick up where Kathleen left off. Sleeping here, getting to know Jesse Medicine, getting to really know him.

A major chill shot through my body. I stood staring at the bed, unwilling to climb under that comforter. Afraid of what or who I'd wake up as.

Bottom line: I couldn't sleep here, not just yet. I started to head for the phone on the glass table beside the bed. Couldn't do that, either. Instead, I fumbled in my bag and, finding my phone, punched in Jesse's number.

"I'm coming over," he said.

"No." That's what I got for phoning him. I was really asking for it. "Just talk to me, will you?"

"What's going on?" he asked. "Are you hearing noises?" Before I could remind him that I heard little, he said, "Sorry. Sometimes I forget."

"I'm just not used to the place, and I remembered what you said about Kathleen being scared." As I spoke, I carried the phone with me to look out over the weathered shingles, the lawn, the long drop to the beach and its black rush of surf below.

"What's happened?" he asked.

"Nothing. It's just a feeling."

"I'm coming over," he repeated.

Before I could object for a second time, he'd hung up.

I saw his car round the curve, and then the head-lights disappeared. Just as I was wondering how he'd missed the turnoff, he pulled up beside the house. He found me on the front porch, still clutching the phone. I hadn't been able to stay inside. At least out here, I'd have options if anyone approached me. Inside, I was as helpless as that homeless woman in the shed.

"How'd you do that?" I asked as he joined me.

"Do what?" He wore a windbreaker that had prob-ably been gray-blue when it was new.

"I didn't know that there was another way to get in here," I said.

"Shortcut." He stood beside me, and I caught a whiff of his sweet, warm scent. It reminded me of being a kid, of rubbing suntan lotion into my skin. But there was nothing sweet about this moment. There was still the discomfort of our dinner last night, of my telling him of my short history with Malc, even though I knew he'd be convinced that I was Malc's motivation for distrusting him. I was no more comfortable with Jesse than I'd been without him.

"What made you decide to stay here?" he asked.

"Annette as much as dared me."

"I should have known."

"No, it was my own fault."

He reached out for my hands, and I gave them to him, the way I'd give them to a doctor bent on taking my pulse.

"You're cold," he said. "I could make a fire."

"About last night," I said.

"Your past is your past." He squeezed my hands. "Come on."

I felt myself nod, found myself turning and following him back into Kathleen Fowler's life. I settled on the sofa. It seemed to expect me, offering up a soft plum-colored comforter that I pulled around my thin sweater.

Jesse retrieved wood from the box on the porch, and soon the space behind the grate filled with the crackle and spit of tiny flames.

"Are you sure they won't go out?" I said.

"No. It doesn't take much."

I noticed that there was a place beside me just big enough for him. He settled into it.

"I shouldn't have called you," I said, no longer sorry that I had.

"It's best that you did." His eyes picked up the glint of the fire. "She always did, until—"

"Until when?"

"I told you how she was at the end. She wouldn't tell me what was happening, why she was so scared."

"What do you think it was?"

"I couldn't begin to guess. At first I thought it was just her own ghosts."

"What ghosts?" I felt as if he'd slammed down a cold steel wall between us.

"Everyone has them." He turned those eyes on me

now, taking the offense. "What about you? What was frightening you?"

"Ghosts, I guess." I stared into his eyes, trying to find the comfort that had been there earlier. What I saw looked like the unfocused eyes of a stranger. "Did you hear?" I asked. "About the homeless woman?"

He nodded, his eyes too fierce to do anything but deepen my sense of uneasiness. "I didn't know if you had, and I wasn't about to bring it up."

"You should have told me," I said. "You can't protect me from this stuff."

"I can try."

I didn't like his kind of protection, and I'm sure that he sensed that.

"Now I've gone and made you mad again," he said, but there was no remorse in his expression.

"Tell me about Kathleen's ghosts," I said. I have a way of staring after I speak that unnerves some people who don't know about me. It didn't unnerve him.

"Not a chance." The way he glared as he said it couldn't be any less intense than the way I looked at the people whose lips I was reading. "I don't reveal things that are told to me in confidence."

"But if they'll help us figure out what happened to her?"

"They won't." I turned away, trying to act huffy, but he didn't buy into it. "I'd do the same for you," he said.

"I feel weird going through her stuff," I told him, "but I've got to try to find out what was going on. I was hoping you could help."

"I've already looked," he said. And when I must have registered surprise, he explained, "We had keys to each other's places. So, yeah, I can get into here as well as the nursery and the locker in San Francisco."

"What locker?" I asked.

"She kept the stuff for the boat there, when she had a boat," he said. "We used to eat in a little dive nearby. I don't think there's much left there now."

A light crept in through the front window, reflecting off the floor. I clung to him. "Easy," he whispered, and left me sitting on the sofa as he went to the window. Then he whipped the front door open. Without warning, he took off into the darkness. I followed as he ran as if chasing someone into the trees.

"Get back inside," he said when I caught up with him.

"What happened? I didn't hear."

"A noise. I think there was someone out here." As he spoke, he looked over toward the front window. A pile of flower pots lay on the porch, some broken. "How long have these been like this?" he asked, and I shook my head.

"Come with me to my place?" His lips curved almost into a smile.

"I can't."

"And you can't stay here."

"I have to, Jesse."

"Then I'll stay with you." I leaned against his shoulder. "Come on," he said as we went inside. "You must be exhausted. I'll keep watch."

"I can't sleep," I said, although my lids were heavy and, in my head, I sounded as if I were speaking in a dream.

His lips touched my forehead. "It will be okay now," he said. "I'm here."

His shoulder was warm, his lips close. I breathed the almondlike scent of him and wrapped my arms around his neck. It would be okay, I thought as we kissed and slipped deep into the heat of the sofa. Jesse would take care of me.

We slid out of our clothes, still kissing. My skin burned wherever it touched his. He rose above me, and the fire caused the shadows to flicker on his flesh like something alive.

"Are you sure?" he asked. But he had to know that there was no stopping now, not for either of us.

I looked up into his eyes. "I'm sure, Jesse. The question is, are you?"

He lowered himself so that we were face-to-face, breath-to-breath. "Why don't you let me show you how sure?"

Nineteen

GERI

I woke stretched out on the sofa in the curve of his arm, and my first thought was *no. Oh, no.* I must have jerked, because a hand shot out and pulled me back down beside him.

"Relax." He squinted up at me through sleepy, long-lashed eyes that gave him a little-boy look. I looked back up at him and realized that we were still alive. Still naked, too.

"I am relaxed," I said.

He stroked my back. "I hope you don't mind that I decided to stay. I just couldn't leave you here alone."

Thank you, I thought. "I would have been okay," I told him.

"Guess I drifted off. I didn't even cover us with a

blanket." He uncurled his long legs from the sofa and watched me warily. He was telling the truth. I felt as if I'd slept on ice.

"Well," I began, uncurling my legs as well, and finally standing.

He stood, too, looking as messed up and uncertain as I felt. "Considering that we spent the night together, you suppose we could share some coffee before I take off?"

Then it hit me. "This is Sunday, isn't it?" I asked.

He nodded. "So what?"

I grabbed my discarded jeans and sweatshirt and threw them on. "Sunday. Sorry. I'll be right back. Wish I could tell you where the coffee is, but to tell you the truth…"

He muttered something I didn't hear, but I was already flying out the door. The paper lay in the front yard.

This would be what I had feared most. I had to read it, had to know how far Doug Blanchard had dared to go. A chill filled the air and seemed to trap me in a pocket of ice.

I pulled the rubber band off the newspaper, fat as only Sunday papers are, and shoved it into the pocket of my jeans. Couldn't throw away a rubber band. Couldn't walk past a pin on the sidewalk. Obsessive-compulsive, I believe Malc called it.

I didn't have to search for the story. My own mug shot glared at me from B1. Beside me, Kathleen looked far more presentable, her arm stretched around a younger Eric, who, although they were cheek to cheek, still seemed to stand apart.

Blanchard's byline gloated back at me. *Half Moon Bay Woman's Life as Troubling as Her Death.* "Kathleen Fowler was loved by all, yet she was still a woman of secrets," the column began. "She lived with secrets and died with secrets, not to imagine considerable wealth—wealth that she apparently left to a woman she had never met. Or had she?"

I skimmed past the gory details of Kathleen's murder in search of my own name. There it was. "Geri LaRue, a second-year reporter at this newspaper, was Fowler's sole beneficiary. When contacted about her connection with the woman, LaRue did not return phone calls."

What a crock. He'd never tried to call me.

The paper was stooping to print this kind of garbage, and not just because I was involved. Marie had approved a similar story a few months before about a former cheerleader and community theater performer who'd gone off to New York to be a star and ended up killing herself. It was written tabloid-style, and the tone reminded me of this one. Now she was doing it again.

I forced myself to read the end of the article, just in case Doug dared to suggest that I was involved in Kathleen's death. I should have known better. Instead, he returned to his favorite subject—himself.

He used Kathleen's murder to remind us of his own murdered fiancée. He continued to beat that drum, a metaphor I didn't mind mixing.

The frozen air melted a little, and I caught the scent of bacon frying somewhere. I stared at the column and wondered what Malc would call it. He'd lay some psychological label on it. Opportunistic, maybe. That's how it felt. Doug Blanchard was using my situation, not to mention Kathleen's death, to revisit his favorite murdered-fiancée subject, the one that had landed him the columnist job in the first place.

And there I was, my face so cold that tears could freeze on my cheeks, trying not to cry. Trying not to care. Trying. I would get through this, and when I did, I was going to demand an explanation from Marie.

The scent of fresh coffee mingled with the frying bacon and made me think of home, whatever that was. I followed its fragrance inside, and came face-to-face with Jesse.

"About time," he said.

"How'd you find the coffee?" I asked, sniffing the air. "I didn't even know where it was."

"I knew." He handed me a cup.

But of course.

"Drink," he said, as if he'd said this hundreds of times before, as if all he had to do was ask and I would respond as the woman he'd loved once had.

I placed the cup carefully on the counter and forced myself to exhale.

"What's the matter?" he asked, and the concern in his face looked real.

"Drink *yourself*," I said, and headed for the door.

He caught up with me before I reached the driveway.

"You're acting childish," he said. "I know this has been hard on you. It's not exactly easy for me. But don't think for a minute that I'm trying to replace Kath with you."

"No?" I tried to read his face but saw only a storm of emotions. Loose cannon, Malc had said.

"No," he said. "No one could replace her."

"I wasn't suggesting…" My hand trembled. And of course I was suggesting just that. "I need to go," I said. "My real life just caught up with me." I snapped the paper toward him. "Take a look at this."

He skimmed the article, his eyes darting back, as if making sure I was still there.

"What's with this guy?" he asked. "You're his colleague, not some criminal."

"That doesn't make any difference to him," I said.

He tried to talk about it, but I couldn't stay there another minute, and I was not going to drink Kathleen Fowler's coffee with him after making love to him on her sofa.

"I'm sorry," I said. "I need to figure out what to do about this story." And, newspaper in hand, I started to leave.

"Why don't you come with me and check out Kath's locker?" He stood on the porch, arms crossed.

His thick brows and dark eyes seemed almost sinister against his stark shaved head.

He knew he'd get my attention, but I couldn't help it. "How long since you've been there?" I asked.

"Years." He uncrossed his arms a little too casually. "I could drive you there."

"I'll take you up on that." I slapped the paper against my open palm. "But first…I've got to check on this."

Although I didn't want to think about a woman being murdered on the nursery property, I knew I had to try to find out if her death had anything to do with Kathleen Fowler's murder. Or Mary Haskins's. It was still early. If the police hadn't isolated the area, I could at least take a look around.

I turned into the nursery driveway and pulled far into the back, by the old house where Eric had lived until he'd moved in with Annette. Through the shadows of the trees, I could see the outline of the building where the homeless woman's body was found. I knew I needed to go there before I left for San Francisco and my confrontation with Marie. Not that I'd find anything, but if I didn't go, I'd always wonder what I might have found if I had.

Sitting there in my car, watching the hopeful blue of the sky breaking through the gray-flannel fog, I realized again that this place fit me the way the right clothes did. Like clothes—mine, at least—it was comfortable. I could move around in it.

Something about the slap-in-the-face scent of the ocean on both ends of the day, and the way the sun felt when it slid out of nowhere and warmed my bare arms, as it was doing now, made me feel bigger, better than I was.

Given a chance, I could grow attached to Half Moon Bay. I realized that's what had happened. I'd been given a chance. Had Kathleen Fowler known that I'd feel this way? Had she cared?

Just as I got ready to review the *whys* of my current situation, a dance I did daily, I glimpsed something—no, someone—out beyond the old house. Glenna Teague walked along the grounds in a sleeveless dress of a gauzelike fabric. Her long gray hair hung in a loose braid down her back. Long pockets were cut into the side of the dress, and she had her left hand shoved in one of them. In her right hand, she carried a plastic bag with the name of a supermarket or drugstore printed on it. I remembered Annette saying that she left out food for the homeless people, and I wondered if that's what she was doing now.

She came from the direction from where the woman was murdered, the same area I'd planned to investigate.

I was out of my car before I thought about it. "Glenna," I shouted. "Wait a minute, will you?"

She stopped, but the way she set her shoulders told me that she was doing so only out of politeness.

Although she wore no apparent makeup, her

beauty was as undeniable as the untamed magnificence of this place in which we stood. Her frown looked pasted on, as if she'd convinced herself she'd try to be gruff with me.

Her voice rumbled, but she could have been reciting the Gettysburg Address, for all I knew. I moved close enough to read her lips and caught a swear word, followed by "You have a problem?" I started to say no, then realized that I did indeed have a problem. More than one, actually.

I looked at the bag dangling from her right hand and knew immediately what she'd been doing. I'd seen her return more than once from that area, always carrying a similar bag. "Were you feeding the homeless again?" I asked.

"*Women,*" she said right back in my face. "They're *women.*" Then she met my eyes as if to dare me to challenge the fact. I wasn't about to. As she spoke, a cloud bank swallowed the sun and shoved the early morning back to darkness. I shivered for just an instant, but I didn't look away. Glenna could be intimidating, and I just wasn't in the mood.

"Women," I said. "Did you ever give food to the one who was killed?"

She nodded and looked away toward the creeping fog. "Sunlight was her name. I talked to her the day it happened. They stayed here every night."

"The homeless people? I mean, the women? How many of them? How many stayed?"

"Just the two in the little shed, a few others in the back field. The other one, her name's Tiny, was in a bad way." She tapped her head. "Someone was after her because of something she saw."

"What'd she see?" I asked. "Who was after her?"

"That's all Sunlight ever said. Just that Tiny had witnessed something really bad. The way those people are forced to live, it's a wonder they communicate as well as they do. How would you like to live never knowing where you'd sleep that night?"

Her pale green eyes bored into mine, angry, I realized. She wasn't just feeding the homeless; she was identifying with them. And she was so into their camp that she was automatically opposed to anyone who wasn't. I probably ought to express similar sympathy. I wasn't that far removed from her. But she was the one who took the time and energy to leave her job and feed these people every day. She'd see through any pretense on my part before the sun crept out again.

"Where's this Tiny now?" I asked.

"In a world of hurt, that's where."

I kept my eyes on her lips and tried again. "Her friend was killed. What happened to Tiny? Do you know?"

"What's it to you?" she asked. Her expression was still wary, but I could feel more than see that she wanted to trust me.

"Glenna," I said. "I need to talk to this woman. I'll do anything."

"Bravo for you." As she said it, I realized how I must have sounded. She shoved the plastic bag farther up her arm and headed toward the walkway.

"I didn't mean to sound arrogant," I said to her back. "Please wait. I'm hard of hearing and can't make out anything you say if I can't see your lips."

She spun on her espadrilles and faced me. "Why didn't you tell me you couldn't hear?"

"Why do you think?" I asked back.

"Didn't want to be different, maybe?" She tugged at her braid. "Did you ever know Kathleen?"

"Not that I know of," I said.

"Too bad. Ever since she died, it's been so screwed up around here." The sun came out again, and she squinted into it. "Tiny doesn't know who you are, does she?"

"No," I said.

"Then I'm not sure she'll talk to you." She pulled dark glasses out of her pocket and covered her eyes with them. So she did know where the woman was. All I had to do was convince her to take me there.

"Will you try?" I asked.

She looked me over again, as if trying to make up her mind about me. "If I do, what are you going to do? Will you try to help Tiny, or are you just going to take her statement and throw her back in the streets?"

"I swear," I said before I thought about anything but what I felt in my heart. "If I can help Tiny, I will— regardless of what she knows. I promise you that."

She grinned, showing even teeth that gleamed as if she'd just run her tongue over them. "And I believe you," she said.

"Will you take me to her?" I asked.

She shook her head. "Can't do that. It's her life. She gets to make the choices and decisions."

"I understand," I said. Then, looking past her to the small building in the distance, "I'd like to go inside there, though."

"Cops have been and gone. Sunlight was killed up in the loft," she said. Then she paused and looked me over, the wrinkled jeans and sweatshirt that had spent the evening on Kathleen Fowler's floor. "You want some company?" she asked.

"Why not?" I said.

Twenty

He hated the holiday season, absolutely abhorred it. No children. And now, no wife. No mother, no father, no family for too many years. Yet, as a public figure, he had no choice. The county coroner had to show up at community events whether he wanted to or not.

This morning it was a visit from Santa, no less, at Blooms nursery for a chamber mixer. And he was Santa. There was no way he could turn down the chamber of commerce committee when they asked him, all at once, it seemed, so that he couldn't confront any single individual. Besides, it was Kathleen's nursery. He'd have done it just to be there.

So here he was, parked outside, waiting for the

nursery to open, wearing a rented Santa suit, padded, of course, and a little tight. He hadn't gained that much weight since Ginger's murder, had he?

"Hey, Santa."

Good Lord, it was Lester Brown, standing right outside his car. He'd hoped Annie wouldn't figure out that Lester was the one helping him. Some, Annie included, were understandably put off by the big man. "You look as if you have news," Chev said.

Brown leaned into the open window. He was wearing that expensive, too-long leather jacket, and his bloodshot eyes looked as if he hadn't closed them all night.

"You'd better believe I've got news," he said.

GERI

Glenna and I talked in that easy way that's a rarity for me, the way it was with Malc at the first. She told me about coming from a family of farmers and loving her work at the nursery. Without shame, she said that Kathleen Fowler had saved her life by taking her off the streets, placing her in a treatment program and ultimately teaching her the business.

The way she talked about her made me wish that I had known Kathleen.

"She knew that you fed the people in back?" I asked.

"Of course. And if I hadn't, she would have. That's the way she was."

"What about Jesse?"

She stopped and met my gaze with those penetrating eyes. "What went on with those two was none of my business." We continued to walk in silence, and then she said, "For a woman who could help others fix their lives, she wasn't always too good at fixing her own."

"Like all of us," I said. She laughed, and I decided not to ask any more about Jesse. After last night, I couldn't pretend that my interest in him was impersonal.

By the time we were inside the small building, I felt that I could trust Glenna, the first hundred-percent feeling I'd had about anyone in this town. I was certain she would convince Tiny, the homeless woman, to tell me what she knew about her friend's murder.

Together, we walked every square foot of the building. It was littered with cop residue. Spiderwebs festooned the first cramped floor. A bathroom the size of a closet contained only a chipped mirror. Unfinished wood steps led up to an even smaller loft.

"What was this originally?" I asked Glenna. "It's too upscale for a toolshed."

"That's all it's used for now," she said. "Too far away from the nursery. Originally, Kathleen stayed out here while she was getting the business going. She slept up there in the loft."

"Not in the old house outside?" I asked.

"No, it was a pile of rubbish when Kathleen started

the nursery. Eric told me that he and his mother lived in this little house for the first few months. It wasn't easy for her, and he never forgot how hard she worked."

"So Eric and Kathleen were close?" I asked, guessing what she was leaving out.

"Very close, until he hooked up with Annie."

"And then?"

She shot me a scowl. "You wanted to look at this place, so let's look, okay?"

"Okay." I glanced around at the meager shelter and wondered about the homeless women who'd felt safe enough to sleep here. Two women. One of them murdered, the other hidden by Glenna.

"There's a lot of dust over here," she said, indicating a wide area to the left of the door. "But look at this. Something was taken out of here recently. A suitcase, maybe?"

She was right. A clean rectangular strip of yellow vinyl was outlined in the grit. I didn't know what it meant, but I couldn't help thinking that what happened to the homeless woman was connected to Kathleen Fowler's murder.

"Maybe this Sunlight woman knew something," I said. "Maybe she saw something."

"Tiny's the one who saw something," Glenna said, "but I don't even know if she understands, poor creature. You know, it could have been a narrow box that was here, a container of some kind, maybe."

She continued to talk, speculating on the object

that had been removed. I headed for the stairs, not really wanting to go. That was where Sunlight had been murdered, right up there. The police hadn't disturbed much. I dropped down on one knee and looked at the wadded plastic shoved up against a large, round, orange industrial fan. That's where they had slept, propped up against this thing in this pathetic excuse for shelter. Glenna was right. They weren't the homeless; they were women. And one of them was killed right in this room.

Something moved, nothing I saw directly, just a sense of motion I picked up out of the corner of my eye. I turned, feeling a sheen of cold sweat break out on my arms. Then, I saw it—a tiny louvered closet built into the west wall, right across from the make-shift bed. The door was slightly ajar, and I didn't think it had been when I'd entered the loft. No, it hadn't been. My obsessive mind filed away facts like that. The door had been inched open after I got here.

No way was I taking one step toward it. But how was I going to get downstairs without walking right past it? Blood hammered in my eardrums, swallowing my thoughts. I stared at the door, almost mesmerized. That wouldn't do. If someone were in there, I'd be announcing the fact that I knew it. I had to get help.

"Glenna," I shouted. "Get up here! I think there's someone in the closet."

The closet door flew open. I screamed and tried to run. Just as I got to the stairs, someone grabbed me from behind. I kicked, screamed, tried to turn around, but the arms surrounding me were solid and angry.

"Glenna," I shouted again, and the fingers dug into my throat. My vision blurred, but I could see what looked like the shape of a woman coming up the stairs toward me. *Glenna. Please let it be Glenna.* Then something sharp and powerful as a shovel plowed into the back of my head, and I went down.

CHEV

Chev felt ridiculous in the Santa Claus attire.

"You understand," he said, leaning out the car window, "I'm doing this for the chamber."

Lester shrugged and blew out some leftover smoke. "Whatever turns you on, man. You've got to be roasting your ass off in that getup, though. Why don't you get out of the car?"

"I'm fine," he said.

Lester laughed and crushed the cigarette with the pointed toe of his boot. "Will you get out *now*?" he asked.

Chev knew that when Lester made a suggestion, it was the same as when anyone else gave an order. Without another word, he opened the door and got out. Lester's bloodshot eyes telegraphed approval.

"So," Chev began.

That was all he needed to say. "You wanted to know about Kathleen," Lester said. "I couldn't get anything."

That was a rarity for Lester. Chev tried to hide the disappointment. "Anything about Geri LaRue?"

"Tried to find her mother, but the old lady moves around a lot. Forget about her, okay? I found out something else about Geri I think you'll like."

"And what might that be?" Chev tried not to sound eager, but his heart was ready to pound right out of the padded red suit.

Lester leaned against the car and grinned, revealing a display of surprisingly white teeth. "You told me to check out Geri LaRue," he said, "and that was a piece of cake for many reasons. I also make it a habit to always check out my client first thing, even before I check out the subject."

"You checked me out?" Chev asked.

"Of course not." Lester chortled. "I did that years ago when I was a little worried about all that foo-foo skating stuff. But calm down, will you? You're not my client, remember. You're doing this for a friend."

"Annette Montgomery," Chev said.

"Annette who?"

"What do you mean?"

"I mean," Lester said, "that there *is* no Annette Montgomery."

The Santa suit felt like a sauna that he couldn't escape. This wasn't making sense to him. He was losing control, and he couldn't handle losing control. "I'm not sure I follow you," he said.

"Of course you can't, man." He clapped Chev on the shoulder. "Because Annette Montgomery is not who she says she is. No fancy East Coast college. No rich-bitch family. No nothing. I'm good, my man, and the first trace of Annette Montgomery I can find is a driver's license when she was sixteen years old."

"Holy moly." Only after Chev said it did he realize it was the term Ginger used to say to avoid cursing. "So Annette—"

"Could be anyone," Lester finished. "Who knows why she really wanted you to check out this LaRue gal?"

"Who knows?" Chev echoed. This was getting worse, not better. He needed advice, and maybe Lester could offer it. Just then, a high-pitched scream came from the path behind the nursery.

"Help! Please, help us!"

Lester covered the distance between the scream and the car in seconds, while Chev just stood there, shell-shocked, remembering. He'd never seen a big man move so fast and with such deadly purpose. And he was frozen, unable to make a step, thinking about that night, about Ginger.

The assistant manager at the nursery, the one

called Glenna, rushed out of the shadow of trees. "Help us," she shouted as Lester approached. "There's a girl back there hurt really bad. Some maniac hit her in the head with a shovel. She's bleeding all over the place."

Twenty-One

PAT

Pat Smith's feet hurt, as they always did after a day at the emergency clinic. If she didn't need the overtime, she'd have been out of here hours ago. Just one more year, she reminded herself. Then Charlie would have his master's, and they could start their family. In the meantime, this was a good job if you could handle the stress. So far, she could.

Right now, she was thinking about the heart attack that was being rushed to the clinic, and the head wound who was stable and improving. Both would be okay, and so would she, if she could just get through the next hour.

Just then, a bald, wild-eyed man in jeans and a

black sweater burst into the room and landed on the other side of the counter.

"Geri LaRue," he said. "Where is she?"

"Are you a family member?" She had no choice. That's what she must ask, and what he must verify.

"I'm a friend." He met her eyes as if daring her to challenge him. "A close friend. Ask her if she wants to see Jesse Medicine."

"As in Medicine Avenue?" Not professional of her, but she couldn't help it. "My husband's an art major," she said. "Getting his master's. He loves your abstracts, Mr. Medicine."

For a moment, he looked insulted, but then a grim smile settled on his lips. "And who's your husband?"

"Charlie Smith."

The expression changed from grim to interested. "He's good," he said. "Very good. Tell him not to sell out to teaching or anything else. Tell him to just paint."

She wasn't sure that she liked that. Charlie wanted kids as much as she did. He'd need a steady income. Still, she felt the truth in his words. Jesse Medicine. She tried to imagine Charlie's reaction when she told him about this chance meeting tonight.

"I will tell him," she said, "and thank you."

"Can I see my friend now?"

It wasn't as if this was a stranger asking. "I think that will be okay," she said. "I'll show you inside."

When she returned, someone else approached the counter. Both the expression and the uniform were friendly.

"Having a bad day, Patricia?" the visitor asked.

She startled at the use of her name, but then remembered that she wore it on her pocket. "That's what they pay me for," she said.

"Jesse can be a handful," the visitor said with no trace of malice. "He's just worried about my sister, Geri, same as I am."

"You're a family member?" she asked.

"She's my kid sister. How's she doing?"

"You'll need to talk to the nurse." Something in the face made her take pity, and she added, "She's doing well, considering."

"Up and running her mouth like always, I'll bet. We never could shut her up at home."

"She's not quite that active yet," she said, then made it clear by looking down at the papers on her desk that the conversation was over. Sensing the unasked question, she added, "Just one visitor at a time. I'm sorry, but that's the rule."

"Not a problem. My sis will want to see Jesse first."

"You can go in when he leaves," she said.

"That works for me. Thanks, Patricia. I appreciate it."

"Anytime," she said.

She went back to the computer, but if was difficult to concentrate on work. Less than an hour now, and she'd be home—in Charlie's arms, telling him that Jesse Medicine said that he was not just good, but very good. Would she add what Jesse said about not selling out? She'd figure that one out when she wasn't so tired.

GERI

I found my way back to light and sound slowly, floating through the colors behind my eyelids. The hammering on my scalp slowed me down. All I remembered was this monstrous something jumping out of the closet and attacking me from behind.

"Geri? Miss LaRue?"

A human voice. A nurse. The throbbing pain in my head was nauseating and constant. "The police officers have a few questions for you," she said.

I didn't remember what I said or how I managed to speak. Only that I conveyed the unhappy information that I had no idea who had attacked me, or why. Then I slept in fits, until another voice woke me.

Familiar, but I couldn't find the source. I touched the back of my head, where all of the pain was. Sure enough, plastic stitches were sticking out of the back of my head. Who the hell had done this? And why?

"Geri, are you okay?"

I could hear the words, straight from the lips of Jesse Medicine.

"I don't know what I am." I turned my head to look

at him and felt as if I were falling off the edge of the world. "Jesse, I think someone tried to kill me."

"Damned straight." His features swam into focus, but all I could make out were his eyes, huge and dark in the moon-colored globe of his face. "You're okay now. In the walk-in clinic. I'll have you out of here this afternoon. I'll take care of you. And if any bastard even thinks about coming after you again—"

I held on to the edge of the mattress, my head still spinning. "What happened to cut me open like this?"

"The blade of a shovel. Your scalp. The nurse said you had nine stitches."

"Ouch. I can feel every one of them."

"Try not to think about it right now," he said.

I turned my head far enough to the left to see the damp, brownish stain on the pillow. "I'm bleeding." I reached for my head again and found it even stickier than the stains on the bedding.

"You're okay." He sat on the edge of the bed and took my hand in his and squeezed. I tried to squeeze back and couldn't. Whoever had sliced up my head had also stomped on my fingers.

"Glenna," I managed to say. I remembered seeing her come up the stairs toward me. I remembered a guy in a black leather jacket, some kind of cop. I remembered a horrified over-the-hill Santa Claus, screaming for help.

"Glenna's fine," he said. "She didn't see who did it, but she did get help right away."

I drew my fingers back slowly. My head didn't feel like part of me. I wondered what I must look like to Jesse, impaired as I was. He looked pretty fine to me. The black sweater—the only color sweater he seemed to own—was retro, a tight knit shot with tiny beige horizontal stripes that only someone with his hot body would dare to put on. I'd bet it was a holdover from the past, not a recent purchase from a trendy vintage shop.

I was obsessing again, studying the weave of his sweater only because I couldn't bear to replay the nightmare I'd just endured. The tape in my head ground on, anyway, without my consent. It was all right there. The slice in the back of my head. The woman, Glenna, I was sure, running up the stairs. The screams. The leather-clad cop guy and the other one in the red suit.

"Who was the Santa Claus guy?" I asked.

"Chev Parnell, the county coroner," Jesse said. "He's a good guy, a little wimpy. They talked him into playing Santa for some chamber event. The other one is Lester Brown, an investigator who used to be a cop. I don't know what he was doing there."

Glenna had mentioned a chamber of commerce mixer. It was starting to come back to me.

I was too tired to focus on what he was saying. I felt off balance, as though if I weren't careful, I could roll right off this bed. "First, Kathleen Fowler," I said. "Then Mary Haskins, the Hanford social worker.

Then, Sunlight, the homeless woman. And now me."
Somehow, in some horrific way, we were all connected.

"What happened to them has nothing to do with
you. And you're going to be okay. No one's going to
hurt you." Jesse's eyes were so glassy with emotion
that I would have bet he'd been drinking. But it was
demons from the past, not alcohol, that lit the fierce
fire there. I wondered if he knew what he was doing,
or if it was only obvious to me.

"I've got to find out why somebody tried to kill
me," I said.

"We'll find out," he said. "But first, I want to get
you out of here."

"I can't, Jesse. I want to visit Kathleen's mysterious
San Francisco locker you told me about."

"I can't let you go anyplace alone," he said. "If
anything happened to you—"

"I'm not Kathleen." I hadn't meant to say it, but
once I had, I couldn't stop. I struggled up on my
elbow and slid to a sitting position. "Protecting me
is not going to make you feel any less guilty about
what happened to her."

The rage in his eyes was directed at me now. "You
really don't get it," he said.

The room was listing like a sailboat in rough water,
but I was determined to leave it without arguing any
longer. "You're the one who doesn't get it, Jesse."

He stood like a boxer in the ring, his arms tense

beneath the long sleeves of his sweater. "Are you saying you don't want my help?"

I swung my legs out and stepped onto the cold floor. "I'm saying that I need to go to San Francisco," I said.

"And there's nothing that I can do to change your mind?"

"Nothing."

"Fine, then." He made it to the door in a couple of steps. "Be careful, Geri," he said. "Be safe." And he was gone.

I tried to follow, but the world tilted and I had to grab the side of the bed. I must have screamed, because he was back in the room as quickly as he'd left it, his arm around me.

"Damn it, Geri, please listen to me." He looked ready to explode. I felt thin as air.

"Do you really want to help me?" I asked.

"What can I do? Just tell me."

"Let me know where Kathleen's locker is."

His grip on me went slack. "You don't give up, do you?"

"I can't afford to."

"The locker," he said. "Then we negotiate from there."

And because it was easier than arguing, I nodded. "The locker."

The doctor pronounced me well enough to leave, explaining that I might have some "post-concussion issues." I was interviewed by two cops I'd seen at the nursery after Eric and I were poisoned. By the time I left, I was wondering if I should have accepted a ride with Jesse.

Once I was checked out, I stood at the front desk, wondering how I was going to get back to the nursery. The pretty blonde at the front desk asked if I needed assistance. I'd already assured the nurse that I was fine.

I glanced at her name tag. "Thanks, anyway, Patricia."

"Call me Pat," she said. "Is Mr. Medicine driving you?"

"No. I'll need to call a taxi. At the moment, I don't think he's very happy with me."

She started to say something, and then checked herself. "Your brother seems very nice. You have nice friends."

Brother, I thought as I stepped outside. What brother? But my head hurt too much for me to wonder more than a moment.

CHEV

The chamber event had gone south, and it was no wonder with all of the hullabaloo. A few politically correct people dropped by with their kids for cider and an obligatory chat with Santa, but most were distracted by what had taken place in the little shed in back. It had happened so fast that he still had no sense of how it had all played out. He was relieved when he heard that the LaRue girl's head wound was minimal.

"She's going to be okay," Glenna told him. They walked back to the nursery, staving off the cold with leftover mugs of cocoa from the event. Although her tone was rich with optimism, her teeth were chattering.

"Want my jacket?" Chev asked, feeling awkward about the invitation but knowing that he must offer it.

"That depends on what you're wearing under it, Santa." Her grin was teasing, no meanness in it.

"A regular T-shirt," he said. "Tell you the truth, Glenna, I'd be glad to get rid of this burden, and you look as if you could use a little warmth right now."

She hugged herself again. "I'm supposed to be working. Can't just run home for a wrap."

He took off the heavy jacket and handed it to her. "You had no idea what would happen today," he said. "None of us did."

"I thought the girl was dead." She shuddered, and he had to fight himself to keep from putting his arm around her.

"What did you see?"

"Nothing. Stupid me. I was staring at a blank space in a bank of dust, trying to figure out what someone had taken out of the place. I heard Geri, that girl, scream from upstairs, and just as I went up, she fell down and her attacker pushed past me. I buffered the fall, thank God. Soon as I could, I settled her down and went out for help."

"That's when you found me."

"Forget the Santa suit," she said. "You were the most beautiful sight I could have imagined waiting at the end of that drive. And when you and your friend charged in there—"

"My friend?" he asked, feeling the guilty heat spread along his throat. "I didn't have a friend there."

"The dude with the leather jacket," she said. "He's not a friend of yours?"

"Closer to an acquaintance." He tried to keep a poker face for her.

Less than a month and he'd be out of here, retired. He'd never have to touch the bodies of strangers and people he'd once known the way he'd had to touch Kathleen's. From now on, it would be only community events and public service for him. His staff could take care of the hands-on stuff, including the homeless woman. He'd hoped to keep it quiet that crazy Lester had been doing favors for him, but that wasn't going to last. Half Moon Bay was too small for secrets.

"Hey, you two." Annie's strident voice broke between them like a wave, and they stepped back at the same time, as if they'd choreographed it. "Aren't you supposed to be in there?" Annie asked, motioning toward the building.

"I intend to," Glenna said. "As you know, we had a few problems today."

"I still need help at the counter," Annie said. She wore the Blooms uniform of white jeans and a white T-shirt with I ♥ Blooms on both front and back in blue-green type. She appeared frazzled. The sun caught her carrot-red hair, which she'd shoved up on her head with a silver clip.

"Okay, then." As Glenna drifted out, Annie moved toward Chev. "Did you get anything?" she whispered. "About Geri LaRue?"

"Just that she was a foster child," he said. "Lester says she's okay."

"Lester?" Annie flushed. "I asked *you* for help. There's got to be a connection between Kath and her. Lester Brown is weird. Maybe you need a better source, someone who will dig deeper."

"Lester did find out something," he said, looking into her eyes.

"And what might that be?" She squinted and smiled when she said it, but he could see the golden reflection of fear there.

Most of the eyes he looked into this way were dead, but he knew fear, terror, when he saw it in a living person.

"It's going to sound a little insensitive," he began. "Perhaps more than a little."

"I don't understand." But she did. The fear was there, clawing at her throat, stifling her voice.

He stopped on the path and glanced back in the direction Glenna had gone. "Why did you want me to have Geri LaRue investigated?" Her cheeks went stark white beneath the freckles, and her eyes looked twice their size.

"You know why, Chev. I told you everything."

"You didn't tell me everything," he said.

He expected her to protest, to play dumb, even to raise hell, call him names, threaten. She did nothing. Only turned away from him. When she turned back, she'd managed to wipe all emotion from her face. He couldn't begin to read what was going on behind those pale eyes.

"How much?" she asked.

"Come again?"

"Don't play games with me," she said. "How much is it going to cost me to keep you quiet?"

There was a coarseness to her speech that he'd never noticed before, an anger that seemed just barely in check. And he was alone with her out on the outskirts of her nursery. Not smart.

"I'm going back," he said. "I don't want anything from you."

"Then why did you have me checked out, you bastard?" Something had broken loose in her. He could see it in her eyes, as the garden lights bounced off and reflected from them.

"You asked me to do you a favor," he said. "I risked my reputation to do that. Now I find out you're not who you said you were. It's your business. I don't care. I've got bigger fires to fight, and I'm leaving now."

"You're not going anywhere." She grabbed him by the arm, stronger than she looked, fueled by the rage that seemed unleashed now. "Who the hell do you think you are to spy on me?"

"Annie, please."

Her palm caught him flat across the face, shooting numbing pain through his cheek, blinding his left eye. "Bastard," she said again.

"Wait a minute." Another voice. Glenna. "What the hell's going on here?"

Chev turned, his face still raw with pain, his vision blurred, to see Glenna shooting down the path. Annie stood before him, her breathing heavy. "Don't," he said to Glenna. "She's…"

He couldn't bear to see this uncapped rage directed at the woman who was only trying to help. Before he could finish shouting out a warning, Glenna frowned, then put out her arms to Annie. "What's the matter, baby?" she asked.

Annie dashed toward the woman. Chev followed. He could not let this happen, could not let Annie attack Glenna as she had him. Before he could move, Annie threw herself at Glenna. Sobbing hysterically, her arms wrapped around Glenna's neck, her head against her shoulder.

"It's okay, baby," Glenna said, patting her shuddering form. "Everything's going to be all right."

She looked past Annie's bobbing head to him, to his eyes, and he knew that she was speaking to him as well as to this girl. "It's okay, baby. It's okay."

Twenty-Two

PAT

Exhausted. Even the squish of her shoes beneath her dull blue scrubs sounded weary. It would be okay, though. The streets were as deserted as the parking lot this time of night. She'd be home before ten-thirty, pass along Jesse Medicine's compliment to Charlie, and save the rest of the discussion for later. If Charlie's art meant that they needed to postpone having a family, that's what they'd do. They were still young, and she didn't mind waiting if it meant Charlie would be happy.

A chill had settled over the town, and she wished she'd brought her jacket. As she approached her van, she heard a car door open beside her. Her chest tightened, but then she recognized the smile, the uniform.

"Hello, again."

She caught her breath. "Oh, it's you. Sorry. You startled me." The brother, only Geri LaRue didn't have a brother.

"Didn't mean to. I was just dropping by to see my sister."

"She was released today," Pat said. "Didn't you know?" Geri had been groggy and disoriented. Maybe she hadn't understood what Pat said about her visitors.

"No, I was called back to work, as you can see. Just getting off."

"All of us are working late this time of year," she said, and started to move toward her van.

"Well, thanks for your help today."

He seemed nice enough. And there was that uniform. "No problem," she said.

"See you around, Patricia."

She met the smile and started to walk away.

"Do you wear contacts?"

What kind of a question was that? "I'm sorry?"

"Contact lenses. I can tell. They're beautiful."

Weird. She wasn't going to stick around for any more chitchat. She could make it to the van. Run. Get the cell phone out of her purse. Without looking back, she dashed across the lot.

She reached the van and pointed the remote control key to unlock it. Sweat poured from her as she grabbed the handle, pulled and crawled inside. Then the door was yanked open and she was knocked back across the seat.

She screamed and tried to kick, but the uniformed body covered her like a tarp.

"Such pretty eyes."

A hand covered her mouth. She felt movement, heard a click. Not a photograph? Not now.

She could make out the face in the dark now, the smile still genuine. Yes, it was a cell phone. "Please," she said against the hand. "Don't." The cell phone disappeared. Maybe it would be okay.

But then she heard a second click. She couldn't place it until she saw the blade wavering too close to her eyes.

"Please don't." She screamed. "Please." But all that answered her in the sudden darkness was laughter.

CHEV

He'd had a little too much to drink, and public inebriation horrified him. He knew better. He'd learned those lessons. Hadn't been within sniffing distance of bourbon since Ginger's murder. But now, after his exchange with the woman he'd thought was Annie Montgomery, he'd known he was in too deep. And he'd slid right into this dark booth, as if attached to it by some invisible cord.

"You're drifting, buddy."

Lester Brown. He'd forgotten that he wasn't alone. "I'm right here," he said, squinting up. Lester slouched in the booth on the other side of the table, black cowboy hat pushed back on his head. Chev looked down at their empty shot glasses, their remnants of beer in cloudy pilsners. "Let me get us another round."

"Don't tempt me." Nothing about his scowl looked tempted. Offering to buy Lester a round was like offering a corpse another round of formaldehyde.

Lester could take it or leave it, but all of a sudden, Chev couldn't. He wanted more drinks, more harsh whiskey mellowed by a cold fusion of Heineken or Rolling Rock.

"I insist." He motioned to a weary-looking server with short black hair and a red skirt that split along her leg. "Two more here," he said.

"Sure thing." She smiled at him, showed him a little more leg. Young enough to be his daughter. If he had a daughter.

She left about the same time Lester's phone rang.

"It's not cool to have your cell phone in here," Chev said, but Lester was already on his feet, pacing and talking at the same time.

"No shit? Are you sure? In the parking lot of the walk-in where the LaRue woman was? Damn right. I'm on my way."

The server returned in a liquid flash of crimson silk. "Drinks all around," she said in a voice too child-like for the age she had to be to work there.

Lester stared at the drinks as if he'd never seen

anything that disgusting. "Sorry, darlin'," he said. "My partner and I have to leave now." He crunched around in one of his jacket pockets and shoved some bills in her hand. "See you next time," he said, and patted her on the butt.

"You dick," she said. "If you ever—" They were out of there before she could finish the threat, Lester muttering something about the days when men were men, and women were women.

"What's going on?" Chev asked, once they were in Lester's Mercedes.

Fresh cigarette smoke answered him. Lester's voice followed. "Homicide," he said, "right outside the emergency clinic where they took that LaRue girl."

"Did something happen to Geri LaRue?" he asked.

"A female," he said. "That's all I know. We'll be there in time to find out, though."

Chev didn't know how much more he was willing to witness. He knew that anyone in any profession could hit the wall. Didn't matter if you were military, law enforcement or coroner. And since he'd seen Kathleen's dead body that day, he'd known the moment was close for him.

Lester drove as if he had a cop light on the top of his vehicle. "Bastards," he muttered, more to himself than Chev. "They always pick on the weak ones."

"I know," Chev said, bracing himself as the traffic lights swirled around them.

"Bastard ain't gonna get away with killing that little girl."

Chev felt as if he could throw up right then. "So it is Geri LaRue?"

"Don't know, man," he said. "Could be someone taking another swipe at her. Could be anyone."

The first person Chev saw as they drove into the taped-off parking lot was Geri LaRue. Hugging a denim jacket around herself, and standing just outside the yellow tape, she looked like a teenager watching a scary movie. Not all that steady, but at least she was alive.

He almost waved his hand off trying to get her attention, not that she'd recognize him without the Santa suit. "Look, Lester," he said. "It's the girl. She's okay. It was all a mistake."

Lester slowed the car, turned to him and tapped his finger hard against his temple. "I didn't say it was her," he said, "so shut up, okay?"

He nodded and tried to look away. Why the hell had he let himself drink tonight of all nights? Never again. Never. *Yeah, right.* A voice in his head, Ginger's maybe, laughed gently.

"Lester," he said, "it was my fault what happened to Ginger, and you know it."

"Bullshit." Lester angled his car into a space between two trees. "So you had a few drinks. So what? Even if you'd been sober, you couldn't have stopped those fucking punks. Know why?"

He shook his head and said the only thing he could. "No, why?"

"'Cause the only thing that stops a creep is a gun." He lifted his finger and shoved it at Chev. Chev cringed. He needed to sleep, to throw up, to forget. And he did not need to be where he was right now.

"Since the LaRue girl is okay," he said, "this murder is probably unrelated, don't you think?"

"Won't know till we look at the body," Lester said with borderline pleasure in his raspy voice. "Won't know till then. Your people should be out here by now."

Yes, his people, and he shouldn't let any of them see him in this condition.

"I don't think this is a good idea," he said. "I'll get the report tomorrow."

Lester's laughter rumbled out of his massive chest. "Stop being a wuss, will you? You've seen hundreds of bodies."

"I'm not—" Chev began, then decided against saying more about that, too. He was no match for Lester. Never had been.

They got out, and as Lester had intimated, stepped right into the crime scene. "Careful," Lester said. "Don't touch nothing. Let me talk to the cops." And then as a black officer approached, "How the hell are you, Jerry?"

"Fine, Duke."

Duke? Chev thought.

"And thanks for the call," Lester added. "Okay if

we take a little look-see? You know the coroner here, don't you?"

"We've done our thing," the cop named Jerry said, squinting at Chev. "Waiting on your people now."

"Where's the body?" It was like a man asking another for directions to a golf course. Chev shuddered. That must have been the way the police, and even Lester, had discussed Ginger the night she'd been killed. *The body.*

He hated the mechanics of murder. Always had, even when he'd had the stomach for his job. But he didn't want any part of this. Alcohol. That's what had gotten him here. On one hand, he should have known better. On the other, he wished he had a whole lot more.

Before he knew it, he and Lester were on the other side of the police tape, staring down at the body of a young woman. Not just any young woman. This one's face looked like raw meat, and, oh God, no. Someone had dug out her eyes.

"Who?" Chev sputtered. "Who is she?"

"Easy, buddy." He felt Lester grab his arm, as if to steady him. But nothing in this scene could begin to put him on solid ground, emotionally or otherwise. How had he allowed himself friendship with someone like Lester, even though he, and not Chev, had avenged Ginger's murder?

"I have to leave," he said. "I can't do this. I can't do it anymore."

"You can't leave, man. You look at this stuff every day."

"Not this." He glanced away from the body, but he couldn't erase the horror of the scraped-out eyes. "Sorry, Lester. Maybe I am turning into a wuss. But I had too much to drink tonight, and too much murder. Drive me back, okay? Or help me find someone who will."

"Oh, shit. I'll drive you."

But he realized that he couldn't bear being back in the car with Lester. "It's okay," he said. "The fresh air will be good for me. It's not that far."

He took off through the crowd before Lester could insist, hurrying so fast that he almost didn't notice who was heading directly toward the gruesome sight he'd just left.

"Don't go back there," he said, but Geri LaRue just kept walking, acting as if she hadn't heard his warning.

Twenty-Three

GERI

I couldn't tell if it was a man's or woman's voice on the phone. I'd taken a taxi to the home I could only think of as Kathleen's. After some coffee and a careful locking of the doors, I was feeling safe, and my equilibrium seemed to be working out its kinks just as the emergency clinic doc had said it would. Now, this call on my cell.

"Left you a present in the medical center parking lot." And then, a giggle. The caller said something else, but shouting in the background drowned out the words. I wouldn't have been able to hear any better regardless of where the call had come from.

Weird. It wouldn't hurt to drive by, I guess. I wouldn't have to get out of the car if it looked suspicious. I needed an excuse to get out of Kathleen's house, anyway. I wasn't going to be able to sleep for sure now.

I could tell the moment I pulled around the corner that the voice on the phone had not set a trap for me. At first, I saw only the people, the lookie-loos, the ones who shouted as if at a rock concert, the ones who watched passively as if sucked into a television.

A red-faced man in a uniform that barely buttoned in front seemed to be the gatekeeper. "Can't go any farther, honey," he told me.

Before I could address the "honey" issue, I looked past him and realized that the guy ahead of me wasn't in cop gear. It was the crazy cowboy.

"What about him?" I asked.

"He's a former police officer." His blond brushlike mustache made it difficult for me to read his lips.

"Oh," I shot back. "He used to work with you folks, so he gets in. I'm only a newspaper reporter, so I don't."

That set him back a bit. "Well," he finally said. "I didn't realize you were a reporter."

"I am," I said, "and I need to go in there." I didn't mention that I was on leave from the newspaper.

He swiped a hand across his shiny forehead. "Come on, then." He glanced over at me again. "Thought I knew all of the reporters in town."

"I'm from San Francisco," I said.

He started to object, but by then we were there,

staring at the uncovered body of a woman about my age.

"You can't go any farther," the cop said.

I couldn't have moved another step if I'd had to. The woman—I couldn't think of her as just a body— wore a light blue uniform, the standard tunic and pants, her blond hair spread out behind her like a fan. I'd seen her before, seen her just hours ago. Patricia Smith. The receptionist from the clinic. *Call me Pat.* No, not her. I couldn't control the trembling and tried to stifle a scream. Her eyes, my God. What had happened to her eyes?

The cop nudged me. I looked up in time to see him say, "Easy, now."

"What did they do to her?" I said.

"Hey," he said. "You're the reporter who wanted to come in here. This is the kind of shit we see every day, honey. Sorry it doesn't appeal to you. At least you don't have to find the sicko who did it."

"But I knew her," I said.

"You knew the victim?"

Wrong choice of words, Geri, but too late now. "She worked at the clinic," I said. "I didn't really know her. She just—"

I started to wobble again. This wasn't a good conversation. I couldn't forget the girl's face. Please don't let me pass out, not in front of this asshole.

He tapped me on the arm. "I asked what you were at the clinic for. You got some kind of problems?"

The sneer beneath his mustache brought me right back. I knew what he was asking.

"If you mean problems with my head, damn right." I tapped at my stitches and realized how soft and vulnerable my swollen flesh still was. "Someone tried to chop off a chunk of it." Although I didn't mean to, I glanced back down at the girl's face. Someone had done more than try to scalp her. Someone had destroyed her eyes. New tears kicked in. "I can't do this," I said, not to him, but to the deceptively silky night, the breeze and the gory, tragic evidence to how vulnerable we all are.

"Cool it," he said. "I'm going to need some information from you."

"Why don't you cool it, Tony?" The raspy voice sounded as if it had blown through a canyon, but I could make out the words. They had the same effect on me as cold water thrown in the face of a sleepwalker. I turned to see the cowboy, eyes glazed and crazy as I remembered from my stupor, long black leather jacket smelling of cloying cologne and the burnt scent of bourbon.

I expected the asshole cop to retaliate. Instead, he said, "Hey, Lester. She knew the victim."

"This little gal didn't have anything to do with what happened," he said. "She was attacked herself today." As if aware of my battle to stay vertical, he offered his arm, and I didn't know whether I should run away or hang on for dear life.

"You know the rules, Les," the cop said. "We need to talk to her."

"Tomorrow," the big man said. "The day after. Not tonight, not after what you made her look at."

"Hey, she wanted to see it. Was real pissy about it, actually."

"Whatever, Tony. She's not going anywhere, and she's not going to be any help, anyway. What you ought to do is go out there looking for the sonsabitches." He slicked back his hair, and I noticed that he didn't have cop hands. His were long, tapered, the hands of a pianist, a sculptor, maybe. "Where the hell's Roger, anyway?"

The cop swallowed so hard that his jowls shook. "You know the chief?"

"Started out together," the cowboy said. "He was my first partner."

"No shit," the cop said. "You wouldn't be putting me on, would you?"

"Tell him to kiss that new baby boy of his for me." The cowboy gave me an evaluating frown that made me feel exposed. "You ready to get out of here, darlin'?"

I took a look at him, a look at the paunchy cop, and one final look at the body of the poor woman just a few feet from me. Where could I go? Back to the house? To Jesse's? And could I drive? The cowboy didn't wait for an answer. "Come on," he said.

I took his arm.

"Name's Lester," he said once we were free of the group and I had stopped to take a breath. "Lester Brown."

He had been handsome once. He still was beneath the deep lines cutting up his face and forehead. Someone had obviously told him that he looked like Johnny Cash. He dressed the part, right down to the sad eyes and black leather jacket.

"Geri LaRue," I said.

It's tough enough for me to read through a mustache, but a mustache as droopy as his is almost impossible. "I'm sorry," I said. "I didn't catch that."

"Sorry." He removed the cigarette and spoke clearly. "I forgot about the hearing thing. I can sign if you like."

"What?" I squinted at him through the smoke. "How did you know?"

We were on the street now, my car just a few feet away. Knowing that this guy was volatile, half drunk and probably packing didn't make me all that comfortable, in spite of the southern gentleman routine he was trying to give me.

"Medical records," he said. "Sorry. I didn't know it was a secret. I'll keep it to myself."

"My medical records?" I asked. "What the hell are you talking about?"

"Easy," he said. His dark eyes were bloodshot, but the gaze he gave me was as penetrating as any I'd ever seen. "I'm on your side. Where you heading next? Let me drive you."

"No," I said. "I mean I'm fine to drive. I want you to tell me what's going on."

"I wish I knew, darlin'. People around here are curious about you. I got a feeling they're not too happy about the Fowler woman leaving everything to you."

"Who hired you?" I asked.

"Nobody spent a dime. Sometimes I do favors. I'm not exactly broke, you know."

"So, whose favor was I?"

"That would mean betraying a friend." He stomped out his cigarette, and I could see the anger simmering barely beneath the surface of his gesture. "I don't betray friends," he said. "I don't let helpless women get hurt, either."

"That woman back there sure did."

"I didn't even know her." His face flushed like a man's who'd just swallowed a straight shot of whiskey. "If I'd seen the sonsabitches, let me tell you, they wouldn't have walked away from here."

"I believe you," I said. "It doesn't exactly thrill me to know you've been checking me out."

"You don't have anything to fear from me. I was a cop more years than you've been alive." He took out the pack of cigarettes, and again, I was struck by his hands, not the type I'd imagine wrapped around the butt of a gun. "Here's what I can tell you," he said. "Big Red back at the nursery has it in for you."

"Annette?" I asked. "That's no secret."

"She asked someone to ask me to investigate you,"

he said matter-of-factly. "That was no problem. The problem was that when I tried to investigate her, I found out that there wasn't any her."

"What do you mean? You couldn't find any record of her?"

"Not a trace," he said. "And, darlin', if I can't find a trace of someone, it's because that person never took a breath."

The news chilled me. I knew that Annette hated me, but I never suspected that she might have secrets of her own. "So, she's someone else," I said. "She and Kathleen worked together for years. Do you think Kathleen knew?"

"Maybe, maybe not," he said. "A lot of people get away with changing identities. She got away with it for a long time."

"Are you sure she really isn't who she says she is?" I asked. I knew the moment the words were out that I shouldn't have spoken.

"Damn sure," he said. "Annette Montgomery doesn't exist. And this woman who says she is Annette Montgomery is trying to dig up something dirty about you." He grinned, but there wasn't anything happy about it. "Instead, she's going to realize that I found out what I told you just now."

I wanted to trust him, but knowing that he'd investigated every aspect of my life was unnerving. I just needed to get away from here, sleep and decide what to do next. "Why are you helping me?" I asked.

"I told you I don't let helpless women get hurt." He nodded toward a black Mercedes. "You look a little rocky to me. Why don't you let me drive you back to the house? I'm right down the road from you."

His words sank in through the exhaustion that surrounded me. I was instantly creeped. "You know where I'm staying?"

"It's no secret," he said. "No secret that you stayed at the hotel when you first came to town. No secret that you're seeing Jesse Medicine." He gave me a slow smile that I'm sure he intended to look humble.

"I am not seeing Jesse Medicine," I said, feeling the embarrassing heat rush to my cheeks. "If you're such a great investigator, you should know that."

"Don't get all pushed out of shape. I'm just telling you what's been observed," he said. "Now, come on and let me do my good deed for the day and give you a lift back to the house."

"No, thanks," I said. "I'll drive."

"Stubborn little thing, aren't you?" he said. "If you need anything, and I'm guessing you will, you just call me." He shook another cigarette from the pack into those long, pale fingers.

I turned and stomped away before he could light it.

TONY

Tony Dexter watched them drive away, Lester and the LaRue girl. She had no business anywhere close to a crime scene, reporter or not. Tony didn't like what was happening to his town. It was getting to him, to Chev Parnell, too. He'd smelled booze on the coroner's breath, a first for him. Come to think of it, that wasn't such a bad idea.

"Hey, Jerry," he asked his partner. "Want to stop for a drink when we get off?"

"Next time," Jerry said. "I've got plans tonight. Woman plans, if you know what I mean."

So, he'd drink alone. Wouldn't be the first time.

Jerry left, and Tony stayed put, protecting the crime scene. That's all he was protecting. The damage had been done.

"What's going on, Officer?" The voice startled him, but then he saw the uniform and managed a smile he didn't feel.

"Homicide. Pretty bad."

"And they say this is a safe town."

"Not tonight, it isn't," he said. "Nowhere is safe anymore. Damned lunatics."

A searching look. "Was a lunatic responsible for this homicide?"

"We aren't releasing any details," he said, keeping his voice gruff to discourage further questions.

"Of course. I understand." Talking a little too fast, edging back into the crowd.

Something glinted from the pavement. Tony reached down and picked it up.

"Hey," he called to the retreating figure, but no luck.

"Hey," he repeated, **loude**r. Finally.

"Were you talking to me?"

"Yeah." He put out his hand. "Your cell phone," he said. "You dropped it."

Uncertain hands reached out, took the phone, pocketed it. "Thanks, Officer."

"Wait a sec," he said. "Is that one of those you can take pictures with? My daughter bought one that looks just like it."

"Yes. At least I think it can do that. Sure glad you found it."

He sensed something was off. "You weren't planning to use that tonight, were you?" he asked. "Not trying to take a picture of the crime scene?"

"Of course not." The voice was steady now, almost offended. "I don't even know how to use it."

"Okay," Tony said. And then, "Stay safe."

"You, too, and thanks again."

As the stranger walked toward the street, Tony returned to the crime scene. Stay safe, he thought. That wasn't such an easy order these days, not even here, in his hometown.

Twenty-Four

JESSE

He'd almost forgotten the beer beside him as he sketched with his favorite Eagle drafting pencil on a newsprint layout pad, the way he did when he had more time than sense. With the side of his pencil and a loose wrist, he laid out light and dark patterns, and opposed positive space with negative space, so that if he ever approached a canvas again—which was unlikely as hell—he wouldn't forget.

The muse came to him at night when he drank. He'd let it go in the morning, even work on the new logo for the frigging coroner's office, but for right now, his life was in his fingers, not his bank account.

He guessed this random sketching was the way a

songwriter tried to find the first notes to a melody, and everything good in him prayed that he'd find his song again. On nights like this, with enough beer, it seemed almost possible.

He didn't want to think about what Sheldon used to say. *Man has drink. Drink has drink. Drink has man.* It was a joke to Sheldon, who could pound them harder than anyone. But Sheldon was dead, and *drink has man* was no longer as funny as it was when he and Sheldon were student and teacher.

He was just about ready to give it up for the night when the doorbell rang. It was close to eleven; he didn't intend to open up to anyone. On the second ring, the thought that it might be Geri was stronger than his woozy resolve. He eased the door open. There she was, a denim jacket wrapped around her so tightly that he knew she must be cold. Her face was pale as an eggshell.

"What the hell?" he asked.

She stepped back, as if having second thoughts that she'd come. "You smell like beer. You know that?"

"It's been a long night. You want one?" But then he saw a look in her eyes, something dark and immediate that hadn't been there before. This wasn't an impetuous spur-of-the-moment visit, no testament to what a great lover he was. Something had happened to shake her to the core. "Come on in," he said. "I'll put on some coffee and fix us something to eat."

She nodded and stepped inside. "Okay, then. I don't think I can stand up another minute."

He put his arm around her. Chicken bones. He heard his mother's voice. *That girl's so skinny, she's nothing but chicken bones.* That's what she'd said about Kath, but she didn't understand that strength didn't come from size. "What happened?" he asked. They stood in his living room now, awkwardly balanced against each other.

"A woman," she said. "From the clinic where I was today. She was murdered." Her jacket couldn't cover the shudder that passed through her as she spoke.

"Who?" he asked. "What woman?"

"Pat—Patricia—the nurse at the front desk."

"The blonde?" Not again. Not another woman murdered.

"I saw her. Her body, I mean." Geri's eyes filled with tears, and she removed her glasses to wipe them away. He pulled her closer. "I can't talk about it. I can't think about it. I just didn't know where else to go. I need your help."

"Coffee, then," he said. "Have you eaten?"

"I couldn't eat to save my life."

Save my life. That's what he had to do. She was following him now, into the house, the cool tiles of the kitchen floor under his bare feet.

"It will make you feel better. I was going to throw together an omelet for myself. The kitchen's right over here. Do you know how to make salsa?"

"Open the jar?" She could be serious, or not. With her, he could never tell.

"Come on, you're from California. You've got to know how to make salsa."

Her smile was a cross between weary and something more secretive. "I like to cook, and I'd like to cook with you, but not tonight."

"Salsa's not really cooking," he said. "It's more like mixing a drink." That's what she needed, a distraction, something to help distance her from the horror she had witnessed. "Besides, you have to eat. Come on. I have all of the ingredients right there." He pointed at the pot.

"I noticed the chiles," she said. "Thought they were plastic."

"It's a salsa garden, and this is a *molcajete*. We have everything we need."

"Sorry," she said, squinting at his lips. "Mocha-what?"

"Het-tay," he said slowly. "Mocha-het-tay."

"Thanks," she said. "Other languages are tough for me. I always called it a mortar and pestle."

"That works, too. I'll do the omelet. You do the salsa. The limes are in the refrigerator."

She didn't move, so he collected the limes and put them on the counter in front of her. Although the haunted look still remained in her eyes, she began to go through the motions, almost reluctantly at first. Jesse kept an eye on her while he beat the eggs with a whisk. She seemed to relax a little as she chopped the cilantro, garlic and red onion. He leaned back against the opposite counter, watching her. With the shadows from the candle flickering across her face, deepening her eyes, she looked like both herself and a stranger, in a way, even Kath. Odd how the way the light changed her features.

"What are you looking at?" she asked.

"You."

"Don't look too hard, okay? Especially not tonight."

"But I like looking at you. You can't imagine how much."

Her smile was sudden and sweet. He could sketch it in a single scrawl. "I hope you mean that," she said. "I like looking at you, too, even in that weird outfit you're wearing. You always work in Medicine Avenue sweats?"

"No, but I didn't dream I'd be lucky enough to have you stop by tonight." He reached for her, couldn't help it.

She let him kiss her, then moved away. "Please, Jesse."

Take it like a man, Sheldon would tell him. *You can't knock every lady dead, kid, or else you'd be a serial killer.* Had they laughed then, sitting in that Albuquerque bar as they drank themselves into a night and the following dawn, where they would never again be student and teacher? Yes, they probably had. Most evenings with Sheldon were woven with laughter.

"I'm sorry," he said. "I'm not trying to be a jerk."

"I know that." She moved closer to him, gave him a one-armed hug and another smile that looked like the real thing. "It's not about you."

"That's some comfort."

"Don't kid with me tonight, okay?"

"I'm not kidding. You're more important to me than you know." Where had that come from? But it was true. He cared about her, beyond the physical attraction. Thought about her more than he should. Worried about her.

Color returned to her cheeks. His unplanned confession had caused her to blush. "All I could think of after it happened was to get to you." She looked directly into his eyes and interlaced her fingers before her as if she were having to gather her courage to speak. "Someone had cut off part of my head. That poor woman had been killed. I don't even know why I came here, but it was the only place I could think of to come. And you—" She stopped.

"What?"

She shook her head, and the flush on her cheeks deepened. "I just needed to see you, that's all. I knew you'd understand."

And he did. If she didn't want to go to bed with him, that's the way it was. She'd come to him, and that was all that mattered. "I'm so glad you came," he said. "Tell me what I can do. How can I help?" At that moment he wanted to help her as much, maybe more, as he wanted to take her into his arms again.

She leaned against his white-tiled counter, and he could smell the cilantro on her, fresh and sharp. "You can tell me what you should have a long time ago."

Her words hit him in the gut, sobered him up on the spot.

"And what might that be?"

She held out her hand, as if waiting for something to fill it. "The locker," she said. "You promised."

He stopped at the *molcajete*, unable to move. What would Sheldon say? Sheldon would say: *Tell the truth. The truth never changes*.

"I told you I'd take you there."

"I don't have to be taken. Just give me the key. You can meet me there."

"Not tonight," he said. "If I thought what was in that locker would give us a clue, I'd send you there with my blessings. But you've been through hell. You don't need to be driving to that part of San Francisco this time of night."

"Tomorrow, then. First thing." Her eyes challenged him, and it hit him again how resilient she was after all she'd been through, how much like Kath. Maybe it wouldn't be a betrayal to tell her what he knew.

"Okay," he said. She stared him down through those rectangular glasses, her eyes dark and challenging. Mahogany. That was the color. They weren't the blue-green of Kath's, but, yes, as penetrating and honest, nevertheless. "Let's go there. Maybe we'll find something, and if we don't, at least we'll know that we tried everything."

"Do you mean it?" She looked ready to throw her arms around him.

He could have gone for that. It wasn't a betrayal. He'd kept Kath's secrets safe, and if Geri found out more than she should know, she'd keep the secrets, too.

"Yeah," he said. "Tomorrow. Let's go and get it over with."

"Thank you. Thank you. I was hoping you'd say that. I knew you would." Then she did throw her arms around his neck, and he could smell the cilantro again, the teary scent of the red onion she'd just diced. No way would he let anybody hurt this woman. In that moment, that thought, she was his.

He hadn't intended the kiss, but the moment his lips found hers, every sense he possessed knew how right it was. Her taste, her scent, the touch of her hot, bare skin under the jacket were all both fresh and familiar. Memories of the night at the house flooded him. She moaned but didn't push him away this time. He held on tighter, kissed her deeper.

"Jesse." Her voice was a whisper, her lips against his neck.

She stood pressed against him, the jacket raked off her shoulders, her heart against his chest pounding. Her eyes were filled with a hunger that perhaps not even she recognized. But there was fear there, too, and exhaustion.

She kissed him again, pressed into him with a moan. "I know why I came here," she whispered. "It's because you make me feel safe."

He pulled her to him, rocked her back and forth. *Safe.* She had no idea how much her words aroused him. He ran his fingers along her neck, up to her crazy hair. Finally, he felt what remained of her earlier reserve melt away. Her lips sought his. Her body pressed against him as if they were both naked. He couldn't take any more. He reached up, gently removed her glasses, put them on the counter, and slid the jacket the rest of the way off. Her skin gleamed in the candlelight. He could barely find his voice. When he did, he said, "You are safe with me. I promise."

How many hours? How long had he blanked out everything but her, him, their bodies? Lying on his bed, the covers long kicked off, he curled around her and buried his face in the sharp cilantro scent that lingered still like desire between them.

"I can't remember being this happy," he said. Then, realizing that she couldn't hear him, added, "I am so glad that you came here tonight."

"It's much better here, more relaxed."

"We should have come here to start with." It was wrong to be with her in Kath's house, and he'd known that then. He just hadn't been able to control himself. Never again. It wasn't fair to Geri or to Kath's memory, either.

She turned slowly, her almond-shaped eyes reflecting a contentment he'd never witnessed in them before now.

"I'm hungry." She ran her finger over his lips. "And I heard what you said, and hope you mean it. You make me happy, too, Jesse."

"Thought you couldn't hear," he said.

"A voice against my ear comes in loud and clear." She was against him now, and they were face-to-face. "Especially when I'm naked." Then she stretched and said, "That's my idea of a joke because I'm just now starting to feel a little embarrassed."

Her vulnerable expression broke his heart. "Don't be," he said. "You just need to eat, and you should have hours ago. You must be starving."

She lifted her bare leg and slid it down along his back, deliberately. "Later," she said. "We have all the time in the world."

She sat across from him at the bar, finishing the last salsa-coated bite of omelet from the black stoneware plate. He couldn't believe that this stark-naked woman was sitting here, as he, with a towel wrapped around his waist, tended to the food as if they were a real couple. The first night they'd been together, they'd both been driven by fear. Even last night had been an accident of sorts. But today in the light of early morning, it had been mutual and real.

"You're a good cook," she said.

"No. We are."

She put her fork down on her plate and studied him in that intense way he'd gotten used to. "For the first time in a long time, I am able to actually relax," she said.

"Then don't leave." Seeing the alarm on her face, he added, "I mean, do whatever you need to, of course. But I'd love it if we could spend time together. Here, I mean." He sounded like an idiot.

"I'd like that," she said. "More than you know. But I have some obligations."

"Geri." He reached for her hand, trying to figure out a way to tell her how much she meant to him.

She lifted it and kissed his. "I need to catch up. I haven't even accessed my e-mail account from work for two days."

"Couldn't you do that here?" he asked.

"Well," she said, looking at the counter then back at him.

"Well, what?" he asked, feeling hopeful.

"Well, I'll get it," she said.

She threw on his sweatshirt, and they retrieved the laptop, brought it in, and booted it up on the counter. Once she'd checked her e-mail, he'd try once more to convince her to stay.

"Anything interesting?" he asked.

"A note from my friend Steffan," she said. "He's doing a solo next week at the club where he sings and wants me to come. He also says he has lots of gossip for me."

"Maybe we could go together," Jesse said.

She grinned and tapped back a response on the keyboard. "I'd love for you to meet Steffan," she said. Then she squinted at the screen. "There's something here from the nursery. I wonder what Annette wants now."

He moved around beside her so that he could see the screen as well. "What is it?" he asked.

"There's no message, just three attachments."

She clicked the first one open, and the screen filled with the photograph of a woman's face. He stared at it a moment, and then realized that the bloody gouges on that face were once eyes.

He grabbed Geri and pulled her to him to keep her from seeing what he had, but it was too late.

She shuddered in his arms, tears streaming down her face. "Who?" she sobbed. "Why?"

"I don't know," he said. "We have to go to the nursery." Still holding her, he started to close the laptop and hide the photo of the murdered woman. Then he remembered. "There were three images attached to the e-mail," he said.

She looked up at him, and he knew that she was thinking what he was. "And three murdered women," she said. "Oh, Jesse. And they were sent from the nursery."

Twenty-Five

ANNIE

"So it's settled," she told Eric as they walked to the front door. "I'm going to tell Geri that she can buy me out."

"I still don't like it." He stopped in front of the door with a frown. "You love this place."

"So do you. Admit it."

That at least wiped out the frown, got her a small smile. "Never."

"It's driving me crazy," she said. "I'm having terrible nightmares. I just need to get away."

"There's no getting away, babe," he said. "Wherever we go, we'll know what Mom did, and we'll never know why."

"It was my fault," she said. "Taking me in was one thing. Letting me marry her son was another."

"I don't believe that. She was all for it until a few months ago. That was when she started trying to get me to leave here and go back to school."

Now they could both leave. She no longer wanted to stay, not with Geri LaRue sniffing around. "I thought I could hold out," she said, "but I just can't."

"Let's talk about it later." He put his arms out.

God, how solid and safe he felt. "I love you," she said.

He released her slowly. "Love you, too. Race you home, okay? First one naked in bed is the winner."

"I'm the winner, but I still need to lock up," she said. "I'll be right behind you."

She watched him walk away, grateful the way she always was that regardless of everything else in her life, she had gotten so lucky to find this man. Maybe they could start their own nursery somewhere else—nothing as big as this, of course.

She'd locked up the back and was at the register when she saw the wash of car lights across the drive. Eric must have forgotten something. She stepped outside to greet him, but it was Jesse Medicine's truck that had pulled in. Jesse jumped out of one door and Geri LaRue out of the other.

"What the hell are you doing here?" she demanded.

"I'm one of the owners, remember?" Geri looked ready to charge her. "Where the hell do you get off sending me that e-mail?"

"What e-mail?" She tried to stay controlled, but it wasn't easy. Her nerves were shot and had been for way too long. "I didn't send you anything."

"Liar. You sent me pictures, three of them, of the murdered women. They came from your computer."

"What are you talking about?" She wasn't getting anywhere with Geri, whose eyes were huge with fear or anger. She couldn't tell which. "I'm telling the truth, damn it." She directed the statement to Jesse, who hovered over Geri like a bodyguard.

"Then why not let us check out your computer?" he asked.

She didn't want them anywhere near her computer, and tried to push down the simmering anger. But she didn't have anything to hide, either. "Fine," she said. "I just turned it off. It'll take a moment to boot up."

"She probably cleaned it off," Geri said as they went inside to the back office.

"Will you shut up?" she said, whirling around. "I've just about had it with you."

"And I've about had it with you." Geri glared up at her as if just daring her to respond. "I know you had that investigator check me out."

That did it. She was too angry to lie. "Damned right I did. You came waltzing in here to this place I helped build from nothing. You didn't really expect a warm welcome, did you?"

"I didn't think that you'd have me checked out."

Geri cocked her head and smiled. "Your investigation backfired on you, though, didn't it, *Annette*?"

Her mouth went dry. The bitch knew. "Lester Brown's a nutcase," she said. "What ex-cop do you know with money like that? People say he got it in a drug bust."

"She's right," Jesse said to Geri. "Lester's pretty far out there."

"He may be far out there, but he was smart enough to check her out, too," she said. "Tell me, *Annette*, what's your real name?"

She bit her lip so hard that she almost cried out. It took all of her control to keep from slapping the smile off Geri's smug little face. "I don't owe you an explanation," she said. "I don't owe you shit."

"Cut it out," Jesse said. She was glad for the interruption. It gave her a chance to breathe and to force herself to calm down. "Let's just look at the computer," he said.

"I told you she cleaned it," Geri said, and this time Annie forced herself to remain silent. She hadn't cleaned out her old e-mails, a nasty habit of hers. There had to be more than six thousand messages that had piled up. Let the bastards sort through those.

She walked into the office, and they followed. For the first time since she'd been here, she wished she'd taken Kath's advice and put in a door. If she had, she'd slam it in their faces right now.

The computer seemed to take forever to boot up. Annie stood behind it, and like the enemies they were, they stayed on the other side. Geri's myopic gaze didn't move from her as if afraid she'd try to alter something right in front of them.

Finally, blue light filled the screen, and Annie was able to open her e-mail program. "Have at it," she told Geri. "This might be the biggest in-basket you've ever seen."

"It's the *sent* basket I want to see," Geri said.

"Go for it." Annie clicked on sent messages and stepped aside, waiting for the messages to appear. Nothing happened.

Geri edged around the computer and squinted at the screen. "Just what I thought," she said to Jesse. "She's wiped them out."

"What are you talking about?" Annie couldn't believe what she saw—nothing but flat white divided horizontally by a thin yellow ribbon upon which was printed: *No items are currently selected.* Because there were no items to select. There wasn't a message in the directory. "That's impossible," she said, clicking the screen again and again. But that's exactly what had happened. Someone had gotten rid of all of the *sent* messages and the deleted items, too. Geri stood beside her, her arms crossed in front of her denim jacket. "I don't know," Annie said. "I didn't touch the computer."

"Someone did," Geri said. "A nurse was killed in

the medical clinic parking lot tonight. Someone sent me a photograph of her face, and the faces of the two other victims. From here."

"I didn't." She felt herself start to unravel. She couldn't take any more of this. "God, how awful," she said. "I didn't know, honest." This was the time to tell the truth. She'd be in worse trouble if she didn't. "I did break into your hotel room, Geri, but that's all. I don't know anything about a dead woman in a parking lot."

"You?" The face before her was a blur, and Annie realized that she couldn't see Geri through the tears in her own eyes. She tried to wipe them away and said, "I was trying to find out more about you. I didn't know you'd come back while I was still in the room." She swallowed and added, "I'm sorry."

"You're *sorry?*" Geri moved closer to her, and Annie nodded. She was. She was sorry about all of this. And she couldn't deal with it. The anger was coming back, the outbursts. "Then tell me who you really are," she said.

"My name's Annie. Annie Raymond. I changed my last name, wanted to leave it all behind me." How much should she say? She was in too deep, maybe it was best to say it all. "Only Eric knows," she said.

"What about Kathleen?" Geri asked. "Did she?"

"Yes." God, it felt good to let it out. "She knew me since I was a kid, before my mother died," Annie said. "She probably saved my life." They looked back at her, both of them, their expressions holding as much sympathy as suspicion now. But there were no more words left in her, and what they wanted from her was too complicated to explain. Feeling helpless, she met Geri's eyes and said the only words she could. "My father."

"What about him?" Jesse's voice now.

Her vision blurred again. She wiped away new tears. "He was a drug addict and a murderer. He tried to kill me." God. She'd said it. She really had.

"And Kathleen?" Geri now, trying to make sense of it, squinting at her lips.

"She saved me. Let me live with her when I was a teenager. We made up the story about how we met when she was in graduate school."

"Was she still with her first husband?" Jesse now, dark eyes so penetrating that she had to look away, the way you'd look away from the sun when it hit you in the eyes.

"No," she said. That was easy to answer. "They split right after they started the nursery. She saw a few men off and on, but she never really got crazy over a guy until—" She saw the look on his face and could barely continue. "Until you."

Geri swallowed so hard that Annie could hear it. Jesse's face went stern and cold, the way that seemed so natural for him and yet so scary. She'd always thought whatever he and Kath called love was far too dangerous a dance.

"And Eric?" he asked.

"At first I thought Kath was okay with us. She seemed to be. But then she changed her mind. She wanted Eric to go back to school."

"She thought of you as a little sister," Jesse said. "She loved you."

The words warmed her. "I thought that was why she disinherited him."

"I don't believe that," Jesse said, and Geri nodded agreement.

"Can you see why I hated you?" she asked her. "It wasn't just the money. It wasn't just because I love this place. It was Kath. I haven't even been able to visit the cemetery. I just keep asking myself, could she? How—" She couldn't finish.

Geri's expression was detached. "It's okay," she said, in that clipped way that made Annie wonder what emotions hid beneath it. "I'm glad you told us, and I understand why you did what you did. We need to talk a little bit more, though. Are you up for it?"

Yes. She could talk about it now. She could. Geri LaRue no longer looked like a purple-haired freak intent on taking away everything she'd worked for, including Kath's loyalty. "Let me put some coffee on," she said. Then after a deep breath that calmed her more than she'd been calmed in years, "I'll need to call Eric, too. He worries when I'm late."

Twenty-Six

GERI

At first, I was embarrassed that I'd spent the first night of my concussion in Jesse Medicine's bed. Still, that was what I'd wanted, more or less, since the first time we'd been together, maybe even the first time I'd stepped foot in his studio. My life changed that night. I no longer felt as lost or as frightened. Jesse cared about me. I believed that. He wanted me to be safe, and I wanted the same thing. Besides, he was starting to chase the ghost of Malc from my mind.

It could work; we could. Everything could work, if it were not for the ghost in *his* life.

The stunned, stoic expression on his face when Annie spoke about Kathleen left no doubt about what he still felt for her. I couldn't even imagine how

I'd feel if a man I'd loved looked like that when someone mentioned how much I'd cared for him.

Malc, maybe? No. He'd be too worried about whether or not I trusted him, and I'd be worried right back. As always I'd fallen for a man with too much baggage to fill the room that was already over-crowded with my own.

Jesse, then? In spite of our personal sparks, our mutual chemistry—not to mention his understanding of my hearing situation—was going to be a long shot. Once Annie had started talking about *Kath,* he hadn't been able to hide where his heart was.

As much as I didn't want to compete with a dead woman, I cared about Jesse and not just for the great sex. I hadn't gone to his house in search of great sex. I'd gone there because he was the only person I trusted in this confusing new world of mine. I still did. Today, true to his word, he was going to take me to the boat locker Kathleen had rented through the end of the year.

Annie—she'd said it was okay to call her that now—had told us everything last night, about how her druggie father and mother had camped outside Half Moon Bay and worked a week or two in one of the canneries. Her father had killed a woman in a burglary, Annie said, only to be shot down by Lester Brown, who was a cop back then. By the time she'd finished, Annie was in tears, and we had to call Eric to come drive her home.

Before I left to meet Jesse in San Francisco early that Monday morning, I went with her to the cemetery east of town. It was located on a bare hilltop, with views of the ocean and windswept concrete plots. I felt odd being there, like a fraud almost, but Eric refused to go, and I knew that Annie really wanted to. She didn't say anything, just placed the blue-tipped tulip-looking flowers with the fancy name by the headstone and wiped away tears. A huge vase of orange blooms was already there, artfully arranged and fresh as if it had been put there moments before. They looked out of place, too garish, maybe. I'd seen flowers just like them at the nursery, but this wasn't the time to discuss the matter with Annie.

I was glad I'd come with her, because she was so shaken that I wasn't sure if she could have driven back. Odd how it works with people. How you can go from hate to empathy and maybe more sometimes, just by talking.

The locker was in China Basin, north of the Bayview District and south of Market. The parking lot was small and had an almost rural feeling. Fragrant flowers of tissue-thin periwinkle-blue bloomed among the weeds leading to a restaurant and oceanfront bar beyond the lockers.

According to the sign beside the chalkboard of specials outside, its name was The Ramp. Its clientele dressed in shorts and tans and those easy, early-morning, already-bored expressions of having it all and wanting more.

But it was the lockers, not the bar or pseudo-hip fish joint that attracted me. They were old, really old, the kind of peeling-paint spaces only boat people would rent to stash their gear and maybe some drugs.

Which one was Kathleen Fowler's? As I stared at the solid beige doors, I saw a shiny black pickup pull into the lot beside me. Jesse climbed out, and it took every gene of reserve in my body to keep me from running to him and kissing his face off.

This thing we'd ignited might not be what I'd had with Malc, which was, like it or not, pretty close to what I always imagined when I tried to imagine love. This Jesse thing was more sudden and, in some ways, more passionate. It was also marathon sex—my definition, at least. In that night we shared, anytime I had a nightmare or a flashback to the horrible scene with the crazy killer responsible for my cracked head, I could reach for Jesse's naked body and erase my fear for a while.

He wore the soft-looking blue chambray shirt I'd kissed him into this morning. I'd never been attracted to men with shaved heads before; I'd never thought about it one way or the other until now. But, yes, there was something appealing, even erotic, about that smooth head, something about how it made his eyes so large and riveting.

I stood beside an ugly, branchless tree beside a broken-down wooden fence as he came to meet me.

He gave me a lingering kiss, then asked, "You ready?"

"Sure am." I tried to find his eyes behind the shadow of his sunglasses. "You?"

"I guess so. This isn't exactly the San Francisco everyone sees, is it?"

"Why would Kathleen choose a locker here?"

"It's close to the water," he said, "and we—she— owned a boat for some time."

The we/she thing bummed me out a little, as had the conversation with Annie. But face it, that's where Jesse was. *We. She.* The chemistry suggested that I might be the *she* in his life, but when he talked like that, I wasn't convinced. I'd like to be convinced, though. For the first time since Malc and I had ended our relationship, I'd like to be—well, needed to be— convinced. If I'd said it once, I'd said it a hundred times. Love sucks.

"Why'd she sell the boat?" I asked.

"Beats me." Even behind the glasses, I could sense the pain in his eyes. "That was when everything started going south."

"When you broke up, you mean?"

"No." His grin was hard, as if he were remembering something he didn't want to. "We were doing okay after the breakup. It was after that, when she started backing off and wouldn't tell me what was

wrong. When she started having all those accidents."
He paused for only one beat, but I felt it, nevertheless. "I knew all of her secrets," he said. "I want you
to promise me that whatever we find in here or
anywhere will remain between us unless it's something that will lead to her killer."

How many ways did I need to hear that he was still
in love with her? How many lessons in the school of
Love Sucks did I have to learn before I decided to
drop out? But I didn't have any choice. I looked
again at him, at the bleak lockers beyond us, and said,
"Okay."

"I brought you something," he said. "I thought it
might help if you saw a photo of her."

"I saw the one in the newspaper," I said, but he was
right. I did need more than a mug shot to try to recognize this woman who'd changed my life by getting
herself killed.

"Wait just a minute, okay?" Before I could answer,
he started toward his truck, then returned with a
folder of photographs. Four of them, to be exact. As
I stood there, smelling bacon and fried fish and
looking at the photos of the woman he still loved, I
didn't know how to react. I froze my face, the way I
did when someone talked too fast and I couldn't
follow. And I just looked.

Kathleen Fowler was cute. I wouldn't call her
drop-dead gorgeous, the way Adrienne Revell, Malc's
new love, was, but she was cute, with thick, angular

eyebrows that gave her a mischievous look. And in every photo, her lips were frozen into the same smile. Her eyes weren't laughing, though. They were haunted shadows hidden in her otherwise open expression. I guessed them as brown, as was her hair, long and straight and filling up the frame of the one head shot in the folder.

In another, she had an arm slung around Annie, the other around Eric, all of them wearing Blooms aprons. In yet another, she was at some kind of costume party holding a sequined mask before her and smiling at a guy in a Santa Claus costume, the same guy I'd seen at the nursery, wearing the same costume.

The final shot was just her face, softened by whatever light was behind it. She looked up into the camera, her shoulders bare, make that naked, her eyes smoldering with emotions I could only guess. In that shot, she was beautiful. I had no doubts who'd been holding the camera.

"Well?"

I looked up into his eyes, wondering what he wanted from me. Was I supposed to say what an attractive woman his dead wife was? Was I supposed to try to compete?

"Thanks," I said. "As far as I can tell from these, I've never seen her before."

"So, why did she do what she did?"

"I don't know," I said. "But I was a foster kid, too. I'm thinking it's got to be connected to that."

I could almost feel him jerk away from me. "I doubt it," he said. "That was in her past."

"And in mine."

But he was no longer listening, only marching toward those bleak lockers.

We found Kathleen's and stepped inside. It was larger than it appeared from the outside, but not much, with a rancid green carpet that grime, dirt and age had turned a dark olive color. A wind fan clattered in fresh air that failed to overcome the commingled scents of oil, dust, moldy boxes and despair. From where I stood, all I could see was boat detritus. A rusted anchor. A couple of backpack-looking things. I didn't like this place, didn't like the smell or feel of it, and couldn't believe Kathleen Fowler would have left anything of importance here.

I charged into the stifling place and started opening the yellowed cabinets. The first one held only boat parts. The second held stacks of musty paperback novels. "Books?" I asked, glancing up at him.

"She couldn't throw one away," he said. "She always stashed a dozen or more paperbacks on the boat." He hadn't moved from the door and barely seemed aware of me. It was Kathleen he was seeing in here, Kathleen he was remembering.

Another cupboard revealed only a white windbreaker and a pair of women's shoes. I stared at the shoes and realized that they would probably fit me. For a crazy instant, I wondered how it would feel to slip my feet into them. Would it be like stepping into Kathleen Fowler's life? I slammed the cupboard door harder than I needed to.

"There's nothing here," I told Jesse.

"I didn't promise you there would be," he said. "Let's get out of here."

I was no closer to what had happened to Kathleen or why she'd left her estate to me than I had been that day at the newspaper when I'd found out I was her sole beneficiary.

He walked ahead, and I reached for the lever of the door. I so didn't want to see or smell one bit of that pathetic place ever again.

That was when I saw it, just as I was getting ready to close the door—a turquoise line peeking out beneath the edge of the putrid green carpet.

"There's something there," I said.

"Where?" He was beside me in a second.

"Underneath the carpet." I crouched down and tried to lift it. Someone already had. A tiny chill crept through me. Someone, probably Kathleen, had slid something under here. It looked and felt like a folder.

"What is it?" he asked again.

I tugged at the slender edge, and slid out a turquoise-colored manila folder.

"Let me see," he said. "Bring it outside."

I carried it pressed against my chest, feeling my heartbeat through it. If this folder was the answer I'd been seeking, I only hoped I was ready for it.

We walked down the blacktop toward the smell of bacon and fish. Did people really eat fried fish for breakfast here? I settled into the first weathered seat and opened the folder. Jesse pulled his chair next to mine and peered over my shoulder. I looked up into those smoldering eyes and said, "Please."

"Sorry," he replied, and backed away.

I placed the folder on the table and opened it.

I don't know what I expected—or what Jesse did. Volumes of confession, maybe. Journals. An outline of who killed Kathleen and why. Maybe a convenient tape or photograph. But no. Only a few pieces of paper were slipped inside the folder.

Jesse had already bounced from the table to the weathered oceanside bar. Good. That gave me a chance to read. The first piece of paper was titled Homes. At first the names and addresses made no sense to me. Then, I saw *Hanford.* I saw *Rev. Coy Nichols,* and I wasn't sure I could go on. Kathleen and I had been at the same home, maybe at the same time. I had known her.

Jesse came back with two mugs.

"Too early for me," I said.

"They're Henry Weinhards." How had he already figured out that nasty little root beer habit of mine? If only for that, I shoved the first piece of paper toward him.

"What's this?" he asked.

"Her foster homes, I think."

The second sheet of paper was more confusing. It contained four addresses and phone numbers. Mama's, at least two towns too late. Mine in San Francisco. Mary Haskins at her former office. And someone named Junior, in Half Moon Bay. I was starting to get really shaky. Why had Kathleen recorded my contact information? I hoped the final sheet in the folder would answer my questions.

It was a printout of an e-mail message. The Blooms logo at the top showed that it had been printed from the nursery computer. There was no return e-mail address.

Hey, Kathy Jo. How does it feel to know I'm getting closer? You know that I can see you reading this, don't you? You know that I'll finish the job when I'm ready. How does it feel to be the one who suffers for a change?

Twenty-Seven

JESSE

"I didn't know," Jesse said. "She never told me."

"So, who wrote this?" Geri asked, pointing down at the paper in front of her on the restaurant table.

"I don't know." The truth of what he was saying burned his gut like whiskey. But not even that would be able to dull his raw emotions.

"I thought that she told you everything."

Was she mocking him? No. Something more gentle than ridicule settled around her so palpable that he could have touched it. But Geri wasn't about touching. Geri was Geri in a cinched-in jacket that in spite of its dark, denimlike fabric, looked too flimsy for the weather. And he was doing a piss-poor job of keeping her safe.

"Guess I was wrong," he said. She shifted in her chair, and he knew that she wanted to leave. "Where next?" he asked, as if he were part of her plan.

She touched the folder, then drew back. "I've got to go back to the foster home," she said. "Whatever caused all of this happened back then." She shuddered, and he knew she was seeing the dead women in the e-mailed photos again.

"Are you driving straight through?" he asked, thinking that at the very least, he'd follow her.

She shook her head. Just then, the sky opened, and the late morning sun highlighted her hair a cherry-soda red. The sun on her face seemed to cheer her as well. Her smile seemed less sad. "I have to stop at the newspaper first," she said. "There's the problem of that trash they printed about me in the 'Off the Record' column."

"Can't you handle that by phone?"

"No," she said. "I've got to deal with Doug Blanchard's backstabbing."

"But you have some money now." Before he could say more, she pushed back the chair and stood.

"I love my job, okay? I wasn't looking for a way out, and I sure as hell don't think that creeped-out house and Half Moon Blooms are the ticket."

"Okay, okay," he said, patting the air with his hand to let her know that her voice was louder than she realized. "Calm down, will you?"

"Sure thing." She imitated his gesture and sat on

the edge of her chair again. Then, leaning across the table, she said, "With the exception of you, my life has been one freaking nightmare since I came here. I'm just trying to dig my way out, understand?"

"I do understand," he said, "but why would you want to go back to the newspaper?"

"Because." Her eyes filled with tears, and she had to take off her glasses. "Because it's all I have."

"But it's not—" How could he say more? And if so, what should he say? What promises could he make this time, to this woman, that wouldn't be broken?

She stood again, and he knew he'd lost another round.

"I'm sorry." She took off her glasses again, her eyes exotic, a visual counterpoint to the rest of her quirky appearance.

"Don't be."

"I don't know how much more I can take," she said. "That poor woman. Pat Smith. She said to call her Pat."

"Let me go with you." He had to try. One more time. He had to. If he'd tried one more time with Kath, maybe she'd still be alive.

"It won't make any difference." Her eyes were dry again and impossible to read.

"Please, Geri."

She turned away as if she hadn't heard him. Maybe she hadn't. So he'd follow her. Wait outside her apartment, tail her to the San Joaquin Valley and the foster homes. The foster homes.

The sky had turned into a bedlam of storm clouds again, and she walked into them, to the lockers and the parking lot beyond as if intent on a new mission. But then so was he.

He saw the blow before he felt it. Silver. A silver bird sailing through the sky. Then the weight of the weapon hit him, and he went down. His last conscious thought was to warn her. "Geri," he shouted, but the silver bird had stolen his voice. Then the blurry form above him swung the weapon again.

He opened his eyes, slowly, by increments. That's how sharp the pain was. Darkness, just darkness, and the musty smell of a locker? This couldn't be happening in San Francisco, not even here. "Geri?"

A girlish giggle answered, and then a kick to his head. Lights exploded behind his eyes. "Geri," he shouted again. He tried to find his feet and instead grabbed the uniformed leg closest to him. A band uniform, he thought. The kind of uniforms they wear in a high school band. No, not that, but close. The leg kicked him free. Light slashed across his eyes, as if a door had been opened.

Moments later he heard Geri's voice. "Jesse!" she screamed. "God, no."

"Run," he managed to shout.

He woke slowly in that same musty place. Someone was pressing fabric against the pain in his head. Jesse cracked an eye. Geri bent over him, her eyes stark with terror and shock.

"I told you to run," he said.

"It's okay. Whoever did this to you got away. I called for help."

He could only groan and curse his own stupidity. "I smell blood," he said. "Am I bleeding?"

"Not badly." She squeezed his hand and tried to look brave. "Did you see anything?"

"Not enough to identify whoever did it."

"Crazy," she said. "To attack you in broad daylight is just crazy."

He looked into her eyes and said, "I think that's what we're dealing with."

GERI

I'd paid no attention to him as we left the funky restaurant and started for the car. I knew that he planned to follow me.

Something had gone wrong behind me, something I hadn't heard. When I turned around I saw the door to the locker standing open. He was right. Whoever had done this had to be crazy.

Jesse was lucky, the paramedics had told us. They were taking him in, anyway.

I drove Jesse's truck. As I sat in the waiting room, I returned phone calls. The first one was from Lester Brown. When I told him what had happened, he wanted to come at once, but I thanked him and said that we'd be leaving soon.

"Let me know if I can do anything to help," he said. "Tell the Medicine man I hope he's better soon, and to be more careful next time."

"He was careful." I didn't like the way he said it, as if Jesse had somehow put me in danger. "We were in broad daylight."

"In the worst part of a screwed-up city of fruits and nuts," he said. "No decent man in his right mind would bring a lady there."

I wanted to come back at him but I didn't have it in me. "There were lots of ladies at the restaurant," I said, remembering the relaxed atmosphere of the seaside café.

"Not by my definition. Takes more than a skirt and panty hose, you know."

I sighed, hoping he'd get my point. "Well, there were people all over the place. I don't know why someone would do this to him, especially out in public like that."

"Only one thing makes sense to me." Lester paused, and I could hear him exhale. "Whoever this is doesn't want to kill him or you. At least not now."

"Oh, that's comforting," I said. But he was right. How many times had I been as alone and vulnerable as Pat from the hospital? Then I remembered something that Malc had told me. "Revenge killing," I said.

"What's that, darlin'?" I heard the unmistakable sound of a cigarette lighter.

"A psychologist told me that Kathleen's murder could have been the work of a revenge killer," I said. "The homeless woman's, too."

"Not bad for a shrink."

I cringed. "Do you think that's what this is all about? Revenge?"

"Could be. A revenge killer gets off by knowing that you know and there's nothing you can do about it."

"Wonderful," I said. "And revenge or not, I'll end up just as dead."

"That's where I come in," he said.

Scared as I was, I didn't like the idea of Lester Brown as a bodyguard. "What do you mean?" I asked. "I don't even know you."

"I swore to serve and protect," he said. "That didn't change when I retired my badge. I'm going to cover your back whether you like it or not."

"Well," I repeated, trying to get a word in.

"Just remember I'm on your side," he said. "Take good care, darlin', you hear?"

I sat in the waiting room trying to make sense out of the conversation. If we were dealing with a revenge killer, we needed to figure out revenge for what. And we'd better do it soon.

I looked up to see Jesse walk through the patient exit and cross the room. Other than the bandage on his head, he looked fine. In fact, he looked wonderful. I got up and ran to him, realizing how worried I'd been. He hugged me, gave me a kiss.

"You okay?" I asked.

"Now I am."

We held hands as we walked to the parking lot, and of the many emotions that swirled through me, relief was a major one.

Twenty-Eight

GERI

Jesse was indeed lucky, although he complained that the cut on his head was enough to make him want to grow out his hair. He had even tried to talk me into letting him accompany me to the Valley, but I made him promise to stay put.

I walked into the newspaper building about eleven-thirty, feeling like an interloper instead of an employee. Part of it was the name tag the security guard at the front desk had helped me clip to my jacket. A guard I didn't recognize, probably hired since my leave, had to phone the newsroom to clear me before I could head down the long corridor toward the elevator. Such was security at any newspaper these days, but I couldn't help taking it personally.

When I stepped off the elevator and started down the hall, all of that changed. I had told Jesse that the newspaper was all I had, and it was true. Bridget lifted her golden head and broke into a smile of welcome. The Yo Boys, Wil and Ricardo, waved as if they were family. I was home, a rat's ass version as Mama would say, but home nevertheless. Steffan looked up from his cube as I passed and blew me a kiss. He knew better than to get up and greet me before I finished the job I'd come here to do. I'd told him when I'd arrived, and he'd set up a lunch after. I could hug him then.

Only Marie, my editor, looked unhappy at my return. No, she looked unhappy period. In her straight, V-neck dress and silver belt, she was the definition of painfully thin. She'd scrunched her hair up in one of those playful fabric clips that stop looking cute on anyone out of high school.

She stepped aside to let me enter and said, "Are you here to extend your leave?" In her dreams.

"You know why I'm here," I said. "I left you a voice mail."

"Are you sure? I didn't get any message from you." She didn't appear to be faking it, just eager to get me out of there. "What's the problem?"

"Doug Blanchard," I said. "How could you let him print lies about me?"

"He didn't print lies." She sighed and took a sip from the water bottle on her desk. "He printed opinions. That's what columnists do."

"I know what columnists do," I said. "I almost was one. And Blanchard did print lies. He never tried to reach me by phone. I didn't fail to return his calls."

"Are you sure about that?" She hadn't expected that one, I could tell. "I'll need to talk to him." She gnawed at her bottom lip as if trying to make a decision. Then she said, "I believe you. I'll do it right away, before—"

"Before what?" I asked, although I already suspected. "Is he running another column about Kathleen Fowler's murder?"

"Yes," she said, her expression suddenly sober. "On Sunday."

She said she'd take care of it. She said she appreciated my coming in. Then she looked at her watch and said that she had an appointment. I followed her down the hall, past the cube across from Steffan's, walking slowly enough that she could get to the elevator first. Just as I stepped into the main hall, Romeo Joey Reynolds slithered up, serpentine as ever, between her and me. "Hey, Ger," he said. "Going down?" Then he winked.

"No." I marched toward the stairs but not before I saw the slapped-across-the-face look he gave me. Good. By the time I got to the bottom, they were already gone, both of them, walking out the front door.

No, I thought. Not together-together. Probably just leaving at the same time. But something about the look on his face when he stood midway between me and the elevator with her holding the door creeped me out.

"Hey." Steffan grabbed me from behind and whirled me around to face him. "Welcome back, welcome back, welcome back." Then, taking a closer look at me, he asked, "What is it?"

"Joey and Marie. They're not…?"

"You got it," he said. "Tell you about it on the way to lunch."

So it was true. I felt light-headed. I'd assumed that Marie's treatment of me was my fault. I'd never stopped to think that it might be connected to something going on in her life.

On the way to the restaurant, I told Steffan about what had happened at the lockers in the Bayview district. I paid close attention to his expression when I told him that Jesse could have been killed. It was important that he know Jesse wasn't as Malc had portrayed him.

"And now?" he asked.

"He's at home," I said.

"What are you going to do?" Steffan asked.

I paused. "You can't say anything," I told him.

"What do you think I'm going to do—run snitch to Doug Bastard so he'll have new column fodder, maybe?"

"I'm sorry," I said. "I know I can trust you. I just—I'm going to go back to Hanford, to the foster home."

He inched the car into the parking lot expertly, then sat there staring at me as if I'd lost my mind. "Hanford, where your social worker was killed?"

"People are getting killed all around me," I said. "It's not a geographical thing." I trembled. "And there's no place I'm safe, Steffan."

He hugged me and said, "Oh, Ger," and I knew that coming from someone who always had all of the answers, that wasn't good.

"Guess we'd better go in," I said. "Marie will have your ass if you aren't back in an hour."

"Not these days," he said. There was a wicked gleam in his eyes. "Our dear editor has other distractions."

"No," I said. "I still can't believe it. Say it's not true."

"Disgustingly so," Steffan said. "She must think it's love, too, because she doesn't care who knows it. They arrive and leave together now. Every single day. Wonder what they tell their spouses."

"And she was going to write me up for taking off early on that Friday," I said, remembering how terrified I was that day I thought she was going to fire me, the day I found out that Kathleen Fowler had named me her beneficiary. "What a freaking hypocrite."

"Welcome to the newspaper biz," he said. "Juicy, ain't it."

"Not really."

"You don't think the fact that TBM and Romeo Joe are having an affair right under everyone's collective nose is juicy?"

I shook my head.

After what I'd been through, gossiping about two pathetic married people screwing around held little appeal for me. Maybe I'd been gone too long.

I knew that Steffan could sense my distaste. I managed to go inside and smile and nod as the members of our group relished the tawdry details of said affair as much as they did the sushi. I could have done without both. By the time the food came, I'd lost my appetite. How had I gone so fast from feeling like part of a family to feeling apart from my coworkers and their concerns? I wondered if I still loved journalism—and the paper—enough to put up with everything that the rest of them seemed to take for granted. Like it or not, Kathleen Fowler's murder had changed me.

After the meal, Steffan and I made up for my previous silence by exchanging enough hugs and air kisses to make me wonder if perhaps I'd accidentally driven to Hollywood instead of San Francisco.

"I'm sorry," Steffan said as we walked through the chilly, still air of early afternoon toward his car. "I should have clued you in about what's been going on here. I didn't mean to put you into a funk."

He gave me one of those easygoing smiles that just

barely covered his true emotions. He couldn't begin to understand how I felt. Sure, he was technically a minority, too, if you could consider a gay, Korean, drop-dead gorgeous man a minority in San Francisco. His charmed life knew few setbacks, except perhaps, like mine, in the romance department. And he'd never had to fear for his life.

"You didn't," I said. "I'm just tired."

"The gossip is just what we do," he said. "What you and I always did. It helps us let off steam. You know how much I love my job."

"And I love mine." Didn't I? Didn't I still love it?

I'd been away from the paper a very short time, but I was already looking from the outside in. Maybe it was just that I had too many life-or-death concerns on my mind, but much of what I saw was about politics and pettiness.

"I understand," I said. "I need to get back to my car now."

He stopped in the middle of the street. "Don't be mad at me, Ger. Please."

Cute as ever. Smart as ever. But he hadn't been through what I had. He hadn't been through attacks, through murders, Mary Haskins, Sunlight the homeless woman, and Pat Smith, whose defiled face I could see even without the benefit of e-mail.

"I'm not mad at you," I said. "I'm just tired."

"No, you're disappointed. I can tell. That's the last thing I want."

"Get out of the way," I told him. "You'll get hit by a car, and my life will get even worse than it already is."

I turned my head, the way he knew I did when I didn't want to hear more, and I walked across the street.

I felt him grab my shoulder before I heard his voice. "Okay, I have an idea."

"What's that?" I asked.

"Why don't you talk to Marie and see if you can telecommute until this is all over?"

"Why would I want to do that?" I pretended to look into the St. John Knits window.

He put his hands on my shoulder and turned me around. "You could do it part-time. You'd still be part of the staff, still come to the get-togethers. You've been living that murder. You aren't yourself anymore."

Yes, I was myself, only this self was far different from the one he knew.

"I love you for thinking of it," I told him. "But I'm not sure I could begin to write anything decent."

"Just as long as you love me again." He flashed me that elfin smile.

"I never stopped loving you," I said.

"But it's different between us with you gone. You've got to admit that. You don't laugh at the same things you used to. You obviously don't care about the gossip."

"Too busy trying to stay alive."

"I hate that, Ger. I just wish you'd come back." He took my hand and we walked past more shops, more fashions only trophy wives could afford to wear, an odd contrast with the street people offering to clean windshields and carry luggage outside of the hotels interspersed among the shops and cafés.

"I've got something that will make you feel better," he said. "Something you'll absolutely love."

More gossip? More office politics?

"You've already made me feel better, Steffan."

"No," he said. "I mean it. I was petty today. Insensitive, too. Let me make up for it."

"And how might you do that?" I asked, and jabbed him with my elbow.

"For starters," he said, "I met Doug Bastard's former girlfriend the other night."

That stopped me. I felt a chill that slid from my neck to my ankles. "Not the dead fiancée obviously. Which girlfriend, Steffan, and where?"

"The club, of course." We were at the car now, but he made no move toward it. "Straight women love me, you know."

"Don't remind me," I said. "Just tell me about the girlfriend." Suddenly gossip was no longer beneath me. I'm sure the fact wasn't lost on him.

"She's an astrology columnist," he said, "but not a weirdo. Guessed my sun sign right off the bat."

"Scorpio," I said. "Big deal. Not that you're way intense or anything."

"No fair. We just celebrated my birthday, so of course you know my sign. She didn't get the Leo moon, though, guessed Aries." He shuddered at the thought.

"Guess she's never seen you dance on a tabletop," I said. "What'd she say about Doug Blanchard?"

"Played it pretty close to the chest, and I didn't ask. Way too *tac-kay* to start quizzing her when she'd paid a cover charge. But…" He eyed me with a grin.

"But what?" I asked. "Did you by any chance manage to obtain her telephone number?"

"Better than that, my dear." He reached for his wallet. "I just happen to have a business card. Now tell me you love me."

Twenty-Nine

GERI

Before I left for the San Joaquin Valley the next day, I visited Tracy Luce in her apartment off Union in the Cow Hollow area of the Marina. The living room was small and spotless with only two straight-backed chairs and a salsa-colored sofa covered in equally colorful pillows. Other than a few crystals hanging in front of the sliding glass doors to my left, there was nothing New Age about it. The music from the CD player behind the sofa was classical; the scent was dark-roast coffee, without a trace of incense.

It wasn't what I expected an astrology columnist to live in, but Tracy Luce wasn't what I expected, either. Tall, thin and hair so dyed red that her short, thick do looked like a hat—but a very attractive one—she could have been twenty or forty. Her jeans were tight, her feet were bare, and her black tee lifted along her slender rib cage when she shook my hand and introduced herself. If it's true that red is the new blond, Tracy Luce was the poster child for it.

She took one look at me, squinted, and said, "Aquarius."

That startled me. "How'd you know?"

"The hair." She tugged at her own. "I'm one, too."

"No kidding?"

"Oh, yes. We're off on a mission to save the world, aren't we? Our heads in the clouds—and our hair," she said in what sounded, to my ears, like a munchkin voice, then paused. "You're not into all this, are you?"

"Not really."

"That's okay." She shrugged. "Steffan's not, either, but I think he could be converted."

"Converted to *astrology* perhaps." I let my gaze linger on hers so that she could get my meaning.

"How true," she said. Then with a cheerful sigh, "The good ones are either married or gay, aren't they?"

"Doug Blanchard isn't."

That stopped her for only a moment. Then she said, "That's for damned sure," and laughed at her own joke. "Steffan said you'd been hurt by him, too."

"I can't say that he's my favorite person at the newspaper." I tried to sound neutral, but I couldn't.

"Give it up, Aquarius," she said. "You know that you hate the sorry bastard as much as I do."

I started to grab the closest platitude: *I don't hate anybody. I'm sure he has good qualities.*

Before I could, I caught the unmasked anger in her clear blue eyes and said, "Okay, maybe there are some hard feelings there."

"I knew it," she shot back. "How'd he screw you over?" I realized from the appraising once-over she gave me that she believed Doug and I had been lovers. Please gag me right now at the very thought of that. But, no, I'd pretend even that to get inside information on him. The only problem was my inability to lie. Make that to lie convincingly.

I stared past her head, at the display of crystals directly behind her. "He did screw me over, all right." *Not a lie, Mama, not even close to one.*

"The bastard. You're young, too, aren't you? I mean younger than I am, right? He's done this before. Young women are so much easier to fool."

The crystals were a blaze of light. "I *am* younger than he is," I said, hoping that I didn't sound like a robot. Maybe I should just leave right now. What facts about Doug Bastard did I really need to know? That he was an arrogant prick and an opportunist? I knew that. No, I needed to find out why he hated me. Or did I? The thought struck me that maybe I was no better than my gossiping coworkers, trying to figure out who was sleeping with whom. I liked Tracy and was surprised that Doug could get anyone this decent, but I doubted that anything she could tell me would help me wake up from the nightmare my life had become.

"Don't be afraid." She thought I was withholding something. I could see it in her eyes. "I just made some coffee. Come on in."

She reached out for my shoulder and gave me eye contact so intense that I started to wonder which one of us was running this show. "Come on now," she repeated. "We need to talk."

And I said, "Okay."

An angular bar in front of the glass doors separated the living room from the kitchen. To the right, a hall led to the rest of the apartment. It was a deceptive layout—gracious, open and full of light until one realized that most of Tracy Luce's living quarters were hidden. Now that I was here, spurred on by Steffan's curiosity as well as my own, I'd listen to whatever I could get out of her and then drive on to the Valley.

The all-white kitchen was as immaculate as the living area. "This is really nice," I said, surveying the countertop with its faux marble surface and the single coffeepot so clean and shiny that the four-cup level of coffee looked painted on.

"You can tell me anything about him and I won't be shocked." She started pouring. "Nothing about that shifty, lying Aries will surprise me."

"Doug's an Aries?"

She handed me a cappuccino-size white cup and said, "Damn, woman. You went to bed with him without knowing his sign?"

I took my place on the other side of the white-tiled bar and sipped the coffee while trying to figure out how to extricate myself from this one. "I barely know my own sign," I said.

That got a laugh from her. Thank goodness. I leaned over the counter and pretended to be involved with the coffee. "This is wonderful," I said. "Where do you find beans this fresh?"

"I buy them green," she said. "Roast them myself." I tried to nod happily, but she caught my eye again. "Let's talk about Doug," she said. "I still resent the hell out of him. I'd love to walk into that newspaper and tell anyone who would listen what a son of a bitch he is."

"He is arrogant, all right," I said. "At the newspaper, they call him Doug Bastard."

She giggled. "So I heard. He cheated me out of my first column."

I nearly choked. "Me, too."

"In an alternative newspaper," she said. "Broke my heart in every way. We met in J-school. It wasn't the *Washington Post,* but it was my first shot. He went behind my back." She faced me from the other side of the bar and slugged down the coffee as if tossing back a shot of whiskey. "He told the editor he didn't think I was up for the job. Can you believe that?"

"Now I can," I said. I felt vindicated. Thank you,

Steffan. I did need to come here after all, needed to know that Doug truly was what I thought he was. "Was that the end of your relationship?" I asked.

She nodded. "You'd better believe it. Now I write three astrology columns, and do charts for private clients. So yes, I do just fine."

But she didn't look just fine and she slammed her coffee utensils on the counter and poured our second cups. She was still angry.

"He stole my column, too," I said. "'Off the Record.' It was supposed to be mine."

"I've read it, but I try not to." She shook her very red head, then, as if the thought had just occurred to her, pointed a finger at me. "You're the chick he's writing about, aren't you? The one who inherited all of that money?"

"Yes," I said. No way out now. I wished there were, though, wished I could run from that look of distrust that shadowed her face. "He did screw me over, but not the way he screwed you over."

"But you let me think so." She took a step back from the bar.

"I'm sorry," I said. "Steffan and I had lunch yesterday. He told me about meeting you, and I just thought that we should talk." I put my cup on the counter. Crikey. What a jerk I'd become. Invading this woman's home on Steffan's coattails. Trying to glean information about a man who was a thorn in my side but big-time trouble for her.

"Digging for dirt?" she asked, clutching her coffee cup.

Before I could answer, my cell phone vibrated inside my bag. "Sorry," I said. "I have to take this."

But it wasn't Jesse on the phone.

"Is this Geraldine?" a shaky female voice asked.

I felt myself nod as I answered. "Yes," I said. "Geri LaRue. Who's calling, please?"

"Mother Nichols," she said. "You remember me, don't you, Geraldine? I remember you."

"Oh, my God," I said.

"Geraldine, please don't blaspheme." She shouted it into the phone as *blast-FEEM*.

"I'm sorry," I said. It was coming back, all of it. Her sturdy little frame, her voice, sometimes harsh, her hymns at night, her hair, the color of oatmeal. Her rocking chair, and me on her lap in it. The rocking back and forth, the woman who rocked me. Mother Nichols. And here I was inside the home of a woman who made her living doing something that would send my foster mother to an early grave.

"Coy asked me to call if I could remember anything," she said. "How can I help you, child?"

I couldn't remember when I'd ever felt so vulnerable. Certainly not any of the years with Mama. I'd been a tough kid. I had to be. Other women—women like Mary Haskins and probably Mother Nichols—made me want to believe that I'd once been more, that I'd once had more.

"Could I talk to you sometime this afternoon?" I asked. "I'm in San Francisco, but I can be there in a few hours."

"Let's see now." She paused only a moment. "There's a newspaper reporter who'll be here around noon to interview me. Could you come after that?"

My limbs went numb and cold. "Man or woman?" I asked. "What newspaper?"

"I'm not sure, dear. We communicated by e-mail. Can you believe this old lady actually has an e-mail address?"

"Cancel the appointment," I shouted. "E-mail or anything else. I'll explain when I get there. Please don't let anyone into your house."

Her sharp intake of breath matched my own. "I think you'd better speak to Father," she said, and I did.

I was more direct with the Reverend than I'd been with his wife. "You can't let her meet with this reporter," I said. "People have been murdered—Mary Haskins, the social worker, included. You're both in danger, especially if you know something about my past."

When I finally ran out of breath and energy, he cleared his throat and said, "I thought you were a good girl when you came to the house that day. Now I wonder."

"What do you mean?" I asked.

"Mother's hurting right now," he said. "You're telling us not to speak, but the reporter's going to pay us to speak. What would you do if you were in our shoes, sister?"

"No reputable reporter will pay you for information," I said. "Please, Reverend. She's in danger. You both are. Call the police. Give them my contact information. I can tell them what I know."

The Reverend, who'd proved adept at dominating a telephone call, said nothing. It took me a moment to realize that it was because he'd broken the connection.

"So." Tracy said it in a voice so strong that I felt she'd just chucked a brick against the side of my head.

I tried to regroup, tried to forget that this was a former foster father, a minister, at that, who'd just hung up on me.

"Sorry for the interruption," I said to Tracy's expectant look, and replaced the phone in my backpack.

She stood on the other side of the counter, her earrings almost touching her shoulders. Moons and stars. The only items in this whole place that suggested her profession.

"What was that all about?" She held her ground on her side of the white tile.

"It was about murders," I said. "I'm going to have to leave now."

"That's probably a good idea, anyway." Her smile disappeared. "When Steffan said he had a friend who'd been hurt by Doug, I made certain assumptions. And you didn't bother to correct those assumptions."

"No, and I should have. You're right that I came here to dig up dirt on Doug Blanchard. He got the column I wanted. He convinced my editor to let him write about me. I just thought—"

"That I was some fruit fly who'd bad-mouth an old boyfriend to get on Steffan Kim's good side?" Put like that, it sounded terrible. She stood in judgment, her coffee cup in her hand.

"I thought that you might be able to tell me why he hates me so much."

"I doubt that he hates you any more than he hates all women," she said.

"Because of what happened to his fiancée?"

"Hardly." She glanced down at the rhinestone-covered bangle on her wrist that I realized was a watch.

I put my cup on the counter and took a step back. This was what I got for trying to be petty. I didn't have what it took to pull off even low-level deception. And now I'd insulted this woman who didn't deserve to be insulted. "I shouldn't have come here," I said.

"You won't find any disagreement from me."

"I don't know what I was thinking," I said. "This murder I'm involved in—it's more than I believed it was, more personal." I fought tears. That's what I really needed—just one sobbing meltdown. But not here. "Please don't hold this against Steffan," I added. "He was just trying to help a friend."

And then before I could further embarrass myself, I hurried out the door.

Thirty

TINY

She had gone from hell to heaven, yes she had. Tiny lay in the bed of soft sheets in this room of flowers and wondered how long she'd been here, wondered how many nights she'd gone to sleep with enough food and warm blankets to make her forget what her life had been before.

She heard a noise and realized that someone else was in the room with her. A lady sat by her bed, a big lady named Glenna. Yes, that was her name. Tiny remembered her long, flowing, silver-streaked hair, those pale green eyes, the tiny granny glasses.

"How're you doing?" Glenna asked.

And because she was still too weak to offer more than "Okay," that was all Tiny said.

"You remember me, don't you?"

She couldn't think of a reason to lie. "You used to feed us, Sunlight and me, and you let me stay with you. I'm in your house right now."

"That's right." Glenna pushed back her hair and talked in that gentle way of hers. "I was where you are once. The lady who used to own the nursery helped me. She gave me a place to stay until I could get on my feet. She didn't judge."

Tiny could tell that Glenna was having a hard time talking, and she guessed it was because the lady was dead. "Is that why you're helping me?" she asked. "'Cause of that lady helping you?"

Glenna nodded. "When you came here that night, I knew that she'd take you in if she was still alive. But she's not."

"Dead?" Tiny asked. "Like Sunlight?"

"Murdered."

"That's terrible." She didn't want to hear it.

"You're going to have to trust me," Glenna said.

"I do. You know I do."

"We'll see about that soon enough, I guess."

She looked sad, ready to leave. Tiny didn't want her to leave.

"Don't go," she begged her. "Please don't go."

"Then you need to talk to me." Her voice was cold. Tiny could feel how impatient she was. She was going to lose this nice lady, the only one who had tried to help her.

"What do you mean?" she asked.

Glenna got up and looked down at her. "You were hurting when you got here."

"Didn't know where else to go," she said. "I came here 'cause you fed us."

"You were in a bad way. You talked about things."

Tiny's skin started feeling clammy. What had she said? What had she gotten herself into? "What kind of things?"

"You tell me."

"About that day, you mean?"

Glenna nodded. "Just tell me all you can remember about what happened. About what you saw."

"I already have. I said everything I can remember."

"No." Glenna gave her that sad look again. Then she put the chair against the wall, the way she always did before she left. "I'll bring your dinner tonight."

"No, please." Tiny could talk about it now. She could to Glenna. "Please," she said again. "I'll tell you the truth. I will."

"That's good." She settled back down in the chair. "Go ahead," she said. "Tell me."

Tiny closed her eyes. She could see it all, everything she'd feared, like images flashing in her brain. Sunlight's murder. The killer in the uniform. "Sunlight rescued me, but we hadn't been long on the streets together," she said. "I ended up there because of something I saw."

"Anything else?" Glenna asked.

Before she could consider it, the answer darted from her lips. "Tiny Alice."

Glenna looked as if she'd been slapped, but Tiny understood now. She could see the poster outside the theater. Albee Week All Week. "Tiny Alice," she said again. "I'm Tiny Alice."

"No, you aren't," Glenna said. "That was only the name you took after you witnessed the murder."

The images overpowered her. Damn it to hell, she wasn't Tiny anyone. She was Alice Lynn Barnett from Tulare, California, and, yes, she'd witnessed a murder. She'd watched a woman get pushed off a cliff.

GERI

I wasn't up to trying to figure out why Mama would let the system suck me up as a child and spit me out at eighteen. It had always felt somehow like my fault. Still did, actually.

I called Steffan after leaving Tracy's, both to tell him how bad I felt about seeing her and to ask if he could check up on Doug and be sure he hadn't scheduled an interview with the Reverend and his wife. I didn't think so, but I had to be sure.

Then, as I drove the flat, slate-gray, uneventful Highway 5, I did what I hadn't been able to do since my life had changed that day in Marie's office. I let myself remember the fosters.

They weren't all bad, and that hurt as much as the

rest of it. I could remember being held, could remember clutching various toys, bears usually, as I fell asleep at night. I was too young to know terms like *foster care system*. I knew only that I was scared, that I couldn't hear very well, and that all of the stuffed bears in the world couldn't keep me from what I was. Alone.

Many of the foster families needed the money. That didn't make them bad, just not necessarily qualified for the job they weren't paid enough to do. A few were quirky, trying to regain something lost in their own childhood, perhaps. Maybe trying to replace a child they didn't have any longer, or one they never had.

Steffan called about the time I hit Lemoore.

"Where are you?" he asked.

"Lemoore." I pronounced it carefully, not *Lee Moore*, even though I found out after I left the Valley that it was named after a guy with that name. "I'm about fifteen minutes away from the Reverend's."

"You don't sound so hot." His voice crackled in my cranked-up headset.

"I'm okay."

"Yeah, right. Well, maybe this will make you feel better. I caught up with Doug Bastard in the café at work. In fact, he caught up with me. He didn't appear to have any plans to drive south."

"I didn't think so," I said. It was the killer, I knew, who'd tried to see the Reverend and his wife. I hoped they'd listened to me. If not—I couldn't even think about what might happen.

"I know what you're worrying about," he said. "You can't keep anything from me."

"Indulge me, then. Call the Hanford P.D., okay? Get someone over there, just in case."

I expected resistance. I expected Steffan to argue, to say I wasn't being rational to think a killer could be heading to the home of my former foster parents.

"I'll do it," he said, and I knew that I was in the middle of something so terrifying that even logical Steffan sensed the danger. "By the way," he added. "Doug is really pissed."

"Why, and who cares?" I asked.

"I guess Tracy Luce called him and chewed him a new one after your little visit."

"Good," I said, but I couldn't be sidetracked by Doug Blanchard right then. "Make that call, okay, Steffan?"

"Will do," he said. "Don't take any chances. Make that any *more* chances."

Even from the end of the Reverend's street, I could see that Steffan had kept his promise. Two patrol cars hogged the parking in front of the two-story house I could still just barely remember. I parked mine across the street and walked over. As I did, I heard gunshots.

Without thinking, I ran for the house. A uniformed officer stood in my way.

"I'm Geri LaRue," I said, my heart racing. "I had a friend in San Francisco call you here."

"Lopez," he said, breathing hard. His mustache was thin, his lips easy to read, his voice soft as mush. "Everything's okay. Just stay right here."

Before I could reply, another officer trotted down the driveway, arguing with a large, leather-clad figure.

"Oh, no," I said. "Lester Brown."

"You know him?" Lopez asked. I nodded.

"I gave you all the ID you need," he shouted at the officer. "I came here to protect this lady and those old people in there. I saw someone in back, and I did the same damn thing as you'd do. When I shouted to stop, he shot at me."

"Hold on," the cop said. "I didn't see anyone in back."

"You heard the shot, didn't you?" Lester Brown said, and parked his massive frame right in front of me. "What other ID would you like me to show? NRA? KKK?" And with a wink at me, "That's a joke, darlin'."

"You know him?" Lopez asked again. But I was too rattled to answer his question.

"Lester," I said. "How'd you know I was coming here?"

"Nothing that a good, old-fashioned phone bug couldn't handle," he said. Then, frowning at the officers, "Geri here knew that social worker who was killed. She also knew these folks. I couldn't take any chances."

They looked at each other and did the eye-contact equivalent of shaking their heads.

"You folks be okay now?" Lopez asked.

"We'll be fine," Lester said.

"Good night, then." The other cop nodded and they started for their car.

I looked Lester directly in those dark, troubled eyes of his.

"What did the person who shot at you look like?" I asked.

"Couldn't tell." He watched the departing officers, shaking his head. "Cops today are wusses. All they care about is getting home safe. In my day all that mattered was getting *you* home safe."

"Was it a man or a woman?" I asked, still not certain I believed him. Maybe he'd just bugged my phone and invented an excuse to stir up the Reverend's quiet neighborhood. He could have been the one who fired the shot.

"I'm not sure."

"Lester," I said. "Why are you following me?"

His black-brown eyes grew moist. "Most cops have gone soft," he said. "If I don't do it, who will? What will happen to nice ladies like you?"

I couldn't answer that question, but I still felt uncomfortable.

They sat in their car. I knew they were watching us. Lester started to leave. "I'll hang around for a while," he said, "just in case. Remember what I said before. Anything you need, I'm here for you."

Was that a good thing or a bad thing? I didn't have a clue.

Thirty-One

GERI

I approached the door on shaky legs. It opened before I knocked, and that same spindly little girl I'd seen last week stepped out. Kayla. That was her name. She was holding that same tangerine-colored piece of chalk I'd seen her use to draw on the sidewalk.

"Hi," I said. "Could I come inside?"

"Somebody shot a gun," she said. "I hate guns."

"Me, too," I said. "But I don't shoot them. Your name's Kayla, right? May I come in?"

"Are you a social worker?" she asked, stepping closer to the door with an air of authority. I could see myself in her deep-set brown eyes, her skinny little legs floating around in the too-big jeans she wore.

"No," I said. "I used to live at this home, just like you."

"You lived here?" She squinted, as if looking for a lie.

"Sure did. But I was younger than you," I said. "Let me in, okay?"

She tilted her head again. "I need to ask Mother Nichols," she said.

"I'm here, child." The heavy-set, white-haired woman made her way to the front door. I recognized her features about the same time she recognized mine. "Praise God, it's Geraldine," she said.

Somehow I got inside, past the girl and Mother's hungry, reminiscent eyes. Past the living room with, I swear, the same rose-patterned wallpaper, past the pacing, oblivious Reverend, whispering prayers not even a hearing person could make out.

Mother Nichols thanked me the entire time for warning them, for summoning the police. "Why?" she asked me. "Why would someone try to harm us?"

"I don't know," I told her. "Unless you know something about me."

"Nothing, child," she said. "We didn't even have you that long. And you were a good girl. I can tell you that."

We ended up on a floral-patterned window seat in an upstairs bedroom.

"Remember him, Geraldine?" she asked, and I shivered. A small, glassy-eyed bear stared at me from one of the three twin beds.

"Did I sleep there?" I asked her.

"No, child." And when I looked into her distracted

blue eyes for an explanation, she added, "We had a crib for you. That was the best we could do on such short notice."

"What happened to me?" I asked her.

It wasn't the right question. Her body stiffened. "All of that took place before you came here," she said. "We kept you for only a short while until you could go to the group home."

"Group home?" The mention of it stirred ugly memories.

"Yes, child. We kept you as long as we could, and we prayed for you a long time after that. I never forgot you, Geraldine. You were such a trusting little girl."

I didn't want to ask, but I had to. "What happened? Please tell me."

"You don't remember? No, of course you were too young. A girl was hurt, you know? You remember that, don't you? You were hurt, too. But that was before you came here. We didn't hurt you. We loved you."

I felt unbalanced, as if the padded seat were shifting beneath me. "How was I hurt?" I asked. Her mulberry scent—or maybe it was just the scent of this house—engulfed me.

"Why, you hit your head, child." She looked ready to reach out for me, but instead heaved herself out of the window seat and opened a closet. "Here," she said, handing me a white plastic-covered photograph album. "I got this down today and found the snap-shots with you in them. You're about in the middle somewhere."

I saw myself right off—a sad little girl with cropped hair and large eyes, holding a half-full jar of dirt. I sat between a white duck and a short, dirty-faced little boy. "Quack-Quack," I said. Mother looked down, then up at me. "And little Leon. You re-member poor little Leon, don't you, child? He got sent to the group home, too."

The little boy's image was as different and as familiar as my own in that photograph. There was another face in the photo, too, a smirking blond girl, standing taller than the rest of us in a low-cut top and a glossed-on pout.

"Who's that?" I asked.

"Her name was Kathy Jo."

"Kathy Jo." It started to come back to me. "She was at the other home. She—" And then I remembered the other girl, small and frail as a shadow. Who was she? Why did the memory of her face terrify me? "Becca."

Mother Nichols shook her head as if trying to shake away a memory too painful to remember. "That happened before you came here. We didn't have anything to do with that."

"With what?"

"With the little girl." She turned before I could read anything else in her expression or on her lips.

Becca. Now I remembered, although it was like trying to remember someone else's life. Kathy Jo, Leon, and Becca—oh, God, Becca. "I remember her," I said. "That's why we got sent to your house. Someone killed Becca, didn't they?"

Thirty-Two

GERI

Someone had killed Becca. I'd been too young to retain much, but I retained that. Becca had died. Mother Nichols said that Becca's brother had stayed at her home the same time I had. She was going to try to contact him, to give him my phone number. I couldn't imagine what it would feel like to talk to Leon again, but I wanted to.

The highway looked as barren and hopeless driving back to the Bay Area as it had driving from it. Storm clouds tangled right outside Highway 99. Los Banos was so black with heavy rain that I pulled to a café and decided to sit out the storm through a root beer (generic and not very good) and a burger, which was so huge that I wished that Nathan, Steffan or both of them were there to share it with me. It was as good a place to fill the gas tank as any. The prices were as outrageous in the San Joaquin Valley as they were in the city.

Becca. How do you really remember something that happened to you when you were a young child? Normal kids probably get told what happened to them, and that props up their memories. But I did have a shadowy recollection of Becca and trashy Kathy Jo. I could remember it now if I just took down the wall I'd put up then.

"Hi, darlin'. Order a cup of coffee for me, will ya? Maybe a bite to eat. You've got to be starving. I know I am."

Damned if it wasn't Lester Brown again, his leather coat glistening with raindrops.

"Go away, Lester," I said. "Go save someone else."

"I think I should be the one to decide that, don't you?" He slid into the booth across from me, shouted, "Chicken tenders and coffee, black," at a passing server, and damned if we didn't have both before I could insist that he leave. Good thing, too, because he was eyeing my burger.

"Lester," I said. "Please."

"Don't you *please* me." He pounded his fist on the table. "I've been looking into this deal with you and that foster home," he said, then chewed his way through a chicken tender while I thought about it. "You know about the little girl getting killed, right?"

"I knew," I said, "but I haven't remembered for a long time."

"Were you there when Kathy Jo killed Becca?" He held another chunk of deep-fried chicken in his right hand, but kept his sunken, sad eyes on mine.

"I don't know," I said. It was the truth.

"She drowned, right?"

"I—I'm not sure."

How could I have forgotten that? How could I have forgotten Kathy Jo there with her boyfriend, in charge of her folks' fosters for the night? Kathy Jo, so drunk that she could barely stand up in that short pleated skirt of hers. The tattooed boyfriend, shooting his pistol into the trees in the backyard. I'd put up a wall that night, let all of the fosters blend together, but right now, the wall was coming down too fast for me to deal with.

Lester shucked his jacket, revealing a black-and-white Hawaiian-print shirt. "How'd Becca drown?" he asked.

"I don't know," I said. "I was—"

In the shed in back, my scrawny body pressed against Leon's, our hearts beating protection against each other, both of us too young, too frightened to survive the drunken party and the rage outside.

"There was a fight, wasn't there?" he asked.

"Maybe." Yes, there had been a fight—Kathy Jo beating Becca, screaming drunkenly against the gunshots in the backyard. I'd run out and tried to help Becca, and Kathy Jo had flung me onto the patio beside the wading pool—the cold water from the hose, the slippery blue plastic I could still feel against my feet. Still, Leon and I persisted, screaming and crying. We wouldn't stop. Then Kathy Jo knocked me to the pavement again, and it was all over. My hearing was replaced by the roar of an ocean that still hasn't left me.

Yes, that was when it happened. I hadn't been born hearing impaired. *So why had Mama…?*

By the time I got to my feet, Leon was leaning over the pool shrieking, and Becca lay still as a chalk-faced doll.

"Becca drowned in the wading pool," I said. "I was moved to another foster after that."

Lester seemed to ponder what I'd just said as he chewed on his chicken, but his dark eyes flashed as if they were hooked up to a computer of scary intelligence. He chased the food with a swig of coffee and said, "You know they drugged you kids in that foster home, don't you?"

"What? What kind of drugs would you give children?"

"Some kind of progressive crap about medicating hyperactive kids, but they used it on all of you," he said. "I've got the newspaper articles if you want to read them."

"They drugged us?" I'd known that I'd had some shaky early years, but I'd never guessed this. I looked into Lester's weary cop eyes and knew it was true. He might be a little crazy, a little manic, but he wasn't a liar. "Why?" I asked him.

"Because they were no damned good," he said. "Like a lot of foster homes today. Because they weren't policed the way they should have been, not much better than they are right now." He downed another chicken strip and poked a greasy finger at me as he swallowed. "That's what you ought to be writing about for that politically correct newspaper you work for, darlin'. Write about what happens to kids once the government takes over their care. It's not pretty, let me tell you."

He was a man with a mission, but I was too blown away to think about what he was saying. "Where's that house?" I asked. "Where's the house where it happened? I want to see it." I had to. I had to look at those people who'd given drugs to helpless children. Those people who'd damaged Leon and me. And Becca.

"It was shut down after the little gal died," he said. "Right after that, it burned to the ground."

I shook my head, unable to touch my food. "Becca was dead," I said. "No one told me that later. I just knew it."

Then I knew why I was where I was, and why what had happened to me had nothing to do with luck. "What was the name of Kathy Jo's family?" I asked.

Lester lifted a French fry soggy with grease. "Why don't you tell me?"

"Fowler," I said slowly, and I knew from his wrinkled brow and sad smile that I was right.

"Close," he said. "Close enough. Kathy Jo Folsom was Kathleen Fowler."

"And Kathleen Fowler killed Becca. She ruined my hearing and then named me her beneficiary all these years later."

"Because she wanted to make it up to you. You and the brother. She never said what she'd done, but anyone could see that she was haunted."

"You knew her," I said, my heart beating so fast that I could barely breathe.

"Half Moon Bay's a small town," he said. "She came to me when the accidents started happening. The threats came later on. She was scared as hell someone would harm her kid. She wanted me to protect him."

"And you found me for her, didn't you?"

"You were easy to find. I didn't know how you fit in, only that you were a good reporter. Nice work on those razor killings last year, by the way."

I could barely respond. I could still see their faces—Becca's and Kathy Jo's. I could still feel my heart hammering against Leon's in that tiny, musty space. "Why would she cut her son out of his inheritance in favor of me?"

"She wanted you to use the money to protect him," he said. "To find out whatever happened to her. She gave me a retainer for the same reason, and that's what I've been trying to do. When I get my hands on whoever's behind this—"

Violence. I couldn't take any more of it. "Why didn't you tell me sooner?" I said.

"Because I could have put you in greater danger. I needed all the answers." He reached out for the last chicken strip and dipped it slowly into the cup of ranch dressing. "Besides, you were never out of my sight for long."

"Do you have those answers now?" I asked.

"Naw." He shook his head and studied the food in those oddly delicate fingers of his. "There's something not right." He glanced down at the bulge in his Hawaiian-print shirt. "When something's wrong, I can feel it in my gut."

"What feels wrong to you?" I asked.

"Don't want to say yet. I like to work alone, always have. I think better that way."

I looked down at my watch, and when I looked up, the strip of chicken had disappeared. "I need your help," I said. "If you know something, please tell me."

"Right now, it's just a hunch."

I'd about had it with his games, his secrets and his hunches. And I was stunned by what I'd just learned. "I'm sorry," I said, "but I've got to leave now."

Before he could respond, I threw some bills on the table and left. I think he shouted something from behind me, but, lucky for me, I couldn't hear a word.

* * *

I called Jesse from the car, and he answered on the first ring.

"Why didn't you tell me?" I demanded, realizing that I was sobbing.

"What is it?" he shouted back. "What are you talking about?"

I couldn't stop the tears now. "You didn't tell me about Kathleen. She was your wife. You had to have known."

"Geri, what's wrong? You aren't making any sense."

"You lied to me," I said. "You knew about Becca, about the fosters."

"We have to talk," he said. "How far away are you? Come to my place, okay? There was an accident at the nursery this afternoon. Eric was almost killed."

"How? What happened?"

"A piece of equipment fell on him in the tool shed. I just talked to Annie. He's going to be okay."

"Where is she?" I asked.

"Going back to close up. Glenna needs to leave early."

"I can close up for her," I said. "And then you're right. You and I need to talk."

Thirty-Three

CHEV

He finished his shift as a bell-ringer on a downtown corner. Like many other public figures, he signed up every year to support this good cause. It was a rewarding feeling, sitting there faceless in the cold, watching the bills and coins slide into the kettle, answering, "God bless you." But it was time to leave, and he had nowhere to go. If things had worked out differently, he might have had someplace, someone. He hadn't even bought a tree yet. Why should he? Ginger wouldn't be there to decorate it, to warm the house with her decorations and the scent of cinnamon and vanilla.

Although cold, the night air was lazy with the smell of food and the tinkling sounds of "I'll Be Home for

Christmas," floating from the patio of a piano bar down the street. Perhaps he should go sit on the patio in front of the open firepit and try to breathe in some of the comfort of the season, however momentary. No, he had more important tasks to complete.

Still wearing his smock and carrying his bell, he walked along the street, looking at the homeless men and women bunched outside the alleyway beside the theater. Albee Week was over, but Jesse Medicine's well-wrought posters still hung. Jesse, that moody bastard, who didn't know what a jewel he'd possessed.

A woman appeared out of nowhere beside him, her body in its short jeans skirt and black sweater pressed against the brick wall. "Looking for someone, honey?" she asked him.

She smelled like bubble gum and alcohol, and looked as if she hadn't washed her black tangle of hair for a week.

"As a matter of fact, I am," he said. "Could we step back there and discuss it? I have a photo."

She grinned toward the alley and said, "Gotta see your money first. Sorry."

"I just need you to look at a picture of someone," he said. "I'm not—" What was the proper way to state it? He was so inept at conversations like this. Had been comfortable speaking with only two women, only two, and only one since Ginger's death. "I'm not propositioning you," he said.

"Then keep moving." She grinned again and, with a poke at his apron, said, "Unless you want to make a donation to the cause, honey."

"I have nothing against compensating you if you can identify this woman for me." Chev lifted his briefcase, and as he did, his bell clanked loudly.

"What the hell's that?" she asked.

"Just my bell. I'll put it in my briefcase. Will you look at the photo? Please?"

"You some kind of weirdo?" she asked, without a glint of interest in her eyes. "You get off watching someone else look at kinky photos?"

"There's nothing kinky here," he said. "I'm trying to find someone. I need your help. I'll pay you. Fifty dollars."

"Okay then. Come on." He followed her into the alley as he'd followed more women than he could count. He knew what would happen next. She would try to double the money. She might have a boyfriend waiting. But he'd remind them who he was, the trouble he could bring down on them, and it would be okay. It was worth the chance to find someone who could help him find the woman.

The scene behind the theater was seedier than what was happening in front of it. The Christmas carols blowing in from the church two blocks down sounded ludicrous in this environment. Two men in stocking caps shared a joint and what looked like a piece of cheesecake. More rummaged through trash bags and boxes around a caterer's van. A couple humped and moaned against the side of a dark blue pickup truck. Even in the darkness, Chev could see the man's naked buttocks shining in the moonlight.

"That bother you?" she asked, smoothing her skirt over her thighs as they walked past.

"No," he said, not wanting her to think him judgmental. "I guess I was just wondering why they had to do it outside the truck."

"Because there's another couple in there, honey, and that john's paying twice what the outside guy is."

"Oh, all right. That has a logic to it, I suppose. But alley or not, it's still a public street."

"You know, you're kind of cute," she said, "in a dorky kind of way, that is. Great hair, too, by the way." Before he could try to hide the flush in his face or to thank her, she said, "Now, let's take a look at that picture of yours."

There didn't seem to be a boyfriend or pimp. He was grateful for that. He opened the briefcase, a nice faux python that matched his boots, which were, of course, the real thing. Willing his hands not to shake, he slid out the photo.

"Never saw her before," she said, and he felt the familiar sigh of defeat sweep through him.

"Thanks, anyway," he said.

But then she cocked her head, drew nearer the photo, then stared back up at him, her eyes wide. "Wait… I seen her," she said, "but she doesn't look like this no more. Somebody's messed her up pretty bad."

"You're sure it's this woman you saw?" He couldn't believe it. "Forget the fifty," he said. "I'll give you a hundred, more, if you just tell me where I can find her."

"A hundred." She put out her hand. "Give it to me right now. I'll tell you more once you do."

He knew the way these people lied. He did not intend to stand there with an open wallet. Nor was he about to count out bills with her this close and whoever else watching from the shadows. Instead, he balanced both bell and briefcase in his left hand and, with the right, took a bill out of his back pocket and held it in front of her. She tried to snatch it, but he pulled it back. "Tell me."

"I ain't seen her for a while, but I know who she was with. The name's Sunlight. Word is she turned up dead. This one, though. Her name's Tiny."

"Where's she now?"

"I don't know, honey, honest. I just know she used to hang out here with Sunlight."

A voice boomed from behind them. "What the hell?"

"Oh, shit." She grabbed the bill from Chev and started to run deeper into the alley.

"Wait." He yanked at her, his fingers connecting with her coarse dark hair. It came off in his hands.

Lester Brown ran up to him, sweating and out of

breath. Stunned, Chev handed him the hair. How could he not recognize such an obvious wig? "Let's get her," Lester said.

"No," Chev told him. "She's told me all she can. She's earned the money."

Lester flung the wig to the ground.

For that moment in the cold moonlight and the misplaced carols, Chev wondered how much Lester knew and how much he'd guessed. "This isn't what it looks like," he said.

"I know." Lester led the way as they returned past the street people. When he passed the couple going at it on the side of the dark blue pickup, he said, "Fucking perverts," loud enough for everyone in the alley to hear.

Chev, who moments before couldn't stand the thought of going home to an empty house, now couldn't wait to get out of there.

"So," Lester said when they reached the street and the safe sounds and smells again, "What were you doing back there?"

He tried to think of a lie, then came up with something better than a lie. "What were you doing following me?" As good as it felt to say it, he didn't like the look in Lester's eyes. He squinted as if he were staring up into the sun. Chev started to say that he'd better be going, but Lester grabbed his arm.

"Tavern over there is still open," he said. "What say we take a little walk?"

And Chev knew that he had no choice. Still, he tried. "I was going to buy a tree tonight. Decorate it the way Ginger used to."

"Bullshit." Lester fired up a cigarette and jerked him toward the patio full of merrymakers he'd envied less than an hour before.

"What's the problem?" Chev asked. "What's wrong?"

"You really want to know?" The way Lester glared at him from below the bushy eyebrows was so intimidating that Chev knew he must have practiced it many years while interrogating real criminals. "You and me. We go back a lot of years."

"I know that," he said. "I know how much I owe you, Lester."

"Then you come clean with me." He shoved his face in Chev's. "And you know what I'm talking about. Kathleen Fowler. I saw you talking to her. I saw those flowers you bought her and helped her plant all over her place. You were crazy for her, admit it, Chev."

He wanted to run. He wanted to cry. He wanted to beg Ginger to save him, as she always had. Only Ginger wasn't here now, just this crazy cowboy.

"It wasn't like that," he said. "I could talk to her. Kathleen and I were friends."

"And you were hot for her, man. Admit it."

"I admired her," he said. "She was the only woman who—" How could he explain to a man like Lester how it felt after all of those years, to meet the second woman in his entire adult life who seemed genuinely interested in what he had to say? Who didn't see just a paunchy, aging coroner who'd been the center of attention only when he was young and on skates?

"She caused a kid to drown when she was young," Lester said.

"I don't care what she did when she was young." That was low, even for Lester.

They stood outside of the patio bar. "Come on," Lester said, and smashed out his cigarette.

"No," Chev said, his voice as weary as he felt. "I don't know if you heard, but Eric had an accident today. I'm going to stop by the nursery on my way home and check on Annie."

He started to turn, but Lester caught him by the shoulder. "Not yet," the big man said.

His skin itched with fear, but he forced himself to meet Lester's dark gaze again. "What?"

"You were showing that whore a photo back there," Lester said. "Had it in that case of yours."

Chev looked down at his python-textured case. If he resisted, Lester could take it away from him easily. Besides, he didn't want to contemplate what fate would befall anyone who defied Lester. "It was just a hunch," he said. "You've acted on hunches before, haven't you?"

"I'm acting on one right now." Lester snapped his finger and held out a hand. For the first time, Chev noticed how white and slender Lester's fingers were.

A woman in a black tunic and matching skirt too short for her heavy legs approached and asked, "Two for cocktails?"

"We'll let you know," Lester said, never breaking eye contact with Chev, his hand still extended.

Chev did the only thing a sane person could. He handed it over. "I was trying to get leads on her killer," he said. "I thought someone might have seen a witness."

Lester opened the case and pulled out the photograph. "Who the hell is this?" he asked. "Looks like one of those homeless people."

"It is. I told you that I was trying to find who murdered Kathleen, Les. What's wrong? You know the kind of person I am. Why don't you believe me?"

Lester shook his head and walked away from the bar. Chev followed, feeling as if he were being led on an invisible leash. How bad was this going to be? How much would he have to say before Lester was satisfied?

It seemed hours before the big man shook out a cigarette and lit it, blowing the smoke into the foggy night. "Here's my problem," he said. "I know you dug Kathleen Fowler, even though she was still hot for her ex."

"They were divorced," he said, and realized how hopeless his voice sounded.

"But together, for all intents and purposes, right? No matter what she might have told you."

"We didn't talk about him," he said through the

searing pain in his gut. He was caught. If not right now, tomorrow. It was just a matter of time.

"Of course not." Lester's smirk made him feel even lower. "Because hot as you were for the Fowler woman, she didn't think of you as anything more than a dorky friend, did she?"

Could that have been all it was with them? No, it couldn't be. Kathleen had told him that she admired him. Said that he was a gentleman. Only he hadn't been a gentleman that day. He'd come there wanting to watch her, wanting a glimpse into her life.

"Who's the woman in the photo?" Lester demanded.

"A homeless person, that's all. Just like you said."

"And why the hell are you showing her photo to every whore and pimp in the alley?" Chev could barely breathe. Lester's huge face was inches from his. "Tell me what really happened that day, and tell me now, you squirrelly bastard. Or else our friendship ends right here."

"I can't— I didn't—" Chev tried to speak but couldn't. Lester would kill him regardless of what he said.

"Tell me," Lester repeated, his voice hammering in Chev's brain. "How'd you get that photo, and why are you doing this?"

"Because—" And then Chev did something he'd done only twice in his life—the night of Ginger's murder, and that day he'd watched Kathleen

Fowler's body roll down that cliff. He cried. "I just wanted to help her," he said, staring up into Lester's unforgiving eyes, their pupils like large drops of black ink. "Kathleen and I had something. We cared about each other, even though we never talked in a personal way. I cared about her very much. The woman in the photo witnessed her murder."

"And how the hell do you know that?"

The question he expected. Chev gave the answer. "You've already guessed it," he said. "I was there that day."

"Peeping through the bathroom window or what?" Lester didn't bother to hide his disgust. "What are you, man? Some kind of perv?"

That stopped his tears. "I used to like to watch her in the garden," he said. "That's all. I'd help her buy plants, and—"

Lester groaned. "Then spy on her when she planted them? You are sicker than I thought."

"I'm not," he said. He'd loved Kathleen. Still did, regardless of what Lester imagined.

"You were there that day, weren't you?"

He nodded. "I saw something fall off the cliff outside the house, heard someone screaming. A woman. When I got closer I saw this one, kind of dazed-looking, standing in front of Kathleen's house. When she saw me, she took off running."

"And why the hell didn't you come forward and tell what you saw?" Lester demanded.

Why hadn't he? Because he didn't want anyone to know that he was there that day and too many days when he shouldn't have been. That he had come there to watch and photograph Kathleen as he had countless times before. But more than that, after having to do the autopsy on Kathleen's body, he'd changed. He'd met his violence quota, the way all sane people in professions like his did sooner or later if they kept at it long enough. He'd already put in for early retirement. He was finished making his living off the dead.

"I asked you why you didn't tell the cops about this." Lester's voice was louder this time. "That woman could be the killer."

"I don't know," he said. "I thought I could find her. Only so many places for a homeless person to hide in these parts."

"You? Lester groaned. "Give me the damned photo. If she's still alive, I promise you I'll find her."

"Go for it," Chev said. He started to walk away but couldn't leave Lester while he still felt like such a failure. "I really did try to find that woman," he said. "I really did care about Kathleen."

"Well, we have it all straight now." Lester gave him a shrug of dismissal. "Just one question."

Chev stopped in his tracks. Sweat covered his body. "Okay," he said.

"You saw the Fowler woman fall and saw this woman in the front yard, right?"

Chev nodded.

"You even photographed the witness, the homeless chick? You had a camera with you?"

He nodded.

"Why? Oh, shit, don't tell me you took photos of her."

"Nothing improper," Chev said, yet he felt the sweat covering his face. "And not all that frequently. Now, can I go?"

Thirty-Four

JESSE

Seeing Geri tonight, answering her questions, was the most difficult thing that Jesse could imagine doing. The only thing worse would be not going, not giving Geri the answers she deserved.

Downtown Half Moon Bay this time of year could rival the sentiment, and probably the sentimentality, of Currier & Ives. Christmas carols collided with beer-bar ribaldry. It would be easy to slip into one of those bars, especially that one with the inviting fire pit, the nostalgic music, and disappear into the warmth of an icy Bombay on the rocks. Not too easy, though, not with Geri just a couple of blocks away.

If his life were a painting, there would be two conflicting slashes of color, two men slugging it out inside of him—the Jesse who cared for Geri, and the Jesse who must be loyal to Kath at any cost.

The time had come to pony up, as Sheldon used to say. The problem, he would have asked—had Sheldon not smoked himself into an early grave, and if they were having one of their philosophical drinking sessions—was how could he help one woman without betraying the other? And what would Sheldon say? He'd answer in terms of painting, of course, the way he always had. He'd speak of technique, integrity, color, texture. And he'd order another round. Jesse realized how alone he was, how alone he'd been even when his mentor had been alive.

For a moment, he considered the cell phone, the last gift Sheldon, who'd hated technology even more than he, had given him right before Sheldon decided to beat cancer to the punch by putting a gun to his head. Jesse hadn't been able to figure out why he'd been gifted with this metaphor of everything they both despised, until, with Sheldon guffawing through his breathing tube, he realized that it was not a cell phone at all, but a flask. A flask loaded with Bombay and waiting in his glove compartment.

Tonight it didn't tempt him in the least.

The nursery lights were still on, although it was nearing seven o'clock. Only Annie's van was in the parking lot. He could see her through the parted blinds in front, her head bent over the cash register, strands of flame-red hair falling down over her face.

As her shoulders heaved, he realized that she was crying. *Let Eric be okay.* The big, screwed-up kid was a pain in the ass, but he didn't deserve to die. A tiny voice that sounded too much like Kath berated him. *Maybe he wouldn't be so screwed up if you'd been a better stepfather.*

Not true. He'd loved Eric. Still did. Loved Annie. Loved Kath. And Geri? Where did she fit? No time to think about that right now. He must love her. He was here, wasn't he?

The door was stuck. He rattled it, and felt the knob turn.

Annie stood directly inside, tears streaking down her pale, freckled face. Before he could ask about Eric, she screamed, "Run, Jesse. Get out of here."

Then she crumpled before him, her body crushed behind the counter.

"Annie!" He went for her, and then something hit him. Explosive bursts of silver and deep, unrelenting black enveloped him. His last thought was Kath, her perfect, vulnerable face. Then the violent weight that had taken him down hit him again, and his thoughts splintered into painful fragments of light.

GERI

Seeing Jesse's truck in the nursery parking lot made the trip almost worth it. He was here. He'd come to see me. Maybe that meant—no, I didn't dare think about what that might possibly mean. I could only allow the knowledge to warm my heart. He knew Kathleen Fowler's secrets. He knew what I'd just learned and probably more. He wouldn't be here if he didn't want to share those secrets with me. Beyond that, I couldn't hope for more.

Although the interior lights were out, the huge Blooms sign was still lit. Usually, Annie turned it off first, before the inside lights. That kind of creeped me out and made me wonder if I should blatantly announce myself or hang around in the cool, fragrant darkness of the place for a while.

I decided to try the door. If nothing else, I could call out to Annie. Before I could do that, my cell phone vibrated, and Lester Brown announced himself in a voice I didn't need special technology to hear.

"Told you I do my best work alone," he said. "Where are you, darlin'? I want to tell you to your face what I found out."

"I'm at the nursery, in the parking lot." For once, I was relieved to hear from him. "The lights are out inside, but Annie's van is in the lot," I said. "Jesse's truck, too."

"Don't go inside. I'll be right there."

I couldn't believe I was letting this nutter tell me what to do. Talk about strange bedfellows. But, face it. I was afraid, and he wasn't. Sometimes that's all it takes to bond an unlikely alliance. "Okay," I said. "Hurry, will you?"

"One more thing," he said before he hung up. "My source was finally able to trace the little dead girl's brother."

"Leon?" The memories hit me in the gut—the two of us, Leon and me, our hearts hammering against each other. Probably drugged, both of us, every day we were in that place.

"Yeah, Leon Cooper. You're not going to believe this, but he works for the post office in Half Moon Bay." He snorted laughter into the phone. "Remember what I said, darlin'. Don't go into the nursery. I'm on my way."

The icy darkness seemed to slide under the neckline of my sweater, and I hugged myself, moving closer to the sign outside, so that it would be easier for those passing by to spot me. This was the beginning of the main drag of Half Moon Bay, not some isolated back street. Most of the businesses, from the restaurants to the candy store and the boutique, were still open.

I'd be okay. I really would, just as soon as my crazy cowboy got here. Tonight I'd talk to Jesse. I'd find out what happened to Eric. And tomorrow, as painful as it would be, I'd try to face Leon Cooper.

A horde of tourists scattered past me like ants escaping a water hose. One of them, a woman even shorter than I and in a pink jogging suit, slowed down and called out a question I couldn't hear. Probably asking if we were open. I shrugged and tried to smile. She shrugged back and hurried to catch up with the others.

I studied the double doors in front. One edged out about an inch over the others. Unlocked, but I'd keep my word to Lester Brown and wait right here.

A figure came out of nowhere, walking briskly toward me. Where had he come from?

"I have a special delivery," he said.

Then I recognized him. He was the mail carrier. The last person to see Kathleen alive had been the mail carrier. Lester Brown had just told me that Leon Cooper worked for the post office. I needed to talk to this friendly-looking man in postal getup. I had to make him understand who I was and what we shared.

As he drew closer, I saw the dead gleam in his eyes, and I knew it was too late to try to convince him of anything. The mail carrier. Leon. Whoever he was, what he wanted from me was darker and more evil than the professional grin on his face promised.

"No," I shouted, and he began to run toward me.

I had no choice. I dashed to the door of the dark nursery, yanked it open and fled inside. Five acres, I remembered Annie saying. If only I could hide until Lester got here.

He was right behind me. Leon, only he didn't know who I was. Probably too far gone to believe me if I tried to explain it.

With only my vision to guide me in the silent dark hole of the nursery, I couldn't begin to find my way.

Trees looked like looming figures. Shadows hid every row. I crept quietly over the pebble-covered dirt. Couldn't run. Couldn't let my fear overtake me.

I remembered the first day I'd been here, when I'd crashed in on Eric and the smell of marijuana in the back. I needed to head that way. Yes. Pebbles and bark under my feet, as I'd felt that day. I was on the right track.

As I passed the display of Christmas tree stands against the wall, I stumbled and almost went down. The stack of metal stands I slammed into saved me from falling. I'd tripped over a body partially hidden by three decorated Christmas trees. I crouched down and strong fingers grabbed my wrist. In that moment, I knew it was Jesse. I touched his face, his lips.

"I'm okay," he mouthed. "Son of a bitch hit me. My leg's caught. Help me get out of here."

"Who?" I mouthed back, knowing the only way we could dare to communicate was by reading each other's lips.

"Mailman. He tried—"

Leon.

"Let me help you up," I said. "Lester Brown is on his way."

"That crazy bastard."

"Don't say anything else. He might hear."

His leg was pinned under a pile of lumber that he must have fallen against. I managed to move one board, only to have the whole pile shift.

I whispered to Jesse, "I'm going to need help."

"I'm sorry," he said.

"It's not your fault."

"It is. I was loyal to her. I had to be. She was my wife."

"Just be quiet."

"No." I could see his features now, the way it's possible to see furniture in a room once you turn off the light and get used to the darkness. "I owe you this," he said.

And I said, "Okay."

His voice faded, but I was able to get the last part.

"Kath told me about the foster homes, how awful they were, how they gave tranquilizers to the kids."

"I know that," I said, stroking his cheek. "It's okay."

"She said that she killed someone once. That she killed a little girl. I should have told you."

In that instant, the lights went on. I heard a clatter that must be footsteps or items smashed from shelves and counters. I scrambled up and dragged the large potted tree—the one decorated with angels—in front of us, but Jesse's leg still showed. What could I do? Cover it with my jacket? No, better. A plush burgundy Christmas tree skirt. Carefully, I unwound it from its base and gathered it into my shaking hands.

I couldn't freak. Had to do this. The clatter continued. It didn't matter. All that mattered was hiding Jesse. Finally, I got the material over his jeans, his shoes, and crouched beside him behind the tree. Sweat ran down my numb face, but that didn't matter, either.

"You'll be okay," I whispered into his ear. "Lester's coming. Just hang on."

Then I felt as much as heard the footsteps, the shoes kicking pebbles as he moved closer. "Geri LaRue," a shrill voice called out. "I know you're here, but don't tell me where. We have all the time in the world." He knew my name, knew me as Geri, but not Geraldine. Leon didn't have a clue who I was.

I had to stop trembling, had to hang on to Jesse. Lester Brown might be a nutter, but he was a reliable one. He'd break every speed limit in town to get here.

From my hiding place, I could see Leon now, the baggy legs of his mail-carrier uniform, his small feet in their odd little shoes. So unlike a killer. I held my breath, held it so hard that I could barely breathe. *Please let him keep walking.* He reached up, pulled an angel from the tree, muttered something, then threw it down. Two other pieces followed the ornament.

But at least he was moving past us, into the humid greenhouse just outside. Then he'd have a whole outdoor area to search, and I'd have Lester Brown to help me get Jesse out from that pile of boards.

Yes, good. He swore and threw more decorations from the display trees. Then he moved past us.

Jesse coughed. He coughed again, moaned and started to pull himself out from the fallen lumber.

The angel tree bounced away from us, like a large football kicked by a maniac. It flew into the metal stands and the crash reverberated in my screwed-up ears. I scrambled to my feet, face-to-face with the victorious grin of the man in the mail-carrier uniform.

Leon.

Thirty-Five

GERI

Leon.

I recognized him now, the reddish brush cut and the slight build. The pale eyes were too weak to confront anyone, not even now, not even as an adult.

Leon.

I tried to shout his name just before he kicked his hard shoe into my knee and sent me to the ground.

I almost blacked out but fought to stay conscious, focused on his expression. No time to cave in. I had to let Jesse get away, to tell Leon who I was.

"You have beautiful eyes," he said. "Take off your glasses." I looked up to see an instrument in his hand. A thin knife. I knew it was the same one he'd used on Pat Smith at the clinic.

"Leon." I struggled to stand, trying to regain my balance.

He paused just long enough for me to grab the Christmas tree stand and hold it out as a weapon.

"Try it," he said, dancing around me like a punk fighter, holding out his weapon with its shiny silver edge. "You tried to steal Kathy Jo's estate. Kathy Jo wouldn't leave it to a nobody."

"I know that, Leon." I aimed the sharp point of the stand at his midsection. "You have to hear me out, though. You've killed people. You killed Kathy Jo."

"I'll kill you, too." He yanked the stand but I held on tightly. He wasn't that strong. I stabbed it into him, and he let out a howl. "Please," I whispered.

Blood stained his uniform. With a burst of strength, he wrested the stand from me, the scalpel falling beside him. He jabbed the pointed end of the stand at my throat.

"Leon, wait."

"No," he said. "Just shut up now. It's over."

"Becca doesn't want you to do this," I said. "She doesn't want you to hurt Geraldine."

"Geraldine?" The shock registered on his face as if he'd taken a blow. "What are you trying to pull?" The stand's sharp point pressed against my flesh, drawing blood.

"I'm Geraldine," I shouted.

"You're lying."

He shook his head like a child having a tantrum,

and in that moment, I knocked the sharp-pointed stand out of his hand. He tried to strike me, but I stepped back. "Leon," I shouted. "Listen."

He charged me then, but before I could react, he stumbled over the discarded ornaments he'd thrown to the floor. His fall was slow, a dying scream that drove him, facedown, over the stand.

Before I could think, I was on the floor, turning him over and pulling it out. The feeling, like removing a skewer from a piece of meat, was as horrible as the sound he made as he dropped to the floor, clenching his bleeding stomach.

I crouched beside him and tried to stop the flow of blood with the tree skirt I'd used to cover Jesse just moments before.

"Why?" he gasped. "Why help?"

I fought the pain and the rush of vertigo that accompanied it. "I lost my hearing that day you and I hid in the shed together, that day Kathy Jo let Becca drown in the wading pool."

"Becca?" He was trembling all over now, the fabric I pressed against him soaked with blood.

"That's why Kathy Jo left the money to me," I said, unable to control the tears sliding down my cheeks. "She wanted to make up for what she did to us back then. She didn't know that you were the one who—"

"*You're* Geraldine?" The dead eyes came to life, and he reached up and hugged me to him, sobbing.

His blood soaked my shirt. "Geraldine. I see it now. Why didn't you tell me? Why didn't you tell me you were here?"

I let him embrace me, this man who had just tried to murder me. His heartbeat was a time machine to our shared past.

"Leon," I said. "We have to get help for you."

"No." He tried to push me away, his voice fading like music in a far-off room. "No more shrinks." His eyes met mine, and I remembered that day, our hearts beating against each other. "I had to kill Kathy Jo," he said. "For Becca."

I needed to remember that and not the little boy. I needed to remember that he'd killed and would kill again.

"It was all I thought about, all of those years. Then she contacted me, wanting to give me money, and I got a transfer here. The others just got in the way. It was Kathy Jo I wanted. I'm glad she's dead. She deserved to suffer."

He started to cough, and I panicked. He was dying.

Shouts filled my ears like thunder. Leon's eyelids flickered open. Yes, I could hear someone shouting. Finally.

Lester Brown burst into the room and froze like a large cat that had spotted its prey. "You okay, darlin'?"

"Don't," I said. "No more killing." I couldn't stop

crying, not for the nearly lifeless body of the killer before me, but because of Leon, who would have died to save Becca or me. Who was drugged in that foster home we'd shared. Leon, who never had a chance.

"Bastard would have taken you out in a heartbeat," Lester said. "Now, get the hell out of the way."

I looked up at Lester's eyes, as pain-deadened as Leon's, and shook my head. "I can't," I said. "I just can't."

"Okay, damn it," Lester muttered. "Let me get some help for this son of a bitch. Don't come crying to me if he gets off with an insanity plea and comes after you again. And where the hell's Jesse? That's his truck outside."

"In the next room, pinned under a pile of boards. He needs help." I tried to say more, but he'd already darted past me screaming about paramedics and sonsabitches. I could no longer make out his words, and didn't care. I was beyond reasoning, beyond pain, beyond anything but memory.

I looked into the pleading eyes of the man in the mail-carrier's uniform beside me, took that frightfully cold hand that had committed hideous murders and shuddered as I tried to speak. "You'll be okay, Leon. Everything will be okay."

Everything wasn't okay for Leon. He died on the way to the hospital. We got the news within ten minutes after the ambulance left. Except for a twisted ankle, Jesse was fine, in pain, but happy to sip whiskey in the coffee provided by Annie.

We gathered around the fireplace. I breathed in the smell of the logs and the mixed scents of flowers and herbs that masked the cigarette no one told Lester he shouldn't be smoking. He'd asked for his whiskey straight, and was sipping from a small cider cup as he paced the room.

"This gal's got what it takes," he said to Jesse, grinning down at me as if forgetting that I'd crossed the line with him not long before.

"I know that." Jesse squeezed my hand, comfortable here, I thought. How many Christmases had he sat here, drinking, talking and watching the fog drift in? How would it feel to have a pattern to my own life and days the way most people did?

Lester patted my shoulder in a way that managed to be both paternal and forgiving. "You were right, darlin'," he said. "Sometimes I think crazy, especially if a woman's in danger, but I'm glad you said what you did back there."

Especially since Leon is dead, I thought. I needed to leave, get some sleep and think about what had happened. To ask myself the questions I didn't want to, starting with: Would this have been easier, would fewer people have died, if Jesse had told me from the start that Kathleen confessed she'd killed a little girl named Becca?

He seemed to sense my distance and pulled me closer. Or maybe it was the bourbon and not Jesse at all.

As if able to read my thoughts, Lester said, "There's something else y'all need to know."

I glanced at the door to see that Glenna had entered. She looked worried, standing there in her long turquoise dress. Probably she'd heard.

I let go of Jesse's hand and forced myself to my feet. "Is it what we talked about earlier?" I asked Lester. "You said something was bothering you."

"Matter of fact, it is about that." He lifted the cider cup of bourbon as if toasting me, but I could see that he was milking the attention for all it was worth. "Something was bothering me, and I finally figured out what it was. Kathleen Fowler was murdered in broad daylight. Someone had to witness it, and someone did. A homeless woman. She was scared and ran off, afraid the killer would come after her."

Jesse made a noise that I either heard, sensed or both. I saw the pain in his eyes, the guilt. He was thinking about Kathleen again, about how he'd failed to save her.

"Where is she now?" I asked. "Where's she been?"

"I've been taking care of her at my place." Glenna stepped forward and faced me, speaking slowly and precisely. "She'd seen a man in a mail-carrier's uniform running from Kathleen's backyard the day of her murder and was afraid he'd recognized her."

"So she let my wife's murderer get away?" Jesse was on his feet, furious. "And you hid her?" *My wife*, he had said, and hadn't even noticed.

"Hold on there," Glenna said. "I did what I thought Kathleen would have done. She took me in when I was scared and homeless and didn't ask about my secrets. Alice only just now told me what happened."

"God." He sat back down as if it pained him to do so. "If we'd known sooner, maybe we could have prevented those other killings."

His haunted eyes met mine, and I knew that he was thinking the same thing. If he'd told me about Kathleen and Becca, we might have been able to find Leon before he killed again. Without looking away from me, he reached for the bottle of whiskey.

Thirty-Six

GERI

Mama used to talk about being on automatic pilot when she went to her job at whatever coffee shop she was waiting tables at. Automatic pilot. That's how I felt. The wound in my throat still oozing blood, Lester Brown had told the story before we left the nursery. Chev Parnell, the lonely coroner, had been infatuated with Kathleen. "A harmless stalker," Lester said, in a way that made it clear that he evaluated his friends far less harshly than he did most of society.

When Chev had been making one of his trips to watch her one day, he'd seen her body tumbling down the cliff toward the ocean. The homeless woman had come from the same direction, stunned. When he tried to approach her she backed away and finally broke into a run, but not before Chev managed to photograph her. He was certain he could locate her and convince her to talk, but by then she had been rescued by Sunlight, who'd taken her out of the alley behind the theater. The woman's name was Alice, he said. She'd changed it to Tiny that day after seeing a poster at the theater for Albee's play, *Tiny Alice.* Jesse's poster, I knew, and glanced at him again. Even that connected him to this tragedy. I wondered if he'd ever be able to untangle himself.

I didn't think that anyone saw me leave, but Lester Brown caught up with me outside the nursery.

"I thought you might need a ride, darlin'," he said. And when I followed him back to his big Mercedes, tears burning my eyelids, he added, "And maybe a drink."

"Right on both counts, Lester," I said. Strange bedfellows, as Mama would say. Strange bedfellows.

Lester provided a ride and a few drinks that night. He explained to me about Chev Parnell, his former neighbor, who'd secretly been in love with Kathleen Fowler and was determined to find his one clue to her killer.

"Leaves her favorite flowers on her grave," he said. "Sometimes the loves that end badly are the ones you mourn the most."

He didn't have to say like Jesse mourned Kathleen. I knew that was what he meant.

As he talked about his other cases and his life face-to-face with violence, I realized that Lester was like I was, someone with no one to take care of, no job, no family.

Not that I agreed with his beliefs or approved of his actions, but I related to him. I didn't fit in because I wasn't all the way deaf or all the way hearing. Lester didn't fit in because he was a dinosaur who'd outlived his simple John Wayne time, when it was easier to tell who the good guys were, and just as important, who they weren't.

We talked a lot, and we drank more than we should have. And Lester finally drove me to the hotel.

He took me out to breakfast the next day before I left for the newspaper. I found myself saying, "Stop by if you're in San Francisco, Lester," and not minding when he said, "I just might."

The story of Leon's capture and accidental death made me sound far more courageous than I was. Marie called me and offered me the columnist position. "Off The Record." How I had wanted that not so long before.

"What about Doug?" I asked.

"Oh, didn't you hear? He resigned."

Along with Romeo Joey Reynolds. The newspaper was cleaning house because it had to. Did I want to go back?

TBM didn't offer more, so I didn't ask more.

Later that day, I tracked down Doug myself. He was writing for a weekly, but from what my friends at work had told me, was also working on a true-crime book about Leon. That figured. Doug, the expert.

He didn't want to see me, but I insisted.

Finally, he agreed to meet me at a Starbucks near my place. "Tit for tat," he said on the phone. "I want to hear about Leon."

I met him outside. His tanned skin shone with the glow of self love and probably a killer moisturizer. In his loose gray T-shirt and ass-hugging jeans, he looked better than he probably ever would again. No doubt already picturing himself on the back of a book jacket, unsmiling, of course, his jaw held the way it was now.

"Good to see you," he said. "I'm glad that we can put the past behind us and work for our mutual benefit."

"Meaning?" I asked, before I could think better of it.

"Meaning I want to hear all about Leon Cooper." He took off his sunglasses, gave me a partial grin and added, "I'll credit you, of course."

When I didn't follow him through the door, he looked back at me, and I could see the anger in his eyes. "I can't," I said. That was the truth. I'd been through too much to deal with his arrogance.

"It's Tracy, isn't it?" he said. "She's the one who soured you on me." He talked fast but was easy to read. He must have been mumbling or something, though. I couldn't hear a word, which was unusual when I stood this close to someone.

"I was soured when you got the column," I said. "Tracy only confirmed it."

"What made you believe what a pissed-off ex-girl-friend had to say? Why didn't you come to me?"

I shivered and stepped inside, after all. What had Tracy told him? What did he think that I knew? "She was pretty convincing," I said.

"Two grande pumpkin lattes," he called to the barista, without asking me what I wanted.

"Don't tell me you've never done it?" he said to me, then headed for the back and grabbed a seat by the window. I picked up the lattes and followed.

After I was seated, I asked, "Never done what?"

"Don't play games, LaRue. I know what she told you. And I know you were going to Marie. I just beat you to the punch and got out before it happened." He sipped his coffee, his smile self-satisfied. "The columns I wrote landed me the book deal. You can have 'Off The Record.'"

"If I want it, I will have it," I said to his dark glasses. "I won't have to write about a dead fiancée to do it."

He yanked off his shades, his ruddy cheeks ablaze. "Don't give me that bullshit. I'm not the only reporter who's ever used a composite to make a point."

A composite. A euphemism for inventing a source, but what source? His only source of material was his dead— No. He couldn't have done that, wouldn't have risked it.

Yes. Yes, he had. And Tracy had made him think that she told me.

"What made you think no one from your past would come forward?" I asked, as if I knew more than he did.

"I moved out here from the east when I was twenty," he said. "Tracy was the only one who knew. We lived together for a while. I talked too much."

"I don't know what you did to her, but she sure got even with you," I said. More even than he would ever know.

"Not really." He tipped the latte cup in the way that Lester Brown might tip a bottle of bourbon. "I win in the long run, LaRue. You and Tracy are working for chump change."

"You're sick," I said, unable to pretend politeness one more moment. "Go ahead and write your book about Leon, or try to. There can be more than one book, you know, and I'm the only one who knows the real story."

"You're going to write your own?" he scoffed. "You'll find out it's not the piece of cake that writing for a newspaper is."

"No," I said, and pulled out my chair. "What I'm going to do is talk to a writer who would be perfect to help me with the book. We've already discussed the possibility."

"Who?" he demanded. "Who the hell is he?"

"She," I corrected. "Tracy." And enjoyed watching his complexion shoot from angry red to almost purple. "I've read her stuff," I said. "She's good. But my helping her shouldn't harm your project. Just keep inventing those anonymous sources of yours."

Then, my heart hammering way too fast to be anything close to healthy, I left.

Once I was outside, I turned and looked back, just in time to see him, his face unreadable, reaching for my untouched pumpkin latte.

Thirty-Seven

GERI

Christmas Eve morning. That's when we exchanged gifts at the fosters.

Crikey.

Everywhere I look, couples—including those old enough to be the grandparents I never met—stroll in the blustery weather, many of them holding hands. They'll walk through their familiar patterns and their traditions today. I wonder how that would feel. Not that I believe everyone is thrilled to the max this time of year. I've read and reported the suicide rates. I just wonder how it would feel to be part of something bigger than I am.

I've been an Altoids-popping fool for a week. I've consumed a lot of root beer, too. And I still can't figure out why I feel so lost. Jesse has to factor in, of course, but I feel that's more symptom than illness.

We talked just once after the day Leon died. Jesse admitted that he was still too overcome with grief and guilt about Kathleen to be in a relationship. But then I already knew that. He said that he had started painting again, that it would either cure him or kill him. I told him I was thinking about going back to the newspaper but hadn't made up my mind.

And we talked about timing, about how ours sucked and about maybe one day—the kind of things two people who have once been close say to each other to soften an otherwise abrupt ending.

Before I left Half Moon Bay, I sat down with Eric, Annie and Kathleen's attorney. Based on what Lester Brown said, she'd left the entire amount to me because she suspected that her life was in danger. She knew I was a reporter, knew about the murder case I'd helped solve last year, and gambled correctly that I would use that money to protect Eric and to find out what had happened to her. And she probably knew that I wouldn't fight Eric and Annie to keep the entire amount.

I had no intention of spending months in court, and neither did they. I settled for the same amount Kathleen had left to Leon, and they agreed. I can buy some time if I don't want to return to the paper, and I'm as uncertain about that as everything else right now.

So, I put the money in my savings account. First, though, I did send a little check to Mama. How crazy is that? It was cashed, so I guess it got to the right address. I still haven't heard from her, though.

When Tracy Luce showed up at Steffan's party yesterday, she ran shrieking across the room in her glitzy bolero outfit to embrace me, a far cry from our initial meeting. When I could get a word in, I told Tracy that she should be the one to write the book about Leon, and that I would talk to her about my memories of him if she decided to. And finally she was the speechless one.

Christmas Eve.

So, the tree's a little embarrassing, but it's also, like Nathan, who happens to be zoned out beside it right now, one of the few things on this earth that's genuine. White wrought iron with lots of twinkling lights. I bought it at Orchard Supply from a display for rich people who were probably supposed to line their driveways with them.

Decorated it with what I have. A purple pipe-cleaner man. Can't even remember where I got him. A bunch of silver snowflakes from Target, or *Tarzhay*, as Mama calls it. Others I've picked up here and there. One from Malc, a topaz-colored jewel that he said reminded him of my eyes.

I cringe when I remember how right he was about the makeup of a revenge killer. And how wrong he was about Jesse. He was worried about my safety, he said when he called to apologize. Adrienne had told him about the horrible shouting matches Kathleen and Jesse would have when they drank, and although he didn't admit it, I guessed that he suspected Adrienne had embellished the story because she hated Jesse.

I thanked Malc for calling. We said good-night and happy holidays, the way people do on an airplane, when they aren't sure of the spiritual beliefs of the other person.

Before I leave for Hanford, I call Mama. She answers in her voice, but then when I ask for her, says, "She ain't here."

"Did you get the money I sent you?" I ask, but a rude dial tone is already filling my ear.

Oh, well. I have stick-to-it-ness. I'll find Mama sooner or later, or she'll find me.

Stick-to-it-ness. Mary Haskins, the Hanford social worker, murdered by Leon. She planted the seed that gave me whatever backbone I do have.

I'm still sticking, Mary. Still sticking. I'm going to need that backbone today and then some.

I've already made the trip to Longs, watching more couples, arm in arm, welcoming the Christmas Eve morning. I bought and used a box of hair dye. Mahogany Mist, and spread it over my hair. Yeah, I dyed my hair, covered the purple, except on my bangs. Last week I bought a pin-striped skirt and a pair of black Mary Janes.

I bought something else, too. A little mustard-colored tin of sidewalk chalk: white, orchid, yellow, red, vivid tangerine, carnation pink, lavender, turquoise, sea-green, melon, brown, gray, blue, green, blizzard-blue, peach and spring green. All of the colors any little girl could imagine. And, yes, a stuffed bear.

Kayla sits through the meeting, answering each question yes or no, her expression unchanged, her eyes birdlike in their starkness. I decide not to push her. After the papers are signed, the seat belts are snapped and I begin to merge my car onto the freeway traffic, she says, "What happened to your hair?"

"I changed it."

"Why?"

For you, I want to answer. Instead I say, "I thought I'd try something different."

"I liked the purple."

"Yeah? So, maybe I'll change it back."

A few more miles in silence, the bear and box of chalk on her lap. I feel her gaze on me and sneak a look. She is staring at me with fierce eyes that could have been my own.

"Where are we going?" she asks.

And I look at her lost, frightened face and say, "Home."

**Two classic stories of laughter and love at
Christmastime from *New York Times*
bestselling author**

DEBBIE MACOMBER

On Christmas Eve, Maryanne and Nolan Adams tell their kids
the story they most want to hear--how Mom and Dad met and
fell in love. It all started when they were reporters on rival
Seattle papers…and next thing you know,
"Here Comes Trouble!"

When three Washington State women are finalists in a national
fruitcake contest, the story's assigned to rookie reporter Emma
Collins (who hates fruitcake--and Christmas). But then she
meets smart-aleck pilot Oliver Hamilton who flies her to her
interviews. And in the end, she falls in love and learns
"There's Something About Christmas."

Glad Tidings

Debbie Macomber "has a gift for evoking the
emotions that are at the heart of the
[romance] genre's popularity."
—Publishers Weekly

*Available the first week
of November 2006,
wherever paperbacks are sold!*

MIRA®

USA TODAY
bestselling author

ANNE STUART

NEVER GET IN THE WAY OF A MISSION.

The job was supposed to be dead easy—hand-deliver
some legal papers to billionaire philanthropist Harry Van
Dorn's extravagant yacht, get his signature and be done. But
Manhattan lawyer Genevieve Spenser realizes she's in the
wrong place at the wrong time when she meets Peter.

Peter Jensen is far more than the unassuming personal assistant
he pretends to be—and Genevieve's presence has thrown a
wrench into his plans. Now he must decide whether to risk
his mission in order to keep her alive, or allow her to become
collateral damage....

COLD AS ICE

"Brilliant characterizations and a suitably moody ambience
drive this dark tale of unlikely love."
—*Publishers Weekly*, starred review, on *Black Ice*

Available the first week of November 2006 wherever paperbacks are sold!

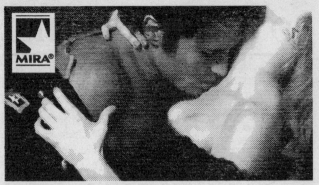

USA TODAY bestselling author

NAN RYAN

Susanna LeGrande lost her fiancé, her brother and her beloved home to the Union army. But her grief only strengthened her resolve to spy for the Confederacy. The once-pampered Southern belle charmed her way through Washington society, falling brazenly into the arms of Rear Admiral Mitchell B. Longley, a commanding Union sailor.

In the heat of ecstasy, Susanna forgot Mitch was her enemy— she surrendered her body and her heart. And now Susanna's dearest love, her dearest enemy, will show her that the sweet kiss of vengeance is a game he, too, can play....

Dearest Enemy

"One of passion's leading ladies."
—*Romantic Times BOOKreviews*

Available the first week of November 2006 wherever paperbacks are sold!

www.MIRABooks.com   MNR2348

BONNIE HEARN HILL

32347 CUTLINE   __ $6.99 U.S.   __ $8.50 CAN.
32339 IF IT BLEEDS   __ $6.99 U.S.   __ $8.50 CAN.

(limited quantities available)

TOTAL AMOUNT $ _____
POSTAGE & HANDLING $ _____
($1.00 FOR 1 BOOK, 50¢ for each additional)
APPLICABLE TAXES* $ _____
TOTAL PAYABLE $ _____

(check or money order—please do not send cash)

To order, complete this form and send it, along with a check or money
order for the total above, payable to MIRA Books, to: **In the U.S.:**
3010 Walden Avenue, P.O. Box 9077, Buffalo, NY 14269-9077;
In Canada: P.O. Box 636, Fort Erie, Ontario, L2A 5X3.

Name: _____
Address: _____ City: _____
State/Prov.: _____ Zip/Postal Code: _____
Account Number (if applicable): _____

075 CSAS

*New York residents remit applicable sales taxes.
*Canadian residents remit applicable GST and provincial taxes.

MIRA®

www.MIRABooks.com

MBHH1106BL